Praise for The Garde

*The Rest Falls Away, Gleason's publishing
romances--on their ear with a decidedly di
heroine who stakes the undead with the best of them.*

-- *Detroit Free Press*

*The undead rise to great heights through Gleason's phenomenal storytelling. She
creates a chilling world with the perfect atmosphere of fear and sexual tension.*

-- Romantic Times

*Gleason keeps upping the ante with each novel, weaving the characters around her
readers with each engaging conversation and narrative, every stage set of all the
appropriate gothic gloom and melting beauty.*

-- Book Fetish

*A promising, enthusiastic beginning to a new paranormal historical series,
Gleason's major label debut follows the adventures of a conflicted young vampire
hunter in Regency England.*

– Publishers Weekly

*Sophisticated, sexy, surprising! With its vampire lore and Regency graces, this book
grabs you and holds you tight till the very last page!*

– J R Ward, best-selling author, Lover Revealed

Witty, intriguing, and addictive.

– Publishers Weekly

*A paranormal for smart girls who like historicals. Buffy in a bonnet takes on the
forces of darkness in Regency-era London.*

– Janet Mullany, award-winning author of Dedication

The paranormal world should rejoice, for a new Queen has emerged!

– MyShelf.com

...Above all, the writing is what recommends this book most. Gleason's writing is sharp and taut, which makes for excellent action sequences, and a plot that travels quickly from the start. The writing strength alone gives me ample reassurance that this potentially plot-heavy series is in the right hands. I'm definitely looking forward to the next installment.

– Smart Bitches Love Trashy Books

...Victoria is the perfect heroine. Smart, sexy, and tough while remaining vulnerable, she is the reason I love this book. Secretly I'm dying to be her, including wearing the fancy dresses and kicking undead butt. Even though Victoria is a very modern heroine for the time period, she works well with the rest of the storyline. Max is another great character, with brooding good looks and full of mystery; there is a lot in his past that I will enjoy reading about in future novels. Then there is Sebastian, but trust me you will want to read about him for yourself....

– Blogcritics Magazine

...The paranormal world should rejoice for a new Queen has emerged! Colleen Gleason has written an explosive debut novel that is assured to please paranormal fans for a long time to come. This is the first in a series that is destined to be one that will go down in history. Very highly recommended.

– MyShelf.com

With its wonderfully witty writing, action-infused plot and sharply defined characters, "Rises the Night," the second in Colleen Gleason's irresistible Regency historical paranormal series, is deliciously dark and delightfully entertaining.

– The Chicago Tribune

A tense plot line and refreshingly diverse supporting characters complete the package, giving series fans plenty to sink their teeth into--and plenty more to look forward to.

– Publishers Weekly

...Heart-stopping scenes and sexual tension. With numerous twists, [Gleason] leaves you hanging, eagerly awaiting the next installment.

– Kathe Robin, Romantic Times

Other Books by Colleen Gleason

The Gardella Vampire Chronicles
Victoria Gardella
The Rest Falls Away
Rises the Night
The Bleeding Dusk
When Twilight Burns
As Shadows Fade

Macey Gardella
Roaring Midnight
Roaring Shadows

The Envy Chronicles
Beyond the Night
Embrace the Night
Abandon the Night
Night Betrayed
Night Forbidden
Night Resurrected

The Draculia Trilogy
Lucifer's Rogue
Lucifer's Saint
Lucifer's Warrior

The Medieval Herb Garden Series
Lavender Vows
A Whisper of Rosemary
Sanctuary of Roses
A Lily on the Heath

Modern Gothic Romance
The Shop of Shades & Secrets
The Cards of Life & Death

The Stoker & Holmes Series
(for teens and adults)
The Clockwork Scarab
The Spiritglass Charade
The Chess Queen Enigma (forthcoming)

THE GARDELLA VAMPIRE
CHRONICLES

ROARING
MIDNIGHT

MACEY BOOK 1

COLLEEN GLEASON

AVID PRESS

A Note to the Reader

This book begins the saga of Macey Gardella, Vampire Slayer.

If you've read the previous books in the Gardella Vampire Chronicles, which feature Victoria Gardella, Max, Sebastian and a variety of other characters, I hope you'll find this series as compelling as the original five. Many of the questions you may have had after them will be answered… and some won't, at least in this volume.

If you haven't read the original five books (listed below), know that you can dive into this new series without feeling lost. This is a self-contained trilogy that doesn't require you to have read Victoria's books. However, because this series does take place about a hundred years after Victoria's books, note that there will be some spoilers for the original five stories.

At any rate, I hope you enjoy the read—wherever you choose to begin.

I love to hear from readers; feel free to contact me with questions or comments through my website (www.colleengleason.com) or Facebook page (www.facebook.com/Colleen.Gleason.Author).

— *Colleen Gleason*
June 2013

For new readers who want to start from the beginning,
the Victoria series is as follows:

The Rest Falls Away
Rises the Night
The Bleeding Dusk
When Twilight Burns
As Shadows Fade
"Northanger Abbey" in the anthology *Bespelling Jane Austen*
(loosely connected).

There is also a short e-story that would have taken place during *The Rest Falls Away*, which acts as a sort of teaser/preview to the series. It's called *Victoria Gardella: Vampire Slayer*.

Happy reading!

Prologue
A Warning

Chicago, 1925

SEBASTIAN VIOGET PLACED HIS PALMS on the bar and leaned forward. The large ruby signet on his left hand glinted in the golden light. On his right five fingers were the ever-present copper rings that had once belonged to Lilith the Dark. Sebastian allowed his eyes to glow just enough to give the man on the other side of the counter a clear warning. "If Iscariot or Alvisi get to her before she's ready, I'll kill you."

The other man was swarthy as a Gypsy, with too-long black hair and jet eyes. He shifted lazily, appearing unmoved by his host's threat. "You'd have to catch me first."

"You know very well I could." Sebastian eased back from his threatening stance. The bastard across from him was nearly as cocksure as his old friend and nemesis Max Pesaro. Damn good thing they were on the same side.

At least, as far as he knew.

He didn't trust the other man any more than he trusted anyone—aside from Wayren. Who, incidentally, had been annoyingly absent for the last decade or so.

His visitor, the last of the night's patrons—and one who could actually leave once it was dawn—chuckled. "Some day, I'm certain we'll find out if that's true. I'll even let you chase me *after* sunset to make it fair, Vioget. I wouldn't want you to cry foul." He lifted the fullest bottle of whiskey from the counter and gestured with it before slipping it into the inner pocket of his overcoat. "This is a far sight better than the hooch Capone peddles. My deepest gratitude."

"The Silver Chalice serves only the best, legal or no," Sebastian replied. "Always has, regardless of what continent it's in." The Volstead Act's prohibition of the manufacture or sale of alcohol was a ludicrous proposition. As if the United States government could control what he chose to ingest.

Hell, Sebastian had a hard enough time controlling it himself.

He refrained from glancing toward the bottles of the other type of libation he stocked—for himself only. Even the thought of the rich, heavy lifeblood filling those vessels was enough to make his gums throb and his fangs begin to unsheathe. The familiar *need* swelled, rushing inside him, pulsing through his body, turning his vision rosy.

He reached automatically for the silver *vis bulla* that hung beneath his shirt, sliding his fingers through the opening to touch the tiny cross. The holy metal burned, but he welcomed the subtle pain. It reminded him he could still feel.

It reminded him why he was still here.

Giulia.

He'd given everything for Giulia.

And for Victoria.

His guest didn't seem to notice Sebastian's discomfort; he was intent on adjusting his enveloping overcoat and hat. He always wore his fedora unfashionably low over the forehead, to the eyebrows. "I'll be on my way then. See if there's any news on Capone, if Alvisi's made any move on him."

That likely meant the man was headed to The Blood Club. Where else would a vampire hunter go to find undead, or to extract information from the undead? Not that Sebastian approved of the way Chas Woodmore went about doing so, but he wasn't a judgmental sort. Not like Pesaro had been. And particularly in this case, when it was so bloody important, he didn't care how depraved Woodmore was.

"The sooner the better. We have to stay more than a step ahead of him and Iscariot. Once either of them find her—"

"I see her every day, on her way to and from her job, Vioget. They haven't found her yet. And they don't have any idea about me. She's safe for now."

"She has the book. It's only a matter of time until the dreams begin."

"And once that happens, you must convince her to accept."

I will.

The other man looked at him with those cold, dark eyes and Sebastian turned away. He didn't need Woodmore to see the desperation in his own gaze. The long promise and the sacrifices he'd made would be for naught if a single woman denied her legacy.

After a hundred and two years, one would have thought it would have become easier to wait. And accept.

But it hadn't.

One

Coincidences and Mistakes

MACEY DENTON WOKE ABRUPTLY, bolting upright in bed.

Her heart was slamming so loudly the sound filled her ears, and cold sweat made the nightgown cling to her skin. She was breathing fast and hard, and felt as if she'd been running for hours.

She *had* been running—scrambling through a dark forest, along the shadowy streets, across grassy backyards...in her dream.

"It was just a dream," she told herself, as if saying it aloud would dispel the last vestiges of the terror.

Moonlight cast wrinkled silver beams across her mussed bed, and Macey glanced nervously toward the window. A gentle spring breeze wafted through the small opening. The sounds of automobiles trundling by, distant shouts and even something far off that sounded like gunshots...just the normal night sounds of Chicago.

Nothing was out there. Nothing with glowing red eyes or gleaming fangs.

It was just a dream.

Moonlight reflected off the face of her alarm clock. It was hard to clearly read its numbers, but she could make out the vague shape of the hands. Three o'clock.

Drat it. She had to get up for work in three hours and she'd already stayed up too late reading that old book. It sat on her bedside table, beckoning temptingly—just as it had when it appeared at the library office yesterday.

The Venators by George Starcasset.

The slender book was ragged and worn, its leather corners bumped and rounded. It was an odd publication, with no title page listing a publisher or even a copyright page. It appeared crude and inexpertly made. That was why she hadn't put it on the pile to be catalogued at the library...yet. She was curious. The printing was awkward and imperfect, unlike the neat rows of letters that came from her typewriter. Clearly, it was more than a hundred years old. And though she had no idea who or what a Venator was, Macey had been compelled to pick it up. She turned through the first few pages, taking care not to crack or tear the delicate paper, and saw unfamiliar words like *vis bulla* and *Tutela*.

And then she shoved it into her satchel to bring the book home. For research.

It turned out to be about a family of vampire hunters. And despite the fact there was, of course, no such thing as vampires, she found herself swept up in the world of the men who risked their lives to hunt the demonic beings.

That was the reason for her nightmares.

As she hurried along the busy sidewalk, Macey tugged the felt hat down over her ears, making sure its little brim curled up saucily in the back.

Well, she would have been hurrying, glad to be on her way home from work, if her feet weren't so darn *sore*. The new shoes she'd sprung for with her first paycheck—shiny black Mary Janes with sassy black and white organza bows—were still a little tight, and Dr. Morgan had had her running errands in them all day long.

Even though she loved books and absolutely adored her job at the Harper Memorial Library at the University of Chicago, Macey normally wouldn't mind being out and out of the office as a break from the re-shelving and filing of catalogue cards—but it had been drizzling since noon today, making it chilly and messy outside.

And because she'd overslept again (thanks to those darn dreams), she'd forgotten her umbrella and dashed out of her boarding house in a rush. Thus her hat and stockings had gotten damp and stayed that way for the rest of the day. Even the rabbit fur around her coat collar had wilted. Thank goodness it was removable.

The top few floors of the Lexington Hotel, where Al Capone lived and reigned, were visible over the rooftops. She'd walked past the luxurious brick and terracotta building on Michigan Avenue many times—and had even delivered an old book there once. (She counted herself fortunate she hadn't seen Capone himself.)

On each occasion of passing the hotel, Macey couldn't help but look for the gangsters with the so-called Tommy guns that were rumored to patrol the place. It was common knowledge that Snorky, as Capone was called, owned the city—from the mayor on down to half the police force, as well as a variety of businesses. Nightclubs, restaurants, meat-packaging facilities, funeral homes, and illicit ones—like breweries—as well.

He was, some said, more powerful than the president of the United States. And despite the violence and countless illegal activities he controlled, Chicagoans were fascinated by him. Capone liked to present that he was a sort of modern-day Robin Hood, providing services to the masses from beneath a repressive, controlling government—and there were some who lauded this position.

Macey didn't have much of an opinion. She'd moved to the city only eight months ago and was still enamored with the tall art deco buildings, countless shops, and variety of entertainment. As long as Capone, Torrio, Moran and the like didn't bring their violence to her, she intended to ignore them.

An old, open-style Model T trundled past her on the street. She dodged when it drove through a shallow puddle, but she wasn't fast enough and the automobile sent water spraying on her legs.

"Drat!" she muttered, pausing to twist around and look down at the back of her flesh-colored stockings. They were speckled with dark flecks of mud.

"Hey, doll, where ya goin' in such a big hurry?" An admiring whistle followed.

Macey glanced down the alley at a man unloading crates. Her landlady, Mrs. Gutchinson, was always complaining about how the latest fashions, with skirts stopping just below the knee and sheer stockings, seemed to give men permission to be vocal and obnoxious. Instead of responding, she continued along, making her way on the sidewalk with scores of other people heading home at the end of the work day. Everyone seemed to be walking more quickly than usual because of the damp April chill.

She passed a second truck being unloaded in another alley and two skinny kids trying to woo a cat out from beneath a porch. There was a man sitting on one corner with a tin cup on the ground as he sang long and low and sad. Occasionally, someone dropped in a coin.

A man walked along ahead of her, holding the hand of a young blond girl in a darling pink coat. She danced and chattered, twirling around on the end of his hand, and pointed at things as they walked along. Her father smiled down at her and nodded, and once even paused to crouch and look at something she found on the sidewalk. They made a sweet picture—the image of a girl with her daddy.

Macey dragged her eyes away, ignoring the dull, familiar pang of anger and grief.

On the block ahead, she saw the shill who regularly enticed passersby to stop and play dice or shell games. His normal crowd was nonexistent, for today there were only two victims trying to outsmart the con as he shuffled the upside-down cups and kept up a patter designed to distract from the movement of his hands. On her first day going to work at University of Chicago's library, Macey had been lured in by his invitation. Ten minutes later she'd walked away—a dollar poorer and late to work on top of it.

Since then, she'd avoided getting too close to that side of the block, even though he regularly called out to coax her back. But one day she was going to try it again, and she'd win.

By now, Macey was almost limping from a blister at the back of her right foot. That would teach her to wear new shoes without giving them a chance to stretch out first. And there seemed to be another sore spot developing over the big toe on her left foot.

Double drat. That was going to make it a little painful dancing at The Gyro tomorrow evening. She'd be hobbling instead of shimmying, which would make for a long night.

She rounded the corner onto Quincy Street in order to avoid the insistent shill and his cups, and plowed into a man standing there.

"Oh, pardon me," she said as he reached out to catch her arm and steady her.

"I'm sorry, miss." He stepped away from where he'd been looking at a sign posted in a bulletin board on the brick wall. "I should have been watching." Beneath his fedora, he had strong, dark brows and blue-gray eyes that were sharp and intelligent. They seemed to take in every detail of her with one sweep.

"I wasn't watching either." Instead of continuing on, Macey took the opportunity to give her sore feet a rest.

And aside from that, he was an attractive man, probably in his late twenties. What little she could see of his hair appeared dark under the shadow of his hat, and he had a solid, square chin that looked as if it had been a day since it was shaved. Taller than she—but what man wasn't?—he wore a dun-colored trench coat that had a button hanging loosely from its threads. Because he wasn't wearing gloves, she could see his ink-stained hands were well formed and sturdy. No wedding ring.

Trying to give the impression she was waiting for a bus or for the traffic to clear so she could cross the street, Macey glanced at the board to see what had caught his interest.

There were some flyers announcing a sale at Thomson's Furniture along with several posters promoting a jazz trio at The Leonine, a vaudeville act at Prego's on Vashner, and some others that were faded and torn. "Planning to go see The Armbruster Trio?" she asked.

"Not at all. I was actually looking at this one." He stabbed a finger at a hand-lettered sign off to the side.

Its ink had run, but Macey could still read it. *Missing: Jennie Fallon. Last seen March 29, 5 o'clock, at Vashner and Michigan.*

The description of the young woman of twenty was partly obliterated by weather and damp, but Macey had seen enough. March 29 was more than a week ago. Her stomach soured and she looked up.

"Do you know her?"

"No." He snatched the paper from its mooring, crumpling it into a ball. "And no one ever will again. Her body was found this morning."

"Oh no," she breathed, her insides tight. The woman had been her age. "Oh, that's terrible. What happened to her?"

His mouth drew up flat. "You'd best be taking care, miss," he said, and for the first time she noticed a bit of the Irish in his voice. "It's not safe for a young woman out alone, especially after dark. I don't know you, but you look just like the sort of girl Jennie Fallon was: young, pretty, one that likes to go out dancing in the clubs and getting into trouble in the speakeasies—"

"I beg your pardon," she said, suddenly a little nervous. Was he a policeman? "Why on earth would you think I know anything about speakeasies?"

He looked at her, his eyes a more intense blue now—steady and knowing. "You can be saving your innocent protestations for the cops, miss. I'm not here to condemn or judge."

"Well, I nev—"

"Her body," he continued, speaking over Macey's breathless indignation, "was mutilated. Throat and chest torn to ribbons."

"My God, that's *horrible*." Her annoyance evaporated. "The poor, poor woman. Do they know what caused something like that?"

"I can only assume that by 'they' you mean the authorities." All trace of his brogue was gone. "As if they have time to investigate the disappearance of a poor young woman when there are gangsters to be cared for. But no, no one is certain what caused such a terrible death."

"Maybe it was a mad dog or some other wild animal. Or… or…a vampire." This last came out as little more than a mumble, but he must have heard.

"A what?" He was staring at her with the same shock she felt coursing through her own body, along with mortification that such a ludicrous comment had come from her lips. "Did you say *vampire?*"

"I…." Macey fumbled for an explanation. She had no idea why those syllables had come out of her mouth. "I was just… joking," she said lamely. "It was a silly thing to say." She shook her head, miserable and mortified. As it tended to do, her mouth had taken on a life of its own, speaking before her brain caught up. She had vampires in her reading, vampires in her dreams, and now vampires reared their ugly fangs in everyday conversation.

He was looking at her differently now. In a way that made her feel prickly and nervous inside her skin. "Joking, were you? I wonder why you'd be joking about something like that."

Just then—and Macey was to be forever grateful for the interruption—someone called, "Grady!"

They both turned to see a uniformed police officer approaching. It was obvious he'd been hailing the man next to her.

Macey was delighted to have the opportunity to edge away as the policeman, who was quite a bit older, walked up. He looked at her, then at Grady, and said, "Is everything all right here? Miss? Is this man bothering you?"

Before she could respond, Grady gave her an assessing look and said with an ironic smile, "Oh, and I'm quite certain I am." Then he turned to the policeman, effectively dismissing any complaint she might have been moved to make. "Any news, Linwood?"

Macey was only too happy to make her escape, sore feet notwithstanding. She didn't look back as she started off down the sidewalk, cheeks still burning over her rash suggestion that a vampire might have attacked the young woman.

And the fact that Grady *heard* it.

Not that it mattered. Surely she'd ever see the man again, and thank goodness for that.

As she rushed along, she continued to berate herself. That strange book had captivated her, and the story didn't want to leave her alone. For the last two nights, she'd been having those same nightmares of being stalked and hunted by red-eyed vampires.

And the oddest thing had happened at the library earlier today. Macey was secretary to the director of accessions (with aspirations of being head librarian herself one day), and Dr. Morgan had received a visitor early this morning.

Although, as it turned out, the visitor hadn't been looking for Dr. Morgan. He was a nice-looking young man, and he came into the office, folding up a very large, dripping umbrella but carrying nothing else. That in itself was unusual, because just about everyone who came into the library was either in possession of one or more books, or was carrying something in which to put one or more books. Or was at least *looking* for a book.

The young man looked intently at Macey, who'd enthusiastically taken a break from typing up the twenty-third card catalogue file she'd done since eight o'clock. Typing up card catalogue files was much more tedious than one would think, as she'd quickly learned. She preferred to be walking among the labyrinthine stacks, discovering or re-shelving books and old manuscripts—or, better yet, poring through a newly acquired tome herself, practicing the classification of the title and where it would go on the shelf. And you never knew what sort of fascinating information you could find paging through a book.

But when she looked up at the visitor, Macey's first impression was that he might be a gangster. She wasn't certain why she had that thought. Maybe it was the commanding way he looked around the room. Or the sense of something being *off,* or even dangerous about him.

A sharp spike of nerves made Macey fumble with the pencil she'd picked up. The newcomer carried himself with confidence and boldness, and he was dressed expensively in spats and a tailored suit. A bloodred handkerchief, silky and patterned with black dots, stuck up from his breast pocket, folded in perfect, fan-like creases. She found herself looking at his silhouette beneath the fitted jacket to see if she could spot the bulge of a gun, and wondered what she would do if he pulled one out.

And the way he looked at her was odd. It sent a gentle prickle over the back of her bare neck and across her shoulders, almost as if a chill draft brushed her skin. In fact, she felt a distinct chill lifting the hair at the back of her neck, and she wondered if he'd left the outside door open when he came in.

"Miss Gardella?" He stepped closer to her desk. No one else was around; the rest of the department was at lunch.

Macey looked up at him. "Pardon me?" she asked, rising while trying to hide the fact that her knees were shaking. What on earth was wrong with her? At least her voice came out calmly and steadily. "May I help you?"

He looked at her more intently, and for a moment, Macey felt as if her insides wavered…as if her vision swung and shivered. For just an instant, she felt dizzy. "I'm looking for Miss Gardella," he said, still focused on her.

She shook her head, and it took great effort to pull her gaze away from his. Her heart was pounding and she felt…soupy. "I'm sorry, sir, I'm not aware of anyone by that name. If you'd like to speak to the director, Dr. Morgan, he might be able to help you. Do you know in what department she works? The university is a large place, and I'm new here."

The man's brows drew together and annoyance colored his expression. His eyes flashed red for an instant, then she dismissed the thought as being due to her fanciful imagination and cloudy head. *Am I coming down with something?*

"No, that won't be necessary. I must be mistaken." The man turned and strode out of the office before she could ask his name.

It was only after he left that it sunk into her thoughts that he'd asked for Miss *Gardella*. In fact, it seemed as if he'd initially called *her* Miss Gardella.

Gardella was the name of the family of vampire hunters in Mr. Starcasset's book.

How coincidental.

The dance club called The Gyro was loud and crowded, just the way the flappers liked. Good music, a big dance floor, tables packed in together on the sides, and, if you were daring and knew the right word or phrase, entrance through a secret door behind the musicians. Not that Macey ever went through that door…at least, not so far.

The wall behind the dais where the piano stood appeared to be an innocent panel of mirrors, but the third one was the secret door. Macey knew this because she'd seen it slide open once, and because Flora had told her.

"Do you know the password?" Macey'd asked her friend, jiggling her foot in time to the music. The ice in their glasses of tea clinked gently on the table.

Flora shook her head, and her tight reddish-blond curls hardly moved at all. "No, but I think Jimmy does."

Jimmy was Flora's older brother, and he often accompanied the two of them when they went dancing—although he hadn't tonight. Macey liked it when he came along because he was a deterrent to anyone who might bother them. And every day in the papers, there were stories about gangster shoot-outs, police raids, and other violence related to the so-called beer wars. Since she and Flora weren't about to stay in like two old maids with their cats (not that either of them had any cats), it made for a more relaxing night when the massive, smashed-nosed Jimmy came with them.

Macey suspected he probably knew more about what went on behind the secret door than he let on, and more than once she was certain she'd seen the bulge of a firearm under his arm, beneath his coat. But he was Flora's brother, and she'd known him for more than a decade because she and Flora had been friends since they were ten. The two girls had grown up on the same street in Skittlesville, walked to the same school, and had the same ferocious piano teacher.

In fact, that was how they'd come to be such good friends—bonding over their mistreatment by Mrs. Pevensey. Macey's mother died when she was very young, and her father—who worked for the British government—had promptly sent her as far away from him as possible. She was shunted off on several family members from the countryside of England to New York, and finally to farm country in the Midwest when she was ten. From then on, Macey was raised by a distant cousin and her husband, who owned a timepiece shop in the tiny Wisconsin town. Then Macey's father had proceeded to get himself killed in the Great War. She was left with only vague memories of him—a tall, dark, and austere man.

Her memories might be vague, but her feelings toward him were not. Loathing, disgust, and pain rose inside her whenever she thought of being shipped off and abandoned by someone who was supposed to love her—at least a little.

"Any luck finding a job?" Macey asked, leaning close to her friend so Flora could hear her over the music and loud conversation. They'd moved here from the tiny town of Skittlesville together, initially getting jobs at the same secretarial pool. They'd always helped and encouraged each other all along the way. But in the last few months, since Macey got her dream job at the university library and Flora lost hers at the pool, she'd seen less of her friend.

"I had an interview yesterday for a position with another typing pool, but I'm not sure if they'll call me back. I—uh—knocked over a mug of coffee, and it spilled everywhere on the lady's table." Flora rolled her eyes and smiled gamely, but Macey could see the frustration in her gaze. "I'm such a klutz."

"I'm sure they knew it was an accident. How was your typing test? From what I hear, those office typing pools want someone who can type fast and accurately, and who cares about spilled coffee? And last I heard, you were at seventy w-p-m!"

"Well, considering the fact that I knocked the cup over *before* I even got to the typing test, and it spilled onto Miss Henworth's light pink skirt and stained it…I never even got to the test."

Macey bit her lip. "Oh. That's not good at all. Do you have any other prospects? I keep looking at the job postings at the university to see if there's anything for you. I'm sure I could get Dr. Morgan to recommend you if we find a suitable one."

"Thanks. But I think I'm going to try looking for something *non*-secretarial. Maybe I'll work in one of the garment factories. I'm going to head over to Ingram's first thing in the morning. And if they don't have anything, I'll go to Chestwick."

Macey tried to keep her expression neutral. Working in the garment factories was tedious, low-paying work. Flora was much too smart and fun and lively to be hunching over a sewing machine at a long table with twenty other women, straining her eyes over tiny stitches day after day after day. "Oh, don't give up yet, Flo. I'll ask around. Maybe there are some jobs that haven't been posted."

"I have to pay rent, Macey. Because I sure as shootin' don't want to move back home. As mean and crabby as my landlady is, she's better than living with my mother." The musicians started a new song, and Flora stood abruptly. "It's the 'Tiger Rag.' Come on, let's shimmy."

Macey rose and adjusted her stockings, which were rolled down to just above her knee. Her shift-like dress was made of robin's egg blue satin, with beaded, flounced layers from the dropped waist to just above the knee. The dress hung loose and straight on her body, which made it easier to dance, and its skinny straps held it in place but left her shoulders and arms bare. She'd pinned a large red rose to the front of one strap, and she'd slipped another on a comb into her dark, curly hair.

She'd chosen to wear an older pair of shoes instead of the blister-inducing Mary Janes from yesterday and was glad she'd opted for comfort over fashion. Surprisingly enough, the blisters had healed overnight and were nearly gone, but she decided not to tempt fate if she was going to be dancing all night.

The dance floor was crowded with other flappers in their shift dresses, high heels, and bare legs and arms, mingling with men in spats and sleek suits. Macey recognized a good many of the regulars in the establishment, including some of their other friends. She waved across the space to Chelle and Dottie, who had found some young fellows with whom to dance. A few weeks ago, Macey met a nice one with a sweet smile and round glasses that steamed up endearingly when they did the Charleston. They'd danced twice and chatted for a while, but she hadn't seen David (she didn't get his last name) since. She was hoping he might appear, and so kept looking around the club to spot him.

As she shimmied, arms and legs flying, long necklaces bouncing, feet skimming and tapping across the floor, she noticed a young Negro woman sitting in a corner near the band. She was about Macey's age, or maybe closer to twenty-five, and had very short black hair that cupped her head like an elegant cap. Her skin was the color of rich caramel. The woman sat alone, observing the dancers, watching the musicians, and seemed to constantly scan the room from the long bar to the entrances and the mirrored walls.

By the time the fourth song ended, Macey was damp with perspiration and joyously out of breath. Her feet hurt, but she didn't care. She was glad she'd recently had her hair cut short in the new bob style that went just past her jaw, because it kept her cooler. It occurred to her the bespectacled David might not even recognize her if he did show up, since she'd had all of her hair cut off.

Ready for something cold and wet, Macey left the dance floor, giving Flora a little wave. As she made her way through the rows of tables crowded together, she felt someone watching her. It was like a cool breeze over the back of her neck, raising the fine hairs there in an insistent prickle.

With a little bump of her heart and a flutter in her belly, she changed direction, walking over to the long bar. Leaning against the counter, she looked casually around the room as she ordered a strawberry lemonade.

She didn't see David's reddish-blond hair and was ready to return to the table when someone jostled her from behind.

"Looking for a vampire?" came a voice in her ear.

Macey's stomach flipped in surprise as her cheeks flamed with chagrin. She whirled to find Grady sitting on a bar stool behind her. "No," was her unimaginative retort as her brain scrambled to catch up to reality. Where had he come from? She'd been watching the entire place.

"Good." His expression was sober, and now that he wasn't wearing a hat, she saw his hair was a rich sable brown. Cut short around the ears and neck, it was deliciously wavy and thick at the crown. He'd shaved since yesterday, but his fingers—which drummed impatiently on the bar—were still ink-stained.

Her cheeks had cooled by now, and Macey made a swift decision to sit on the stool next to Grady instead of going back to her table. She didn't want him to think he'd scared her away, especially since she'd fairly run off yesterday.

"Are you with the fuzz?" She leaned her elbows on the counter and looked at him. He had a solid, square jaw and elegant nose. His was a very good-looking face.

Grady's eyes, which had taken to scanning the room, settled back on her. There was a trace of impatience in them. "No, chickie, I told you—you've got nothing to worry about from me. If you're wanting to go through that mirrored door back there—the one that's not as much of a secret as Hownley-Joe thinks it is—and sample some of Capone's hooch, I won't be telling anyone."

"That's not why I asked," she replied, refusing to allow him to annoy her. The man seemed to have a chip the size of the tragic Titanic on his shoulder, and something compelled her to find out why. "You seemed well-informed about Jennie Fallon, and you greeted that officer by name yesterday. I thought you might be a plainclothes detective or something like that." She shrugged and noticed the way his attention followed her movement. She could feel his gaze sliding over her bare shoulders, and a warm tingle shivered through her belly.

"You do know what they say about the cat and curiosity, don't you, chickie?"

"Is that a threat?" she asked, keeping her voice light even as her heart started to pound a little harder. For the first time, she wondered if he knew so much about Jennie Fallon because *he* was involved. He could be a gangster. Or a rapist. Maybe she should go back to her table and forget she'd ever met Grady.

If you could call their interactions "meeting."

He shook his head. "I'm not with the fuzz, lass. That was my uncle yesterday, if you must know. It seems as if you might be as inquisitive as I am, so I suppose I can't be faulting you for that." His eyes met hers, and Macey felt her concerns ease. Possibly in part because of the lovely rhythm of his brogue and the crinkles at the corners of his eyes. "I'm a newshawk for the *Tribune*, so naturally I have an interest in news in the city. Good news or tragic news," he added ruefully. "Like Jennie Fallon."

"I haven't been able to stop thinking about her," Macey confessed. That, along with three nights of dreams about vampires chasing her, had made her feel even more jumpy and nervous than when she heard machine guns in the distance.

"Can I get you something?" asked the bartender, approaching them for the first time.

Grady grimaced. "Sure and I wish you could. You don't have what I want."

"Welcome to the club." The bartender set a short, heavy glass on the counter.

"That's flat." Grady met the bartender's eyes. He gave a brief nod, then returned to looking around the room.

Macey slid off her stool. Obviously, their conversation was over.

But she hadn't taken one step when those ink-stained fingers reached out and landed on her bare arm. "So why did you say that yesterday?" Grady leaned toward her.

He came close enough that his shoulder bumped her bare one, and an intriguing, masculine scent came with him. She almost replied *Said what?* but caught herself in time. Edging away so she could look at him, she answered as honestly as she could. "I was reading a book about vampires, and they were on my mind. That's all. It just slipped out." She sat back on her stool, the fringe from her dress shifting and sliding into place.

"Do you believe they exist?" He watched her steadily.

"Of course not." But even as she said so, that little prickling at the back of her neck grew stronger. Discomfited, Macey twisted in her seat, looking over her shoulder at the jumble of people in the club.

Her breath caught when she spied the glimpse of someone in the shadows...the flash of a face that seemed familiar, that reminded her of someone...but then he was gone, slipping behind a decorative pillar and then into the crowd.

"What's wrong?" Grady craned his neck to look as well.

Macey turned back and tucked her curly, bobbed hair behind her ear. "I thought I saw someone I knew." Why was her heart thumping so hard? "I've got to stop reading that book."

"The book about vampires?"

She noticed he was holding that heavy, short glass in his hand. It was filled with an amber liquid, and as Macey watched in shock, Grady tilted his wrist and tipped the contents into his mouth with a practiced flick, then swallowed.

"But that's—that's—" *Whiskey*. He was drinking *whiskey*! She could even smell it. Macey exhaled in a big huff, for she dared not say the word for fear she'd be overheard.

"Apple juice?" He was looking at her with a bemused expression. "What's wrong, chickie? Cat got your tongue?" He placed the glass on the counter, and it disappeared just as quickly as it had been filled.

"What would your uncle say?" she managed to sputter.

His eyes lit with real humor for the first time, and he laughed. "You surely don't know much about how this city's run, do you, lass?" Then his good humor dissipated, and that sober expression returned. "You must be reading *Dracula*."

Macey lifted her chin. "Of course that. Excellent book, but much too obvious."

His lips twitched briefly. "*The Vampyre* by Polidori."

"No," Macey replied, even as he added, "But that's not precisely a book. Just a story. You distinctly said 'book.'"

"And so is *Varney the Vampire*," she said, surprised he was so familiar with vampire literature. "Which I am also not reading. Currently."

"Thank Jesus," he replied. "What a piece of drivel that was."

Privately, Macey didn't disagree—but as a librarian at heart, she felt it was inappropriate for her to publicly criticize any literature.

Instead, she looked over at the musicians and saw the Negro woman she'd noticed earlier was now standing at the microphone, singing to the accompaniment of the piano. The low croon of the saxophone mingled with her dusky voice, and everything seemed to slow and quiet. Even the lights dimmed.

"I suppose you're wanting to dance," Grady said. "That's not a bad idea, chickie. At least then I can see what's going on from down there." He stood and turned to her expectantly.

She looked up but made no move to join him. He might be attractive as sin, and he might have the smoothest, most velvety voice and the thickest head of wavy cocoa hair, but the man was bordering on being a complete jerk.

"My name is not chickie or lass, and I don't have any desire to dance. With you. Thank you anyway, Grady." She stressed his name just enough to point out that she did, indeed, know it.

"And you clearly have the advantage of me, then, don't you? Knowing my name and all, my profession too. Clever girl," he said, nodding. A little smile played about his mouth and there was a hint of crinkles at the corners of his eyes. "And I don't know a thing about you except that you read about vampires and believe they exist. Oh, and you wear shoes that are too tight and cause blisters. You're very literate but not so great at math, live in or near Hyde Park, and don't have a boyfriend."

She blinked. How did he know all that? "I don't believe in vampires." Macey slid off the stool. Despite her heels, that only put her eyes at about the level of his nose.

"Is that so?" His gaze scored over her again. "Then you'd best be taking my advice to stay out of dark alleys at night. It's hard to protect yourself from something you don't believe exists."

She started to slide past him, but he stepped to the side, half blocking her path. "Aren't you going to tell me your name?"

"Can't you find that out on your own? You figured out plenty of other things."

His smile returned. "I could, but it's easier to ask. And I'd like to think of you as someone other than 'chickie' later tonight… when I'm remembering those velvety brown eyes of yours." His voice had gone silky again, thick with the Irish.

"It's Macey." With a quick shift to the side, she went around him and walked away, trying not to imagine Grady lying in his bed thinking of her *eyes*. Trying not to imagine Grady in his bed at all, in fact.

But it wasn't an altogether awful thought, she admitted privately, wending her way toward the table she and Flora shared. He did have broad shoulders and probably a very fine chest attached to them. And his mouth, the way it tipped up at one side when he was debating vampire literature with her, and slightly fuller in the bottom lip, was a very tempting shape.

Macey was about halfway to her destination when the music stopped abruptly, and most of the lights went out. Someone gave a surprised little shriek, and a hush fell over the club as everyone stopped.

Then all at once, shadowy figures burst into the room and everything turned to chaos. "Raid!" someone shouted.

People were running, pushing, and screaming, and Macey felt someone brush past her. Another person shoved her, and someone else stepped on her foot as she started to make her way toward one of the exits.

The club was lit with a dull brown illumination by the few lights that burned near the entrance. Everyone was shadowy and muted, and Macey, with her imagination running wild, even fancied she saw the faint glow of red in twin pairs. Like eyes.

It was the first police raid she'd ever experienced, and even though she'd done nothing wrong, her heart was slamming in her chest. That prickling chill washed over the back of her neck again, colder and stronger now, as if someone had left a door open to a winter's night. She felt almost nauseated by it, unsettled and upset.

There was an awful scream, suddenly choked off in a sort of gurgle that had the hair rising all over her body. Then a soft, ugly sound that seemed to fill her ears—*kuh-kuh-kuh*—like someone drinking.

She didn't want to know what was happening.

Her hands clammy and her insides upset and churning, she waited for the sounds of gunshots or the *stt-stt-stt* of machine gun fire. Why hadn't they brought Jimmy tonight?

"Flora!" she called, knowing it was in vain—there was too much going on, too many people shouting and shrieking. The last time she'd seen her friend, she'd been on the other side of the dance floor. "*Flora!*"

More screaming. More shouting. More awful, ugly gurgling, suctioning sounds. People pounding on the walls, or doors, on the floor…

She became aware of an odd smell, earthy and pungent— like…*blood?* Macey went cold and weak. Then someone else screamed long and shrilly, the cry ringing in her ears. She again saw twin flashes of red and watched as one of the shadowy figures seemed to fly across the room.

This was not a police raid. Or gangsters.

Icy fingers seemed to curl around her heart and lungs. She froze behind a pillar, her heart pounding. Red eyes. Superhuman speed. *Blood.*

Vampires?

No, no, impossible. Imposs—

Someone grabbed her arm, and Macey shrieked, jolting in surprise. She whirled, hopeful and yet terrified. But it wasn't Flora, and it wasn't Grady. In the dim light, she saw it was the elegant Negro woman who'd been watching the place.

"This way." The woman tugged at her arm. "Hurry. Hurry!"

Macey had no argument with that, and she stopped pulling and allowed the woman to direct her toward the back wall.

Her companion was tall and quick, and very agile, and Macey found herself stumbling as she rushed along with her. She crouched as low as she could, as if that might keep the…whatever they were from seeing her. Nor did she ask where they were going. She just followed.

The next thing she knew, her guide had led her into a dark corner, and all at once the wall moved. Macey followed her into a dark room, suddenly nervous.

"Move it," said her guide, as if sensing her hesitation. "They can smell you."

Macey swallowed back the question that rose to her lips as the wall moved back into place behind them. The other woman knew where to go, despite the darkness. They rushed along until suddenly there was cool, clean, crisp night air as they erupted into a back alley lit by stars and a waning moon.

When Macey would have paused to drag in her breath, the tall, caramel-skinned woman refused to let her. "Come, it's not safe yet," she said in her throaty voice, propelling her through the alley.

"But what about the people still inside?" Macey turned to go back. She couldn't leave without Flora, and what about Grady? And Chelle and Dottie—

"They're either safe, or it's too late by now. They'll be out after you as soon as they realize you've escaped."

Macey shook her head, trying to understand the woman's confusing speech. Obviously, the two "theys" referred to two different sets of people, but what did the rest of it mean? "What do you mean, they'll be out after…*me?*" Her throat went dry and her stomach heaved. "What are you talking about?"

This gave the woman pause, and for the first time, she stopped and looked at Macey. "You don't know?"

"Know *what?*" she demanded.

"Lordy Moses," breathed her companion, shaking her head. "This is going to be worse than I thought. Come on, sister." She started tugging her again.

"I'm not going anywhere until you tell me what's happening."

"For Christ's sake, Temple, just pick her up and carry her. She's only a bitty thing. Vioget's going to be bloody damned fit to be tied if he has to wait any longer." A voice from the shadows caused Macey's stomach to plummet, and she whirled.

"Chas. What are you doing here?" demanded the Negro woman, whose name was obviously Temple. She didn't sound very pleased.

A figure emerged from the darkness like a wraith. He was tall, wrapped in some enveloping dark coat with a hat and high collar that obstructed most of his face. All Macey saw was a flash in the moonlight of straight white teeth.

For a moment, she imagined they were fangs, and Macey smothered a shriek as she stepped back. Then, annoyed, she collected herself and shook away the absurd thought.

He chuckled, his laugh soft and low in the night. "Ah, I'm everywhere. You know that, Temple. Now get Macey out of here before they find her."

As if his warning had conjured them, suddenly the door through which she and Temple had emerged reopened.

"Run!" he hissed, and Macey didn't have the chance to argue as Temple grabbed her arm and towed her off down the alley.

A quick glance over her shoulder showed the man standing in the alley facing their pursuers, his coat flapping gently in the breeze.

He was holding something that looked like a wooden stake.

And somehow, he knew her name.

Two

The Silver Chalice

T EMPLE DIDN'T RELEASE MACEY'S ARM as she ran down
an alley and around the corner. Somehow, though she had
much shorter legs, Macey managed to easily keep pace with her.

But she wasn't thinking about the fact that she was running
at full speed in her chunky heeled shoes, the beaded layers on her
dress bouncing and swaying. She was remembering the horror of
the raid in The Gyro and the silhouette of the cloaked stranger in
the alleyway. He'd been holding a stake, she was sure of it.

"This way," Temple said when they burst out of another alley
onto Vashner.

But Macey stopped and pulled free of the other woman's grip.
They were on a busy street with lights and automobiles and even
a few people—although most of them looked too busy to help a
young woman in distress.

"Who are you, and where are we going?" Macey panted. She
glanced behind to see if any of their pursuers had followed them,
but the alley was dark and empty of everything but mounds of
trash.

Temple was breathing hard, and her skin shone faintly in the
moonlight. "It's very complicated. I thought—we thought you
knew. Didn't you get the book?" She was looking around, peering
down the alley. "And what about the dreams?"

"I don't have any idea what you're talking about. I think you
have me confused with someone else."

"No, I definitely don't have you confused with anyone," Temple said with a short laugh. She'd caught her breath by now. "And if I had any doubt, tonight clinched it. You're Macey Gardella, and I'm taking you to The Silver Chalice. That's the only place you'll be safe."

Macey took another step back, her heart pounding. This was screwy. Not only was the woman the second person to think she was named Gardella, but also weirdly enough, The Silver Chalice had been mentioned in *The Venator*. It was a pub in London, or so she'd gathered. "You've got the wrong person. My name isn't Macey Gardella. So I'm going to be leaving now," she said, looking around for a cab.

Temple blew out a long, irritated breath. "Look, I'm not about to get myself flayed by the likes of Sebastian Vioget—although there are other things I wouldn't mind that man doing to me… not at all. If you get my drift. But that's neither here nor there. My job was to deliver you to him and keep you safe from the Guardians they sent after you tonight. And so far, so good, thanks to Chas. But I'm not about to shirk my job—"

"I don't know what kind of line you're trying to hand me, but I'm not Macey Gardella. My name is Macey *Denton*, and I don't know who Mr. Vioget is or Chas or who the Guardians are. And I'm just going to go home now. It's been a long night."

"You *can't go home*." Temple was obviously beyond frustrated, and while Macey felt bad for her because it sounded as if this Sebastian Vioget wasn't a very nice person, she was tired and more than a little frightened from her experience in The Gyro. "It's too dangerous. They're probably already there, waiting for you. I don't think any of them know me yet, which is why Sebastian sent me after you, but if any of them made it past Chas, word'll be out before dawn." She shook her head in irritation. "I told you this was complicated, and I'm not the best one to explain things to you—I just got here a week ago from New Orleans. Come with me to the Chalice and let Sebastian tell you about it. And if you still don't believe it, then it's his problem. Not mine."

This woman is cracked in the head. Macey wanted to take off running, yet there was something deep inside that made her stay and listen. Maybe if she went and met this Mr. Vioget she'd be able to clear up the mistake, and they'd all leave her alone. And the fact of the matter was, the memories from the raid—the ugly sounds and smells—still made her feel queasy.

If there was any chance those red-eyed creatures (she refused to think they might truly be vampires) thought *she* was Macey Gardella—whoever that was—and they were waiting for her at home … well, it would be best to clear all of this up sooner rather than later.

"All right. I'll go to The Silver Chalice with you."

"Then let's go," Temple said, irritation in her voice. "It's still two hours till dawn—plenty of time for them to find us."

Macey followed the tall, dark woman as she led the way through alleys and along busy streets, wondering how she knew her route so well if she'd just arrived in town. But then she noticed Temple glancing up at the moon and stars, and peering at street signs, and realized the woman was carefully navigating her way. And for all Macey knew, they could have been going in circles.

"Here it is," Temple said at last.

Macey looked around and saw a few disreputable looking buildings with dark windows and shaggy signage, a butcher shop, and something that looked like a pawnshop.

"Are you coming?" her companion asked, her hand settling on a wrought iron railing in front of the butcher shop. "It's down here."

Macey saw the railing enclosed a staircase that led from the street level down into a dark space, and she stepped back. "Down there? Are you looney? I'm not going down into the dark. That doesn't look like a pub to me." Now her hands were clammy and it occurred to her that maybe this woman *wasn't* her friend, and that she'd helped her escape from the raid for her own nefarious purposes. She began to edge away, wishing she'd not followed a screwball woman into this dark, deserted part of town.

What the hell had she been thinking?

Temple muttered something under her breath, then jabbed a finger at the railing. "See? The Silver Chalice."

And then Macey recognized the ornament on top of the railing's newel post, gleaming dully in the moonlight. The finial was, indeed, a silver chalice—unnoticeable unless one was looking for it. Since she still wasn't wholly convinced, she walked to the railing and looked over, down into the darkness. She realized she could hear noise coming from there, and then a door opened far below, spilling light into the cavernous stairway.

"Temple! What the bloody hell are you doing standing up there? Are you coming down or not?" The voice wasn't as angry as its words sounded, and it was slightly accented with a European flavor—a little French mixed in with a little British. "Do you have her?"

"I have her all right," she replied grumpily. "But she's a little hesitant to go down into dark places. I don't know how the bejesus she's gonna be a Venator if she won't go into dark places."

A *Venator*?

Macey's heart stopped and she let go of the railing, backing away. Even though the night air was still, a chill breeze swept over her shoulders and lifted the hair at the back of her neck. Little prickles settled there, cool and irritating. This was getting too strange. It was time to leave. If they thought she was a Venator, they were sadly mistaken. It was impossible, anyway. She wasn't a Gardella, vampires didn't exist, and thus there was no such thing as a Venator.

Even if they did, *she* wasn't equipped to fight the superhumanly strong demonic creatures. She could hardly lift a case of books!

But before Macey could leave, a man appeared before her. Well, he didn't exactly appear, but he came up the steps more quickly than a man should be able to move. Almost as if he *flew*. Or jumped.

"Sebastian Vioget." He gave a little bow. "At your service, my lady." Even in the faulty light, she could feel the weight of his gaze scoring over her.

"Thank God," murmured Temple, starting past him down the stairs on her long legs. Then she paused, looking up at the man whose features were too shadowy to see clearly. "I hope you've got something for me to drink down there that won't send me to the grave."

"Be my guest." His mellow, silky voice was tinged with a little French. "Macey Gardella," he said, his attention never having left her. "There is no doubting it—even if I had, now that I've seen you I know there's no doubt about it. Come below, please, *cherie*, so we can talk. It's not safe for you to be so visible out here. At least, not yet."

His tone and demeanor were compelling and warm, and Macey felt a little tug deep inside her as their eyes met. She thought she saw the glint of red in his gaze, but it was brief and she was so discomfited by everything that had happened tonight she dismissed it as another fanciful moment.

"I told Temple, my name isn't Macey Gardella." She tore her eyes away from where they seemed to be captured by his. "There's some mistake."

"No," he said, smiling broadly now, as if she'd done something unexpected and miraculous. "Oh, there is definitely no mistake. Now come below, *ma cherie*, for I have other things to attend to."

Again, she felt that compelling tug deep inside her—right in the center of her chest, luring her closer, coaxing her to step down into that darkness. And again, she tore her eyes away, aware of her heart beating harder and her breathing coming faster. "No." But she moved slowly toward the top of the stairs. He stood waiting, hand outstretched for hers.

When she got close enough, Macey took a deep breath and instead of taking his hand, she gave Mr. Vioget a great shove. Taken by surprise, he toppled backward, tumbling down into the darkness. At the same time, she turned and was running, running away, faster than she could ever remember running in her life.

Nevertheless, she heard his exclamation of irritation and surprise in her wake. It sounded as if he shouted something like "*Victoria.*"

✝

Macey didn't know where she was or how to get home, but fortune smiled upon her and presented a taxi cab that returned her to her apartment. She rented a one-room flat with kitchenette and full bath on the third floor of a large house. She'd lost her small pocketbook sometime during the night, most likely during the raid, and so she had to go inside to get money to pay the driver.

It was with great trepidation that she crept up the stairs to her flat, Temple's warning ringing in her ears. *You can't go home. They're probably already there, waiting for you.*

Heart thudding, stomach stirring unpleasantly, she went slowly and quietly, listening and watching for she wasn't certain whom—or what. But when she got to her door and unlocked it, holding her breath and waiting to see if some horrible fate awaited her, Macey found her efficiency apartment just as she'd left it: a lamp burning low, a few items of clothing strewn about, a cup on the counter in the kitchen area. The room was silent and empty as a tomb.

Nevertheless, she had the instinct to wait a moment, to listen and to…*feel*…whether she sensed anyone—or anything— present. Just like the Venators in the book, she thought with a nervous smile. If Temple and Sebastian thought she was one, she might as well act like one.

When it seemed obvious no threat awaited her, she made her way to the small box on her bureau and extricated a few bills for the cab, then rushed back down to pay the driver. Then, at nearly three o'clock in the morning, she trudged back up the steps to her living quarters and bolted the door behind her.

It took only a few moments to make certain all the windows in her one-room apartment were closed and locked. Fortunately, it was only April, and it was still cool. But even if it were the height of summer in July, she would have kept the windows shut.

Then, her thoughts in turmoil, her feet throbbing from all of the running in heels, and her pulse leaping at every sound or shadow, Macey climbed into bed.

Temple was wrong. She had a moment of wry amusement, followed by relief borne from logic. *I'm perfectly safe here. There's no one after me.*

She closed her eyes, her mind whirling with memories and information from the night.

Had there really been vampires at The Gyro?

Absurd. Ridiculous.

She shook her head in irritation, and in the darkness, she willed her body to relax, her thoughts to stop spinning, and prepared to slide into repose.

But what about Flora? What if she'd been injured in the raid? Macey drew in a deep breath. There was nothing she could do now, but first thing in the morning, she'd go down and beg Mrs. Gutchinson to use her phone and call. Just to make sure Flora was all right.

Macey drew in another long, slow breath and closed her eyes.

Just then, an eerie chill brushed over her shoulders, raising the hair at the nape of her neck. Macey's eyes popped open and her heart began pounding. Her insides churned because she was lying on her back and the window was closed. There was nowhere for a breeze to come, stirring the air.

And she'd felt that odd prickling feeling earlier tonight, at The Gyro. Just before the raid.

Like a sign of approaching evil.

Her palms grew clammy, and her throat went dry. Macey lay there, staring up into darkness, willing herself into sleep.

But her eyes were wide open, unable to blink, and she couldn't dismiss the uncomfortable chill over the back of her neck.

Slowly she sat up, her heart pounding, her palms clammy and her insides in turmoil. Breathing shallowly, she looked around for something…for a weapon.

Why do I need a weapon?

The night was silent but for the distant city sounds, along with a cat's yowl. Still, she couldn't dismiss the thought that she needed a weapon. Her eyes lighted on the baseball bat she kept behind the door. Jimmy had told her it was the best thing for a young woman living alone.

The chill persisted, growing even stronger and more eerie. Silence settled heavily, expectantly, over the world. Macey's eyes darted around the room, to the bolted window, to her door…

She leapt out of bed and dashed across the rug-covered hardwood floor, snatching up the baseball bat. Then, crouching there in the dark corner, she waited, heart pounding, listening and…waiting. Just waiting.

Nothing. She heard nothing.

Macey forced herself to breathe again, even emitting a short, derisive laugh for her nerves. Then she looked over at the window next to her bed and screamed.

There was a face there, dark, shadowy…and with burning pinkish-red eyes.

Three

A Shattered Broomstick

For a moment, Macey was paralyzed, pinned in place by the glowing eyes of the face at the window.

Glowing *red* eyes.

Vampire eyes.

She shook her head violently, as if to dislodge the absurd thought, even as another part of her mind registered the baseball bat in her hands—heavy, solid…the way her bare feet staggered across the cold hardwood floor—toward the door…and the leering face at the window. With long, white fangs, fully exposed, gleaming like small ivory daggers.

The glass separating them shattered, vaulting Macey into full motion. Choking back a scream, she stumbled past the tiny kitchen table toward the door, banging into the umbrella stand on the way, then fumbling with the deadbolt she'd just slid home.

But all at once, he was there. Behind her. The chill at the back of her neck turned sharp and icy. The hairs there lifted, as if in anticipation of fangs sinking into her skin. Macey stifled another shriek as she spun, swinging the bat toward him with all her strength.

It connected with his face, smashing into his cheek with such force that his head snapped aside. He reeled back in surprise, hands flailing. Macey attacked again, this time jabbing the bat viciously toward his midsection. She caught him at the side of the torso and sent him stumbling back against the bed.

By now his eyes glowed a light ruby pink, blazing with fury, and he rolled to his feet as she staggered away.

The door. Get to the door.

Macey tripped and surged against the wall, knocking over the old broom and tipping the trashcan onto its side. Scrambling to her feet, she flung the metal can up and at him as the vampire leapt toward her. It clanged into his arm, and she barely dodged his grasping hand as she rolled away.

A stake.

The words blazed into her mind. *A stake. Find a wooden stake.*

He came at her again, and now she was trapped in a corner of the small kitchen area with nothing but a baseball bat. Trash littered the floor, and the broomstick rolled under her palm as Macey tried to spring to her feet.

Broomstick.

Slender. Wooden.

The thought crystallized in her mind with shocking force, shoving itself through the terror that nearly paralyzed her. As the vampire lunged toward her, she swung the bat once more, but it was in such close quarters that she had little room to put force behind it. Her weapon slammed against his shoulder, and he hardly seemed to notice it.

His fingers curled around her arm, yanking her up and off the floor. Macey's bare feet scrabbled helplessly, brushing against his trousers and the cool tiled area.

But she had the broomstick in her hand. The old, round-tipped broom.

Not a stake. Not yet.

Her heart surged into her throat, filling it, along with a scream, as he pushed her back against the wall. One clawing hand grasped the hair at her temple while the other pressed against her chest, holding her there immobile.

She smelled heat and sweat from the creature, and the pink-red eyes burned bright and hypnotic as he bent closer to her. A little hum of pleasure came from deep in his throat. Her pulse was rampant, surging through her veins, making her head light and her body hot.

"Venator." He smoothed one hand over her throat, holding her by a clump of hair with the other. "I have so longed for a taste of the Gardella blood." He smiled, running a tongue over the tips of his fangs, his lips full and glistening.

Macey still clutched the broom and used every bit of strength to keep her gaze from being captured by his. Instead, she focused— not on how close he was, not on the strong, sharp fingers digging into her skull, not on the slender hand sweeping over the flesh exposed by her nightgown…but on the broomstick.

She felt around it with her foot, finding the broom's bristly bottom, closing her eyes so she could picture it…shutting herself off from the hands, the fingers, the hot breath that spread over her sensitive skin. He yanked her head to the side, pulling it toward one shoulder so far she couldn't hold back a moan. Her neck was exposed and she felt his hot breath on her skin. Closing her eyes, she moved one foot up along the length of the broom.

"Now," he said, and she felt something warm and slick on her neck. Her body lurched with revulsion, and evil things began to crawl over her flesh as he used his tongue to trace the tendon on the side of her throat.

Macey squeezed her eyes shut tighter, closed her fingers on the slender wooden handle, and pictured the position of her foot. It took all her effort not to buck and twist, trying to fight him off. Instead, she battled away the sensation of her attacker's lips, the suffocating grip on her head, her chest…and under the guise of trying to kick him, she slammed her heel down against the broomstick.

It was old. Thank God it was old. And it broke.

She had a stake.

He was forcing her tighter against the wall, pushing his body against hers, pinning her like the butterfly specimens in the museum. His fingers firm, his breathing heavy and hard, filling her ears. Her world swam. The tower weakened. Heat licked at her neck.

Then all at once…*pain.*

Warmth, and pain, and…a burst of release. Something hot and ugly flowed from her, surged free, and Macey felt her lifeblood draining, drawn into the hot, slick mouth that covered her neck and pierced her flesh. It was a dark insidious *pleasure* that made her insides roil and her pulse trammel, and yet it was lush and dark, beckoning to her to slip back…to enjoy, to allow…

Enjoy. Relax. *Submit.*

The stake.

The voice was back in her head, strong, urgent, insistent. *Be strong.* Macey's knees trembled and her head was swimming, but the words were clear. Urgency swarmed her and she dragged herself from the dark, deep well. She focused on the slender, jagged wood in her hand.

Help me.

Help me.

Something surged through her, some strength and energy she didn't know she possessed, and all at once she could *move.* Macey raised her arm, pulling it free from behind her, and with a cry, she slammed it over and down. The point penetrated the vampire's back with sickening ease.

He jolted into paralysis, gave a little hiss, and then all at once…he *exploded.*

Poofed. Into foul-smelling ash.

He was gone. Just like that.

Macey let the stake fall from a trembling hand and looked around. There was nothing. No one.

Nothing but a scattering of dust.

Her knees gave way and she sank to the floor, trembling and nauseated, gasping for air. Her nose and mouth were filled with the scent of old, moldering ash, and she felt the grit under her fingers. The rapid sound of her breathing and the slamming of her heart filled her ears, chasing away the internal roaring that had blocked all sound from the moment she saw the glowing red eyes.

Reaching for the stake, Macey closed her fingers around it and staggered to her feet. Cold, gray moonlight filtered over the room, and a gentle breeze fluttered the curtains at the broken window. In the distance, beyond the jagged cityscape, she saw the faint gray of dawn lightening the lower portion of sky.

The night was so still. So silent.

Had no one heard her struggles? Had no one heard her scream? Surely Mrs. Gutchinson, who lived below, would have been awakened by the battle. Or the Duchovny couple, who were on the same floor.

But no one had come.

She was alone.

Macey leaned against the counter. Cold settled over her: the chill of solitude, of loneliness. Pain throbbed in her neck. When she reached to touch the wound, her fingers came away glistening with blood.

Blood.

Bile surged in her belly. The creature had *fed* on her. Had drunk from her veins, violating her with his odd lips that were cold and warm at the same time. He attacked her with his tongue and fangs. At the memory, her vision tipped and wavered with shadow. Macey squeezed her eyes closed and breathed deeply, curling her fingers deep into her palms, still gripping the stake.

No. I survived.

Her eyes flew open, determined. She looked around her small living quarters, seeing the space with different eyes. It was no longer her cozy sanctuary, but it was still a symbol of her independence. She'd defended it. And herself.

Her gaze fell on the old book, still sitting on her nightstand. A rush of clammy heat, like fever, surprised her. *The Venator.* The vampire hunter. She felt lightheaded and dizzy.

Macey reached to touch the side of her neck again, feeling four small bumps beneath sticky, iron-scented blood. Still staring at the book, she tottered over to her bureau and scrabbled through the small jewelry box, feeling around for…yes. There it was.

She pulled it out—a rosary she'd been given by an old lady as she walked by Old St. Patrick's Church just last week. She checked: yes, it had a cross on it. A big silver one, dangling from the end.

Glancing at the book as if for confirmation, Macey walked over to the shattered window, skirting the shards of glass with her bare feet. She arranged the holy object on the unfettered windowsill, ignoring the drop of blood that fell onto the white paint.

She was safe.

She curled up on the bed, wrapping her arms around her legs like a small shield, and stared into the waning darkness.

She was safe, but she'd never felt so alone.

"You didn't get there in time? How the bloody hell could it be that you *weren't there in time*?" Sebastian barely controlled himself from lunging across the counter and grabbing Woodmore by the throat. His vision tinged red and he curled his fingers into the sleek mahogany bar as he forced his breathing to slow and his fangs to retract.

If something happened to Macey Gardella, everything he'd sacrificed over the last century would be for naught. *Everything.*

Chas Woodmore, his features obscured as always by the shadow of his low-riding fedora and the high collar of his trenchcoat, rested a gloved hand on the bar. "She's alive and well," he told Sebastian in a mild but unrepentant voice. "If she'd needed help, I would have interfered. But you know as well as I do a Venator must slay his—or her—first vampire unaided before being considered worthy to receive the *vis bulla*. I simply gave her that opportunity."

"By allowing a Guardian vampire to get past on *your watch*," Sebastian replied evenly. "Such a convenient excuse, but I suspect that only happened because you were otherwise distracted, *non, mon ami*?" He found and held the other man's gaze. "Too long at the damned club, weren't you?"

The other man's dark eyes flashed, then turned flat and cold as he eased back. "If you want my assistance, Vioget, you'll get it in the manner I choose. If you don't care for my methods, then you can—"

"I see now that dawn has broken," said a voice flavored with Creole, "all the entertainment has moved in here. And I thought The Silver Chalice closed when the sun came up."

Sebastian glanced over at Temple as she strode across the room. Her heavy, chunky heels clunked purposefully on the wooden floor as the interior door slammed closed behind her. She'd come from one of the freight tunnels rather than street level. She met his eyes, unmistakable invitation lingering in their coffee-colored depths, and he smoothly pulled his gaze away. She was lovely. Elegant. An amazing specimen of woman.

Sebastian didn't normally like to mix business with pleasure, but in this case, he might make an exception. And he could, without fear. Temple was lovely, but she wasn't Giulia.

"The entertainment is long done, Temple," Chas said sharply, pushing away from the bar with a violent gesture that revealed a flash of skin between glove and sleeve. Sebastian wasn't surprised to see a small, crusty wound in that brief moment and he drew in a long, deep breath.

Everyone had their own demons. Some of them just weren't as visible as fangs and red eyes.

And copper rings.

"Is Macey here, then?" asked Temple, positioning herself between Chas and the exit. "I'll see to her—"

"No," said Sebastian in a carefully modulated voice. "Macey Gardella isn't here. She remains at her flat, I believe. Alone. Unprotected, and—"

"Surrounded by the dust of an undead," Chas finished, striding smoothly past Temple. "That she staked herself."

"She did? With no training? Fancy! Then she's ready to—"

"One can hope," Sebastian interrupted, and the ever-present rings on his hand glinted, "that now she'll be more interested in listening to what I have to tell her, yes, but I suspect she's inherited more than a bit of stubbornness and independence from her great-great-grandmother. It might not be quite as simple as we might think."

A reluctant smile tugged at his lips. When Macey turned on him, pretending to acquiesce to his invitation to enter The Silver Chalice before shoving him down the stairs, her expression had been very much like one Victoria would have worn: determined, annoyed, and more than a little arrogant.

The arrogance, Sebastian acknowledged as his smile faded, would have been Max Pesaro's contribution to the family line.

"Since we can't be certain when—or whether—to expect Macey Gardella, perhaps it would be prudent for both of you to venture out into the day to determine whether Count Alvisi is aware that he's lost one of his Guardians."

"How do you know it was Alvisi's and not Nicholas Iscariot's?" asked Temple. "Or both?"

Chas snorted. "Alvisi and Iscariot hate each other. They wouldn't cooperate on anything—even this."

"So you'll visit the club to see if there's any news?" Sebastian said to him.

"It would be my pleasure." Chas was already at the door.

Sebastian narrowed his eyes. "I'd express my gratitude for your assistance so far, but I'm not convinced you did anything particularly beneficial."

"I did find out Capone hasn't been turned. Yet. He's still as mortal as you and—well, as I." Chas's smile was bland.

"Ah. Well, then, I cannot fault you for your other transgressions," Sebastian said, making no effort to hide his sarcasm.

Chas cast the low rumble of a chuckle over his shoulder as he slipped out the door, striding into a pool of faint yellow daylight.

Sunshine. A place Sebastian had long ago forgotten.

Four

The Grim Reality of Day

MACEY DIDN'T EXPECT TO SLEEP. But she must have done so, for all at once, she opened her eyes and found bold, hot sun streaming through the window.

The events of the night before were uppermost in her mind, and she realized she was still holding the stake. As she looked down at it, rolling it in her fingers, a chill washed over her. *I killed someone with this.*

I took a life.

Macey squeezed her eyes closed and tried to block the memories of the attack, of the pinkish eyes and grasping hands, the pain…the desperation as she lashed out. When she opened them, once again her attention fell on the stake. She saw for the first time that there was no blood on the jagged end.

She'd driven it into flesh, and there was no blood? A deep, violent shiver took her by surprise. As if it were happening again, she remembered the feeling: shoving that slender wooden pike down through clothing, into skin and muscle and organ. There'd been a brief resistance at first, and then, with a little *pop!* the point slid down deep with sickening ease.

It was like stabbing butter. Macey swallowed hard and looked at the stake again. Clean.

Something shiny drew her attention to the window. The rosary, its holy beads glinting in the light, was still arranged carefully on the windowsill. Whether it had worked for the rest of the waning night as a protective barrier, she'd never know, but Macey decided it was staying there for the foreseeable future. If there was any truth to the stories in *The Venators*, holy objects would repel the undead.

The nagging ache on the side of her neck had Macey rising from the bed on shaky legs. She tottered to the mirror and examined the image reflected there. Her curly jet-black hair was a wild, tousled mop with its blunt ends brushing her chin, covering her ears, and leaving her long, slender neck bare and exposed. Crusty red rivulets curved over the shape of her throat and down over her chest, and she closed her eyes for a moment, grateful it had mostly stopped bleeding.

Didn't people die from vampire bites? Her eyes opened then, wide and large in a pale face as she stared at herself.

"No," she told the reflection firmly. "There are no such things as vampires." Then her shoulders sagged. "Except the one I killed last night." She still couldn't believe it.

It was *impossible*.

But it had happened. She had four puncture marks in her neck and an ash-tinged apartment to prove it. And as if that wasn't enough, the musty, foul smell still lingered, leaving her to wonder if it would ever go away.

Someone rapped loudly at the door of her apartment. Macey whirled, heart pounding. Then she drew in a deep breath. A vampire wasn't going to be knocking on the door of her apartment. Especially in the light of day.

"Macey? Are you in there?" The knocking became more insistent and the vocal tones sharper. "I'm sure I heard you moving around in there. Macey?"

Her landlady, Mrs. Gutchinson, was not only stubborn, but filled with a sense of entitlement in regards to knowing the comings, goings, and habits of her tenants. "I'm coming, Mrs. G." She yanked on an old flannel robe, wrapping the collar high around her neck so as to hide the vampire wounds.

Holding the robe tightly in place, she opened the door to find her landlady peering at her from behind thick glasses. All sharp angles and gangly limbs, Mrs. G stood on the landing of the stairs looking like a near-sighted scarecrow wearing a housedress. "There you are." She arranged herself so as to see behind her tenant and into the one-room apartment, her large-knuckled hand grasping the edge of the doorway.

Macey knew from experience if she moved even a smidge to one side of the entrance or the other, despite her arthritic hip, Mrs. Gutchinson would breeze right into the room faster than a breath of fresh air.

"Where else would I be on a Saturday morning, Mrs. G?" She hoped the odor of exploded vampire flesh wasn't noticeable. Not that the old woman would recognize it, but the last thing she needed was her landlady thinking anything unusual was going on in her apartment.

"I didn't see you last night," Mrs. Gutchinson replied with a note of accusation. "When they came and evacuated us."

"Evacuated you?" Macey blinked.

"Yes. Overnight."

Well, that explained why no one had come to investigate her screams and the sounds of struggle. "What happened?"

"A man came through on as about ten o'clock last night and said as how we all had to vacate the building for the night. He claimed it was a gas main leak, but I'm sure he was lying. I think it was just a cover-up for a gangster shoot-out." Mrs. G leaned closer—either for confidentiality purposes, or to get a better look inside the apartment.

Macey was certain it was the latter, and she tensed a little when her landlady sniffed experimentally. Shifting to block the doorway as much as possible, she replied, "A gas main leak?"

"That's what he said. Once I let him in, he even posted notices on the doors of each apartment. Said we could return after six o'clock in the morning. Now how would they know the leak would be fixed by then?"

Macey didn't find it necessary to mention there'd been no notice on her door. A little shiver ran down her spine.

But Mrs. Gutchinson didn't seem to notice. She waved her large-knuckled hand in Macey's face. "As clean as the nose on my face, it warn't no gas main leak. I didn't smell it, and my nose always knows. I've suspected that man across the street is involved in something illegal since the moment I set eyes on him, and I wager the agents were coming in to arrest him. They didn't want anyone to get caught in the crossfire." The fact that her eyes sparkled behind their heavy glasses suggested she wouldn't have minded being caught in the crossfire at all.

"I see. Well, thank you for the information. I'm sure we'll find out soon enough whether your suspicions are correct. Have a nice day, Mrs. G." She started to close the door and found it blocked by a well-placed black-shoed toe.

She should have known it wouldn't be that easy.

"Late night, I see," Mrs. G said, sniffing as she looked pointedly at her tenant's robe. Macey gripped the collar to hold it high and in place. "Now, you don't have a young man in there, do you, Macey Denton? You know I don't allow those sorts of goings-on here. My Fred would roll over in his grave if he thought there was fornication happening under the roof of his parents' old house!"

"No, Mrs. G, of course I don't have a young man in here." Macey made her expression as innocent as possible.

"It's one thing to go dancing at those music clubs," her landlady barreled on, "or joyriding in those new-fangled closed cars—but drinking spirits and indulging in immoral practices is not to be tolerated." She pointed a finger at Macey. "Do I make myself clear?"

"Yes, ma'am, of course. Thank you so much for checking on me, Mrs. Gutchinson." She began to ease the door closed. Then she remembered. "Oh, could I possibly use your telephone? Flora and I—" She stopped. "There was a fire at the club last night and I lost Flora in the ruckus. Could I call her just to make sure she's gotten home all right? You can add the cost to my rent."

To her surprise, Mrs. G agreed without any further questions or demands. Or maybe the old bat thought she'd find out more information about her tenant by eavesdropping on the phone conversation.

But if that was her plan, it didn't work out. Macey called the main number of Flora's boarding house, and the landlady answered. "Flora? I ain't seen her since yesterday."

Macey's stomach dropped. "Truly? There was a—" She glanced over her shoulder and saw Mrs. G carefully adjusting the figurines in her china cabinet—within close earshot. "There was a fire and we lost each other."

"She mighta come home. She mighta not. She don't always check in with me. But she ain't here now."

That didn't really mean anything, as Macey well knew. Mrs. G might be nosey and directive, but Flora's landlady was mean, and a drunkard who made her own hooch in a basement distillery and hardly remembered what she did or said from one day to the next. Flora did her best to avoid the woman whenever possible. "Would you have her call me or send word if you see her?"

"Call you? On *my* phone? Why, I'm—"

Macey listened to her rant for a few seconds, then hung up the phone. She was still feeling jittery and nervous, but told herself not to worry—at least not yet. Surely if something had happened to Flora, Jimmy would know. He was the next of kin—at least, here in Chicago. He would have come to tell Macey. Maybe Flora was really out looking for a job, like she said she would do today. Or maybe she was just not answering the door to her despised landlady. Macey sighed, trying not to be too concerned. Flora needed more than a job. She needed to move somewhere nicer, with a decent landlady.

"Thanks Mrs. G. I've got to get back upstairs. I was just getting ready to wash up because I have to go into the library today. Dr. Morgan scheduled me overtime," she lied.

The landlady sniffed, but apparently an obligation at her place of employment was a good enough excuse for Macey to leave without further interrogation. "Very well, then. I'll be sure to tell you if anything else happens."

I'm sure you will. "Thank you so much, Mrs. G."

When Macey got back into her flat, she looked longingly at her bed. But sliding back into it wasn't an option. The old bat would be peering out her lace-curtained window (lace allowed for less obvious spying than calico or linen) to make certain Macey actually left for work.

Aside from that, she couldn't stay cloistered in her apartment all day. At the very least she had to try and find out if Flora and Chelle and Dottie were safe. And she had to try and find The Silver Chalice again and speak to Monsieur Vioget. Clearly, there was some mistake about her and who she was, and until she straightened things out, she could be in danger of more terrifying and unwanted visitors.

She just hoped there was a way to put an end to the misunderstanding quickly and permanently.

A short time later, Macey was arranging a white crocheted cloche hat over her mess of short curls when someone knocked on her door.

Flora!

She turned and started toward it, then stopped in the nick of time and spun back to her dressing table.

"Just a minute," she called, snatching up a white scarf that matched her hat. After arranging the scarf to hide the wounds on her neck, she swiped on a bit of pink lipstick. Like most of her generation, Mrs. G didn't approve of rouge or lipstick, but it was a light enough shade so as not to invite criticism. She hoped.

Then Macey picked up her handbag and a light wrap and started to the door. At least if it was Mrs. G, she'd be able to make the excuse she was on her way out and didn't have time to talk.

The knocking had ceased, and when she opened the door, Macey found not only Mrs. Gutchinson on the threshold, but another, completely unexpected visitor.

"Do you know this man?" demanded the landlady.

Grady was standing in front of her door.

"I—uh…" Macey didn't know what to say. *What are you doing here?* was only going to send Mrs. Gutchinson into a tizzy.

"Top of the morning, Miss Denton," he said smoothly, his brogue thicker than she remembered.

He was dressed in a gray coat and vest, stylishly baggy flannel trousers, a white shirt that could use an iron, and black scuffed shoes. The same hat she'd seen on him the first day they met covered his sable hair, tipped back into a more stylish position on his head. His square chin and jaw were dusted with dark stubble, making him look a little disreputable, a little dangerous…and a lot attractive. "I see you're on your way out."

"Indeed I am," she said with as cool a tone as she could muster. Her mind was darting in a myriad of directions: he'd learned her full name *and* address since last night, he hadn't been thrown in jail (or killed) after the raid at The Gyro, he was acting as if they knew each other much better than they did, and he'd washed the ink off his hands.

She wasn't certain whether to be flattered or annoyed he'd tracked her down so easily.

"I could be giving you a lift," he said. "My automobile is parked on the street below."

"Do you know this gentleman?" Mrs. Gutchinson demanded again, casting irritated glares between them. She despised being uninformed. "He says he's from the *Tribune*."

Macey detected conflicting notes of suspicion and interest in her landlady's voice and decided Grady was the lesser of two evils—at least for the moment. He did, after all, have a car. "He's from the *Tribune*," she said, hoping it was true after all, "and he's interviewing me about a new collection we just received at the library. And he's *late*. I expected you thirty minutes ago," she added with a sharp look at him.

"My apologies, Miss Denton." His eyes glinted with humor. "We'd best be leaving, then, so you aren't any more tardy than you already are."

Macey had already pulled her door shut behind her, and she quickly locked it. "Have a nice day, Mrs. G." She started down the steps to the main floor.

Her landlady might have said something, but Macey wasn't waiting to be accosted further, and the sound of their feet clunking down the stairs drowned out Mrs. G's voice.

Once outside, she paused and, of necessity, waited for Grady to indicate which automobile was his. It turned out to be a dark blue Ford Model T, one of the closed models that kept the dust and weather out. It was neatly parked, gleaming in the mid-morning sun.

She looked back and wasn't surprised to see the lace curtain twitching at Mrs. G's window. The elderly woman could certainly move quickly enough when she wanted to. *Nosy thing.*

Grady opened the auto's door and Macey hesitated. She didn't really know this man. And after what had happened last night, she was more than a little apprehensive. Things were all off-kilter.

"My uncle's a cop," Grady said, amusement tingeing his voice. "He'd be about punching my lights out if I so much as ruffled your skirt or mussed your hair."

She gave him an exasperated look. "Only if he knew about it. You could stash my body somewhere in an old house or freight tunnel, and no one would ever know the difference."

He laughed and she climbed into the car, adjusting her scarf to make sure it still hid the vampire bites. And she couldn't help but notice the admiring look he gave her stockinged legs just before he shut the door. Macey smiled to herself.

Settling into his seat, Grady pushed the electric starter in the floor and the car rumbled alive. "Thank Pete we're not having to crank these lousy things anymore." Then, one wrist resting casually on the steering wheel, he turned to look at her. "Where are we going?"

"Harper Library at the university." Her voice was clipped, for she was irritated he'd still given no explanation for his appearance—and didn't seem to have any intention of doing so. And here she was, following his lead with no questions asked. Macey's irritation turned inward. She'd played right into his plans...whatever they were.

Nevertheless, she waited until he started driving before asking, "And…?"

He stopped at an intersection and turned to look at her. "And…you're wanting to know why I'm about showing up on your doorstep today."

"The thought *never* occurred to me. Why, it happens nearly every day that a man I don't even know, and who doesn't even know my name, tracks down my home and appears there, offering to give me a ride somewhere he doesn't even know where I'm going."

Grady chuckled and accelerated the automobile. "I didn't figure you'd be wanting to stand and discuss all this while your hatchet-eyed landlady observed from her window."

"Hatchet-eyed?"

He shrugged. "I'm a writer. Hazard of the trade." The remnants of his smile faded, and he took his eyes off the road just long enough to glance at her. "I was wanting to make certain you'd gotten home all right last night. That was an awful…thing that happened, and I lost track of you in the melee."

"But you didn't know my name," she said, mollified by his confession. Although he'd figured out where she lived and that she didn't have a boyfriend…

"What do you think took me so long? I would have been here sooner if I had. It helps I have a cop for an uncle, and I have access to all sorts of information. And there aren't very many young women named Macey in Chicago."

Which was probably why someone had apparently mistaken her for a different Macey. Macey Gardella.

"How did you know I lived near Hyde Park? And that math isn't my thing? And what makes you think I don't have a boyfriend?"

He grinned, the corners of his eyes crinkling in that charming way. "I saw you get on the trolley toward Hyde Park that day we met on the street. Figured you had to be going home at that time of day. And when you went to pay for your drink at The Gyro,

you had to calculate the change. Twice. As for the boyfriend…
well," he said, glancing toward her, "I was just hoping it was true."

Macey's cheeks were pleasantly warm. "I see."

Still smiling, he turned down a side street and began to
maneuver into a parking place.

"This isn't the library." She frowned at him.

"I thought since I was so-called 'late' coming to pick you
up I owed you at least a cup of coffee," he said. "Maybe even a
sandwich?"

"I'll bite. We can do the interview over coffee and a sandwich.
Yes, it's the least you can do—write a story about the library for
the *Tribune*. We're trying to renovate the book processing rooms
and could use some publicity for our charity dinner next week."

Part of the reason she accepted his invitation—if it could
even be considered an invitation—was because she was putting
off deciding whether she should try to find The Silver Chalice
again. But the memory of those glowing red eyes and long, lethal
fangs left her no choice. The thought reminded her to adjust the
scarf as she waited for Grady to open the car door.

Once again, he gave her legs a long look as she climbed out.
"Maybe you'd like to get a photographer here to take a shot," she
said as he closed the door.

"For the interview?" He looked at her quizzically.

"No," she said. "Of my legs. You seem fascinated by them. A
photo would last longer, you know."

His confusion disappeared into a smirk. "And then I could
hang it in my office. An excellent suggestion." When she huffed,
he added, "You should be flattered, lass. You've got gams worth
taking a second look. Not to mention other assets." His voice
dropped a little at the last bit, and his smile turned warmer.

More flustered than she cared to admit, Macey declined to
respond as they walked into the small diner. Earlier, she hadn't
been certain she'd be interested in food any time soon, but now
she smelled something good to eat and realized how empty
her stomach was. Adjusting her scarf, she nodded when Grady
suggested a table in the corner by a window.

Their attention was taken up by perusing the handwritten menu on a chalkboard and ordering from the waitress. But once that was accomplished, Macey settled in her seat, looked at Grady, who was flipping through his notebook, and contemplated her situation. Strange and unsettling—for here she was, sitting in a cafe with a mysterious man who'd tracked down her identity and home, and with whom she'd had an absurd conversation about vampires…the morning after she'd been attacked by one.

Could it be coincidence?

Grady removed his hat, and she couldn't help but notice how thick and rich his hair looked—like swirls of chocolate-colored velvet. He had brilliant blue eyes that, in the short time she'd known him, had ranged from light and twinkling with humor to sharp and serious, as dark blue as Lake Michigan on a wintry day.

He looked up at that moment, and his eyes were currently colored in the serious, midnight blue tones. "Miss Denton—"

"What happened to 'Macey?'" she asked, trying to diffuse the sudden tension that had settled over her shoulders. "Why so formal?" She hoped her grin came across as breezy as she intended. She wasn't particularly adept at flirting.

"Macey, then." The seriousness didn't ease from his gaze. "Do you know what happened last night?"

She opened her mouth to ask what he meant, then stopped. She didn't want him to think of her as fairy-headed, because she knew damn well what he meant. Her palms had suddenly become damp. She wanted to talk to someone about what happened in her flat—she *needed* to tell someone. Someone who'd believe her.

But…he'd probably think she was loony.

"At The Gyro? There was a raid." She chose her words carefully.

He started to respond, but the waitress approached and set two cups of coffee in front of them and so he waited. When she walked away, he spooned a single scoop of sugar into his cup and stirred slowly, looking down as if fascinated by the vortex the swirling coffee made. "A raid? Is that all you think it was?"

Macey poured a large dollop of cream into her drink and used three spoonfuls of sugar. She didn't seem to be able to form the words that needed to be said. What if he thought she was loco?

He dropped his spoon onto the saucer with an impatient clatter. He leaned across the table, his face intense as he said in a low voice, "Macey, there were vampires there." He speared her with his eyes. Her heart thumped.

"I…know." The words came out in a whisper as she looked straight at him.

Grady settled back in his seat, relief evident in the way his shoulders sagged. He looked at her, that deathly serious expression still there…but now it was tinged with satisfaction. "Thank you."

She accepted and understood his gratitude for her acknowledgment. But she was still so confused and overwhelmed by everything that had happened, she wasn't certain what to say, or even where to begin. As she contemplated how to respond, she noticed a man being seated nearby.

His smooth, spare movements as he made his way between tables in the wake of the waitress caught Macey's attention. Something about him seemed familiar. She caught just a glimpse of his face, but it was obscured by a low-riding fedora, and he was angled away from her.

"About last night…how did you know? Did you see a… vampire?" Her voice dropped low.

"I wasn't certain until I saw the—one of the victims."

Macey stilled. Her body went numb. Oh, God, yes, there had been *victims.* An ugly chill crawled up her spine and clamped around her insides. "Oh God," she whispered as her eyes grew wide. "*Victims? How many? Do you know their names?* Flora! I've got to get to the—to the—morgue or wherever—"

She bolted from her chair, drawing the attention of everyone in the diner…except, noticeably, the man who'd caught her attention earlier. His back to them, he continued to peruse his newspaper as if he hadn't a care in the world.

"Macey." Grady grabbed her arm as she spun blindly toward the door.

She paused, her blind fear and capriciousness ebbing into practicality. Dashing out of the diner in an area of the city she didn't know wasn't going to help answer her question. She'd get Grady to take her to Flora's, or to the morgue, or wherever. She drew in a deep breath and returned to the table.

"My best friend." She sank into her seat, holding Grady's gaze desperately, as if he'd have the answer. "Flora."

The other diners were still watching openly, as if ready to spring to her assistance if it was her companion who'd caused her to bolt…or, perhaps more likely, they were merely interested in the entertainment of a potential lovers' quarrel.

"There were three female victims. " His expression was serious and compassionate.

Her heart in her throat, Macey tried to keep her thoughts calm. "Did you see any of them? Were any of them identified? Flora McGillicut has bright red hair. We called her Carrot Head when we were younger."

His concern eased. "I don't know their names, but none of the three were redheads," he told her, just as the waitress appeared with two bowls of soup and a basket of crusty bread.

Macey exhaled, weak with relief. Yet, as she looked down at the potato chowder, her appetite faded. Three victims from the vampire raid last night. Plus the attack on her. She could have been a fourth casualty. There could be even more. A chill snaked up her spine, and she looked at Grady with sudden realization. "Jennie Fallon."

He was already three bites into his soup—which, judging by the amount of steam curling from the bowl, had to be scalding—but he glanced up. His sharp nod was all the affirmation she needed.

Jennie Fallon. Three from last night. How many more victims? And what could be done to stop there from being more? If there really were vampires…and she had no choice but to accept there were…they couldn't be killed with Tommy guns or stopped by being put in jail. She suspected the likes of the undead didn't give two shingles about the laws of mortals. And would a jail cell even hold them? From what she'd read and experienced first-hand, the creatures were unnaturally fast and strong.

For the first time, Macey felt truly afraid. Gangsters were one thing—for unless you accidentally happened to be caught in a crossfire or tried to encroach on their territory by selling booze or setting up a gambling house, they tended to keep their violent tendencies among themselves and rival gangs.

But vampires…they were a different story. They *fed* on mortals. According to *The Venators*, they lived only to kill.

Macey glanced down and realized her soup was still sitting untouched in front of her. She might as well eat. It smelled good, and she was hungry—and besides, there wasn't anything she could do about the situation.

Or was there? A shiver zipped up her spine.

"What is it?" Grady asked, pausing with a crust of bread half-lowered into his chowder. "Are you cold?"

Macey hesitated only a minute before asking, "Have you heard of The Silver Chalice?"

His eyes narrowed as he shook his head. "What is it? Some sort of vampire artifact?"

"Shhh." Macey glanced around the room. "It's a…a bar or a dance hall. I think," she added quickly. "I've never been there." Literally, that was true: she'd been *outside* the establishment, but hadn't set foot in it.

"I've never heard of any place called The Silver Chalice. But it would be easy to find out. Why?" His eyes narrowed, focusing on her.

"I thought…I thought I heard someone say something about The Silver Chalice last night. During the raid."

"You are a terrible liar, Macey Denton," Grady said flatly. "But regardless, I can find out if there's such a place in the city."

She looked at him primly. "Thank you."

"And if you're not going to eat that, I will." Grady had already finished his own soup and clearly had designs on hers.

"I'll eat it."

He looked disappointed, but placated himself with another piece of crusty bread and his cup of coffee. When Macey finished her soup, her companion rose to pay the bill.

"I'm going to wash my hands," she told him, thinking it would be a good opportunity to adjust her scarf and make sure no blood stains were showing. The last she checked, the wounds were still oozing.

Grady went up to the counter, and she went in the opposite direction to the washroom in the back of the restaurant. Inside the handkerchief-sized room, Macey checked out her reflection in the small mirror. Her white crochet hat looked smart and jaunty, and her inky curls peeked out just below. The scarf had some streaks of blood from her injury, and she vigorously pumped the foot-lever below the sink. The pipes squealed and groaned loudly, and water splashed into the basin.

She was dabbing at the two punctures when the door behind her flew open. Macey stifled a shriek and spun around. It was the familiar-looking man from the restaurant.

"All right. You're done here," he said. "Time to come with me."

Five

Of Venators and Vis Bullae

MACEY THOUGHT HER KNEES WERE going to give way, but she had the presence of mind to swing her handbag at him. "Get *out* of here or I'll scream."

He held up a hand and caught her bag in mid-wallop. "Scream? A Venator doesn't scream." His laugh was short. "Let's go. I don't have as much patience as Temple does."

"Venator? Temple? Who are you?" Macey was still jittery, but her panic had begun to subside; he sounded familiar. She suspected he was the stake-wielding Chas from the alley last night, but she hadn't had a good look at him. Even now, he seemed particularly adept at keeping his face in shadow, with his fedora riding unfashionably low over his forehead.

"Let's go. We're going to give your friend the slip. He's not invited." He flashed a humorless grin and, taking her arm, directed her firmly out into the cafe's back hallway.

By now she was certain her assailant was indeed the trenchcoated man from the alley behind The Gyro—that was why he'd seemed familiar when he walked into the diner. Temple knew him, and he was obviously another person who thought she was the mysterious Macey Gardella.

"I can't just leave him—"

"You're going to have to."

"No." She yanked at his grip, and to her surprise, she easily pulled free. "I'll...get rid of him."

Leaning against the wall, he sneered, looking at her from beneath his hat. "A Venator with a conscience. That won't last long."

Venator again. "Who are you?"

"Hurry, or I'll make a scene."

She believed him. But even as she walked out on trembling legs to ditch Grady, Macey wondered whether she should go with Chas or not. Maybe she should ditch both of them.

No. I'd better go with Chas and clear this up.

"What took you so long?" Grady asked as she met him near the front door of the cafe. "You didn't have to primp for me, I already think—*hey*. What's that on your neck?"

Damn. She'd forgotten her scarf. Her hand whipped up to cover the wound. "Nothing. I have to go. I forgot I'm supposed to be somewhere. Thanks for lunch."

"What the hell are you talking about?" Grady moved in, grabbing her elbow with his hand and, pulling her close to his side, maneuvered her toward the door. He was still staring at her neck, and his eyes had gone dark. "If that's what I think it is—"

"Problem here, miss?"

Suddenly Chas was there, blocking the way. Macey's heart lodged in her throat. He looked like a mobster: sharp and dangerous—and not in good humor.

A glance behind told her the attention of the cafe's occupants was riveted on the scene in the entrance. Two male customers stood and, grim-faced, began to make their way through the labyrinth of tables toward them.

"Grady. I need to go," she said in a low voice. She'd already attracted attention once before. What if someone pulled out a gun and started shooting?

"Go? With this goon?" Grady looked from her to Chas and back again. "Are you all right? You don't have to go anywhere w—"

"It's okay. He's a friend." She hoped he was, anyway. "Don't make a scene. I really do appreciate lunch, Grady. Thanks so much, but I *have* to go."

She thought he wasn't going to move, even then. Macey could feel the tension zinging in the small foyer as the two men took measure of each other. They appeared well-matched in size and strength, crowding her into the small space, and neither seemed ready to back down. She could feel the battle of wills vibrating between them.

"Need some help here, miss?" One of the men who'd risen from his meal interrupted.

"No, thanks," Macey told him. "It's fine." She looked up at Grady, whose blue eyes were cold and flat. "It's okay. Really. He's a friend."

He muttered something under his breath. After one last measured look at Chas, he released her arm, stepping away just enough for her to slip by.

"Good Christ," muttered Chas as he ushered her away from the diner. "Next time can we forget the niceties and chit-chat? And you need something for that." He gestured abruptly in the general direction of her neck.

"What I need is to get everyone off my case. There's a misunderstanding, and I want to clear it up. I'm not this Macey Gardella you and your cohorts keep talking about."

Chas's only response was a short laugh.

Instead of leading her to an automobile or cab, he directed her briskly down the street and around the block, then into an alley. She hesitated, pulling away when they came upon the black, imposing entrance to a tunnel.

"I'm not going in there."

"Freight tunnels are the fastest way to get where we need to go—without being seen. You said you wanted to get this problem cleared up." Chas stood there, hands in his pockets, his fedora still shading his brows.

"Why should I trust you?" Macey backed away. What sort of fool would go down into a dark tunnel alone with a strange man? Her heart pounded and she looked around to see if anyone was nearby.

"Have it your way. But if we're followed, you can explain to Vioget." Chas whirled on his heels and stalked off, apparently expecting her to follow.

And darn if she didn't. At least they were still on the street, in the daylight. And his acquiescence went a long way in making her more comfortable going with him. Besides, she wanted to see where they were going—whether to The Silver Chalice or someplace else.

Chas led her through such a maze of backstreets and narrow alleys Macey lost track of where they were. Since they didn't travel on the main throughways, she didn't see landmarks or street signs other than the Drake looming in the distance.

By the time they reached a street that looked vaguely familiar, she was not only completely lost, but had more than once seen men loading up trucks in back alleys…with things Macey knew were illegal. Barrels, clinking jugs in crates, and other things she didn't want to see or recognize.

She averted her eyes—just like most Chicagoans, including the fuzz— and marched along with her escort. Better not to take note of anything.

"After you." Chas pointed to an iron-railed stairway that led beneath the street.

Macey noticed the small finial on top of the railing, shaped like a chalice—exactly like the one she saw last night. Since she and Chas were on a different street, she could only assume there was more than one entrance.

Heart pounding, palms slick, insides churning, Macey looked around. Scads of people were about on their way to market or other errands, but no one seemed to take particular notice of them. It seemed a normal Saturday morning in Chicago for everyone except her.

"For the love of God, you're not going to your execution," Chas said, gesturing again. "And that bite needs to be seen to, sooner rather than later. You wouldn't want to scar that long neck of yours."

She couldn't argue, for the warm trickle of fresh blood had begun to seep more freely into her collar, activated by the brisk walk. Hoping she wasn't about to make a fatal mistake, Macey drew in a deep breath and started down the steps. As she descended, leaving the sunlight and familiarity behind her, she felt a chill settle over the back of her neck.

At the bottom of the stairs was an iron door with a knocker in the center. A small goblet was imprinted in the center of the metal, and above it was a peephole.

Chas crowded into the small space next to her, and Macey felt a trickle of alarm. In his black coat and hat, he was big and dark and dangerous—and she was trapped by three sides of brick wall below the street. But he didn't even look at her; instead, he used the knocker and waited. Macey shivered as the nausea-edged chill surged stronger over the back of her neck.

"You feel that, do you?" Chas looked down at her, grim satisfaction in his tones. "Not bad for a novice."

She had no idea what he meant, and might have asked if the peephole door hadn't swung open at that moment. Two amber-colored eyes looked out at her, blinked, then shifted to Chas. "About bloody time."

The door to The Silver Chalice opened and there stood the most handsome man Macey had ever seen. He had blond-tipped tawny hair, rich golden skin and hot amber eyes. His full lips formed a sensual smile as he looked her over, *slowly*, then nodded. His gaze grew even warmer. The hand that gripped the edge of the doorway had rings made of braided copper on each finger.

"Sebastian Vioget, at your service."

If Sebastian had any lingering doubts Macey Denton was the young woman he believed she was, his first good look at her in full light would have wiped them away.

She very much resembled Victoria—not merely because of her thick black hair, curling wildly around her jaw and earlobes, or the lush, wide mouth he'd known so well—but also in the way she carried herself, in the lift of her stubborn chin, the tilt of her head, the shape of her striking face.

But not her eyes. And that was what clinched it. Macey Denton had the Pesaro eyes: large and dark, thick-lashed. They were extraordinarily beautiful and expressive, bright with intelligence—and laced with suspicion.

Except for the glint of wariness, it was like looking into Giulia's eyes.

For the first time in a hundred years, Sebastian felt something inside him *move*. Something warm and tantalizing. *Hope.*

Something dangerous.

Oh, indeed. This woman was exactly who he needed. Precisely whom he'd been waiting for.

"If you keep us standing out here long enough, a shaft of sun will fry you where you stand, Vioget."

Sebastian realized he'd been staring. Flaring a burn in his eyes at Chas, he moved, gesturing the pair into his private parlor. As she walked past him, he scented the essence of fresh blood at her neck. The shock of awareness took him by surprise, causing him to salivate and his pulse to speed up. Fresh blood. *Her* blood. *Dangerous.*

But he quickly regained his head and gave a little bow. He'd controlled himself for more than a century. Now that he was so close to his goal, he must be even more vigilant and strong.

"Ah, *cherie*, I'm delighted you've returned. I'm afraid you took me by surprise during your exit last night—otherwise you would have been safely ensconced here, and wouldn't have had to attend to your unexpected visitor." He smiled at Macey and closed the door. The scent of her blood tugged at him again.

"Unexpected visitor?" she said, looking around the room. "Is that what you call it? I was nearly *killed*, and I only came here to clear things up. I don't want anymore unexpected visitors climbing through my window at night."

"I'm quite cert—climbing through your window?" Sebastian frowned. "But the undead cannot enter your home uninvited." He looked at Chas, his eyes burning hotter with displeasure. By

God, if that man's negligence had caused harm to Macey Gardella, Sebastian would have killed him. Venator or nay.

The other man ignored him, walking over to the liquor cabinet. He opened it without waiting for an invitation and Sebastian gritted his teeth. Chas had many beneficial qualities, and he was a damned good Venator, but all too often, it was impossible to remember them. If Wayren hadn't sent him, Sebastian would have divested himself of Chas's presence years ago.

"Well, someone must have invited him—or it—or whatever it was. Because he climbed in through my window. And I'm on the third floor." Macey, so delicate and petite she would barely reach Sebastian's chin, was indignant. And yet there was an underlying fear beneath her bravado. "I don't know how he could have gotten up there."

"But you staked him." Chas turned, holding a glass of Sebastian's best Scotch—contraband smuggled in via the Great Lakes with great difficulty. "And now all is well."

"All is *not* well. I came here so I could make you realize I'm not this Macey Gardella everyone thinks I am. I don't want to be involved in—in whatever is going on here." She was still standing, using her hands and shoulders for emphasis. "I've got a job and friends and—and things to do. I don't want any of my friends to get hurt."

"Too late," Chas told her abruptly, and downed his drink.

Sebastian wanted nothing more than to send the man away, but he couldn't. Not yet. Instead, he turned his full attention on the young woman. The scent of her blood still lingered, but he had himself under control and the aroma became little more than a faint tease.

"Please, *cherie,* sit, and I will tell you all. But first—ah, Chas, something for her bites if you please. You must surely carry salted holy water with you…but, oh, of course, you wouldn't. How *foolish* of me." Sebastian's smile was cold and false, and he was rewarded for his parry and thrust when the other man's expression darkened. The whiskey bottle clinked as Chas poured himself another generous drink, and this time, Sebastian didn't care. He turned back to Macey. "Did you receive the book?"

For a moment he thought she would ask what he meant. But then before his eyes, she wilted…and then straightened up, drawing her shoulders back. He nearly smiled. *By God, it's like Victoria come to life.*

Except for the eyes.

Oh, the eyes. He could drown in them. And if he was not careful, he would.

"I assume you are speaking of *The Venators*. By George Starcasset."

"Indeed. And have you read it?"

"Much of it. Which is how I knew what to do last night. When the…whatever it was…came in my room."

"*Vampire*. It was a vampire. You can say the word." Chas had a small, dark vial in his hand, and he brought it over to Macey. "Pour this on your wound. And take care not to splash. You might injure someone." He slanted a suggestive glance at Sebastian.

"Salted holy water." She looked at the vial, which was the size of her small finger, then began to work the tiny cork free. When she poured it on her neck, Macey's eyes widened in shock and she gasped, then began to pant, flapping her hand as if to ward off the pain. "You didn't tell me it was going to burn!"

Chas's lips twitched behind his glass and his only response was to drink. Long and heavily.

"Now that we've attended to your injury, I shall tell you everything. Please, *cherie,* sit." Sebastian patted the sofa near his chair and waited while Macey settled in. Though over a hundred years old, he was still most definitely a man. Thus he couldn't help admiring her slender, shapely legs and elegant ankles.

One of the things about living an immortal life was the experience of radical fashion shifts over the decades. He'd been born in 1790, and thus had seen—and unbuttoned, unlaced, untaped, unhooked—everything from high-waisted Empire gowns with bosoms spilling out over low necklines to tight corsets and full skirts with cagelike hoops that made it impossible to discreetly make love to a woman while tete-a-tete at a party or ball. And then there were the ridiculously narrow skirts and ungainly bustles of the late previous century…

Current fashion provided tantalizing views of sleek, silk-stockinged legs and bare ankles, but the dresses were little more than shapeless sacks, hiding the curve of breast and hip. And for these reasons, Sebastian found flapper fashion both titillating and disappointing. In the past, he rather enjoyed the chase, the coaxing and seducing…and the pleasure of finding out just what was beneath the complicated package of skirts, corsets, and petticoats.

As Macey smoothed her skirt over a pair of shapely knees, Sebastian conceded privately that one shouldn't complain about the lovely sight of bare legs, at least—and offered so readily.

"I received the book—or rather, the library received the book. It was only by chance I happened to read it—otherwise, I would have been completely offguard last night." Again her eyes were troubled.

"But no. Not at all. You have Gardella blood—Venator blood—and you have instinct. All born Venators do. The book surely helped you, but it was your own skill and innate abilities that came alive when it mattered."

Macey was shaking her head. She'd removed her close-fitting hat and set it on the sofa next to her. Her hair was a jumble of dark curls. "But that's the problem. I'm not a Gardella or a Venator. There's been a mistake."

"No, *ma petite*, there is no mistake. You are most definitely a born Venator. You've been having the dreams, no?"

"Dreams?" Her expression was arrested. "What sort of dreams?"

"About vampires. Being chased or attacked by them. Every born Venator has a series of those dreams when it is time for them to be Called."

"I…" Her eyes were huge and her lips slightly parted. "Yes. But that doesn't mean I'm a Venator. I was reading that book and it put me in mind of the vampires." She glanced at Chas, who, for once, actually seemed interested in something other than his own bloody needs.

"You are a Venator," Sebastian told her again, holding her with his eyes—but without his thrall. "There is no doubt. You look so much like Victoria Gardella, there can be no denying it—even if I wasn't already certain." She opened her mouth to speak, but he continued, "Do you know what happened to your parents?"

Those deep, dark eyes fastened on him. "You wouldn't ask if you weren't aware they're both dead. So you must know my mother died of a blood disease when I was a baby, and I—my father sent me away." Her voice became clipped and flat. "Then died in the war."

"I knew your father. He was the infamous Max Denton, my darling. Known throughout Europe as a fearless Venator of great skill, named after his great-grandfather. He certainly did perish in the Great War, but not on the battlefield, regardless of what you might have been led to believe. He was an assassinator of vampires and was quite instrumental in bringing about an end to the war. Unfortunately, that was his final mission. And as for your mother…" Sebastian reached over and closed his fingers over her slender hand. "A blood disease was a kind way of saying Felicia Denton died at the hands of a team of vampires, bent on avenging the work of your father. They kidnapped her and…well, I'll spare you the details. But suffice to say, your father was devastated. I've never seen a man so destroyed, yet still alive. He was never the same after, and he did indeed send you away—to protect you."

She stared at him, her mouth half open, her eyes wide with confusion and disbelief. The pulse drummed in her slender neck, her skin a soft, dusky rose. Sebastian swallowed hard and forced his attention from the temptation of her throat and the delicate blue vein therein. Her expression hardened, and she pressed her lush lips into a hard line. "To protect me? If he was an—what did you call him?—'infamous vampire hunter,' why didn't he protect me himself?"

Sebastian hesitated, uncertain whether to explain and attempt to heal what was obviously a deep wound. "Max Denton was no fool. He knew you must be well hidden, and he dared not visit or have any contact with you for fear the undead would find you. It took me more than ten years searching throughout Europe and America to find you, and I was aware of your existence."

Her hard, skeptical expression didn't ease, and Sebastian felt as if his chance was slipping away. "Chas. Pour me one before you've emptied that whole bloody bottle. And perhaps Macey would like something to calm her as well. Clearly, she has much to digest."

She was shaking her head. "I don't believe any of this. It's...I'd say you were completely looney if I hadn't seen a—" She glanced over at Chas and drew in a deep breath. Then exhaled. "Vampire. Last night."

"Get used to it. You're going to see a lot more of them." He handed her a glass, leaning his hip against the sofa behind her. "You'll become intimately acquainted with every aspect of the undead. The smell of musty, putrid ash will permeate your clothes and hair, and you'll have to determine how to keep a stake hidden on your person at all times." Chas's eyes glinted as they skimmed over her slim-fitting skirt and blouse. "Unless, of course, you elect to refuse your Calling."

By God. It took great effort for Sebastian to keep from taking the man by his neck and giving it a good, sharp twist. *Damn him.* Macey Gardella couldn't refuse her Calling. It wasn't an option. Not for him. Not for his soul, and not for Giulia's. And God *damn* Chas Woodmore for bringing it up.

Instead of hurting the man, Sebastian sipped calmly from the golden liquid. Yet, as warm and lush and smooth as it tasted, whiskey was a poor substitute for what he truly wanted. He closed his eyes and swallowed, touching the *vis bulla* through his fine linen shirt. The answering sizzle calmed him.

"My Calling. You mean...to be a Venator?" Macey looked up at Chas, who loomed over her like a dark shadow. "You can't be serious. I'm not a vampire hunter."

"You slayed one last night, without any training—*and* without the protection of a *vis bulla*." Sebastian kept his voice steady and easy, allowed his eyes to soften warmly. He was very skillful at coaxing a woman to do what he wished—even without his thrall.

"*Vis bulla.* That was mentioned in the book—the strength amulet the Venators wear. Was George Starcasset a Venator too?"

"Good God, *no*. Which is why, incidentally, there are many incorrect assumptions and missing facts in the book. I don't believe your great-great-grandmother is even mentioned. In fact, Starcasset barely escaped with his life when Max Pesaro found out he'd written the treatise and meant to reveal the secrets of the Venators and vampires. That's why there are so few copies of it. They were all destroyed—or so we believed. Until Chas acquired one—and I'm not precisely certain how that happened. He's never felt obligated to share that minor detail."

Chas flickered a glance at him and lifted his glass in acknowledgement.

"Are you both Venators?"

"Of course." Chas leaned closer, his hand shifting on the sofa behind her shoulder as his voice dropped low and suggestive. "Would you like to see my *vis bulla,* Macey?"

Sebastian was familiar with that technique: if she were wearing a low-cut gown, he'd have an excellent view down the front. As it was, her buttoned blouse was a shallow vee-neck that showed only a hint of healthy cleavage.

"I…"

"Perhaps another time, Woodmore," Sebastian cut in. "And Macey will soon receive her own *vis.*"

"If she accepts the Calling."

"Indeed." Sebastian kept his smile easy with effort. "But why would she not? She might not yet appreciate it, but she *is* the daughter of Max Denton, and the great-great-granddaughter of Victoria Gardella. She is born to be a Venator…unlike others in this chamber."

Chas's smile turned humorless and cold. "Indeed. And then there are those who wear the *vis* but are no longer worthy of it."

Sebastian's vision flushed red and hot. A blaze of anger rushed through him, and his fangs shot out before he could stop them.

He gripped the heavy red-stoned signet ring on his left hand and summoned calm before Macey noticed his slip. By God, Woodmore was more of a thorn than Max Pesaro had ever been, the bloody bastard.

"What does it mean to accept the Calling?" Macey's question caused a shaft of clarity to break into his flaming vision.

"You will receive your own *vis bulla*—a small cross forged of silver from the Holy Land, steeped in holy water from the Vatican. It's worn pierced through the flesh and provides strength, speed, protection, and healing."

"And then what happens?"

"And then…you hunt vampires."

Six

Revelations of a Family History

MACEY'S BREATH CAUGHT. *Hunt vampires.*

"I can't hunt vampires," she managed to say, shaking her head. "That's ridiculous. I'm a library assistant. I'm a…I'm a *woman.* And look at me—I'm not big or strong or tall, and I have no idea how to…do that. This is the silliest thing I've ever heard."

Yet, even as she said the words, Macey felt a little tingle inside. Almost like a sizzle, a *zing.*

Confused, frightened and—yes—curious, she lifted her glass to drink and froze with it halfway to her mouth. Its scent was sharp and pungent. "This is—this is *whiskey.*"

The man named Chas laughed softly. He'd removed his fedora, finally, and now she could see his eyes. They were emotionless and gray, set in a surprisingly handsome countenance. She'd imagined him to be as craggy and sharp in appearance as he was in personality, but he looked like an exotic Gypsy, with jet-black hair and swarthy skin. "Indeed it is. And an excellent vintage if I do say so. One thing about Vioget—he always has the best."

For some reason, she remembered Grady tossing back a gulp of the same cider-colored liquor last night at The Gyro. Guilt nudged her for leaving him at the diner. She hoped he wasn't too worried about her. She hoped he didn't have reason to be. "Whiskey's illegal. I can't—"

"I beg to differ, *ma cherie*," Sebastian Vioget said mildly. "The sale, production, and distribution of spirits is explicitly prohibited by Volstead. But not the actual imbibing of it."

He smiled warmly at her, and Macey felt another different sort of sizzling tingle in her belly. She tore her eyes away, her cheeks warming. Sebastian Vioget exuded sensuality, heat, and danger. Yet, even though a look from him caused warmth to shimmy up her spine, she still felt a chill over the back of her neck. As if a constant breeze settled there.

She looked down at the whiskey, pretending to consider taking a sip. In reality, Macey was trying to organize and control her racing mind. *A vampire hunter? Me?*

Father as well? Her insides turned cold at the memory of his stony heart. How could a man send his daughter away after she lost her mother? To place after place, home after home...and never ever see her again?

Vampire hunter or not, Max Denton was not a person she wanted to emulate. Or respect. Or even remember.

My father...a vampire hunter. Impossible.

But perhaps not as impossible as she would have believed only yesterday. Before she'd seen a vampire.

Since vampires do exist, there must be those who hunt them. The police are surely incapable of doing so.

But me? Impossible. Crazy.

Macey set the glass down. Her heart thudded harder as she stood. "I'm going to leave now." It occurred to her that perhaps they wouldn't allow her to leave, these two dangerous—silkily dangerous—men. Her palms were damp and she could hardly breathe, fearing what would happen.

She suspected facing Al Capone or Bugs Moran would be a cakewalk compared to a showdown with the two in this room. Her heart filled her throat and she thought she might choke, but she walked steadily toward the exit.

"Macey."

She was at the door. Hand on the knob, she turned, not expecting to see that Sebastian and Chas had remained in their seats. Neither made a move to stop her.

But as her gaze was caught by Sebastian's, she felt a funny tug in the center of her belly. And had the impression he'd changed somehow. His eyes were…warm. Hot. *Glowing?*

"Now, now, Vioget…let's play fair." Chas moved suddenly, his arm jerking in front of Sebastian's eyes. Macey blinked and the tug inside eased.

Then all at once, realization jolted her. Her knees wobbled. She clutched the knob as they buckled a little, then caught herself before her legs gave way. "You—you're a *vampire.*"

"*And* a Venator." He wore an odd expression—a little chagrined, a little wary.

"But…how can you be both?"

"That is a damned good question," Chas said brightly. "How can you be both, the lady asks?"

"Get *out*," Sebastian growled. "Now." His eyes burned—literally—red and glowing, just like those of the man who attacked Macey last night. Her pulse jerked when she noticed fang tips pressing into his lower lip.

"Very well. If that's what you wish." Chas set his glass down and it clinked gently against the whiskey bottle. "Good luck convincing a Venator to help a vampire."

"Wait." Macey held up her hand. To her relief, it wasn't even trembling. Maybe she was made from sterner stuff than she realized. "I'm leaving. I'm going to think about this. And I'll let you know…in a few days."

"Of course, *cherie*. But do you truly wish to place yourself in danger overnight? Now that the undead know who you are and where you live, you're no longer safe. Particularly since you've already slain one of them—the clock has begun to tick. All has been set in motion." Sebastian rose, but the glow in his gaze faded, and he looked at her with mortal eyes. "Whether you wish to accept it or not, whether you *believe* it or not, you *are* Macey Gardella. Daughter of Max Denton, great-great-granddaughter of

Victoria. You are the heir to *Il* Gardella—The Gardella—line, and destined to change the world in this era. The undead know this. They've been waiting for you. And Count Alvisi will do whatever he must to destroy you."

"Now you're scaring the girl, Vioget."

Chas's voice wasn't particularly kind, but Macey couldn't disagree. She had no feeling in her legs, and her insides were a jungle of nerves. "But I don't have to accept the Calling. You said I didn't have to accept it." She looked at him, uncertain whether she'd find help with him or not. "What if I don't?"

"If you don't…well, first, you'll live in utter ignorance of this very conversation, of this very place and even our identities," Chas said, speaking before Sebastian could.

His lackadaisical attitude had evaporated. Gone was the insolent, testy man who'd drunk half a bottle of whiskey in forty minutes. Now his words were sober, matching his expression. "And the undead will continue to do what they have always done. What they must do to survive: take from mortals, feed on them, rape and maul them. For that is what they've been created to do: to take. Without reservation.

"If unchecked, they'll grow in large numbers, as the likes of Capone and Torri have done—but these are immortal beings, not gun-toting mortals. Someday soon, instead of being run by gangsters, Chicago will be controlled by vampires. Particularly if they convince Capone and the others to join them. And there is nothing—not one thing—redeemable about one who is undead. They cannot be saved, they cannot be corrected. A vampire is unadulterated evil. They must *take* in order to live. That is the core of their existence. Rape and violation."

Macey couldn't breathe. Not so much because of Chas's speech, but because of the expression settling on Sebastian's face. Tormented, dark, burning with fury.

"Ah. But there is one exception," Chas added casually. He hadn't looked at Sebastian, but surely he felt the antipathy rolling off him. "And that is our host here—the fine proprietor of The

Silver Chalice. He has a chance for redemption. And he needs you to help him."

Grady had no intention of allowing Macey Denton out of his sight—particularly with the gangster she'd somehow attracted. He knew how to take care of himself, but more importantly, he knew how to read a man. That bastard made his skin crawl and his instincts go very sharp.

He's a friend. It's fine.

Like hell.

But Grady made the fatal mistake of going to his automobile, assuming they'd get into a car and he'd follow. Besides, his gun was under the seat.

Instead of getting in their own vehicle, Macey and her escort turned down a pedestrian alley a block away and across the street. By the time Grady got there, they were out of sight.

Sonofabitch.

He looked around for a while, talked to a few witnesses who'd seen them, but he'd lost their trail. Now Grady sat behind the steering wheel and cursed. *Hope to hell you know what you're doing, lass.*

But he didn't have a good feeling at all. Especially since he was pretty damned sure that had been a vampire bite on her delicate neck.

He swore again and pushed the ignition, engaging the engine, considering his next move. Then, his mind made up, he pulled into the street.

Fifteen minutes later, Grady was out of his car, knocking on the front door of Mrs. Gutchinson's house. There were many ways to go about finding answers, and thanks to his work during the War, he knew a hell of a lot of them. Some techniques were legal, and others…not.

He decided to start with a legal one.

"What? You again? Where's Macey?" The spirited landlady, who was hardly more than skin and bones, was already demanding answers before the door was fully open. Though she'd probably watched him approach alone, she peered around as if to spy Macey lurking in the bushes.

"She's at the library. But she left a book here and begged me to fetch it for her since I have an auto. I told her I would, if you'd allow me." He gave her his warmest smile, knowing just how to make his eyes sparkle.

"What book? Where is it?"

"It's a volume of *Gray's Anatomy*," he said without hesitation. "So will you be letting me in, or do I have to go back and tell her my Irish charm wasn't working on you today?" He made his eyes glint with levity, knowing they'd be crinkling at the corners and that his dimple would be showing.

Mrs. Gutchinson stepped back and gestured him into the foyer with a large-knuckled hand. "I suppose I could let you. But I'm gonna be watchin' you every bit of the time. Don't want you pawing through that girl's drawers."

Good thing she was already climbing the steps ahead of him and didn't see the expression on his face. *And just what sort of lacy things does Miss Macey Denton have in her drawers?* That thought was enough to keep him smiling to himself, despite the landlady's skinny, sagging behind creaking slowly ahead of him—precisely at eye level.

However, the slow progress up the creaking steps gave him the opportunity to arrange for the second part of his plan. Mrs. Gutchinson was so enamored with her own voice, she didn't notice when he paused to balance a small can of pebbles between two spines of the staircase railing. Precariously situated, the container would tip with the slightest bit of encouragement.

So just as Mrs. Gutchinson finished unlocking Macey's door, Grady bumped hard against the railing at the top of the steps. The apartment door opened as the railing jolted and the can went tumbling.

"What on earth?" Mrs. Gutchinson whirled, looking behind her. One thing he had to say—the woman had excellent hearing.

Of course, the rattling sound all the way down the steps and ending metallic clunk was hard to miss.

"I don't know what that was. Sounded like it came from down there," Grady said helpfully. He stepped neatly aside as she turned, allowing her past him to make her way down the stairs as quickly as her elderly body would allow. "Be careful now, Mrs. Gutchinson. No need to hurry. You don't want to take a tumble."

He slipped into Macey's apartment. Her scent—something floral without being cloying—lingered, along with the layer of another musty, nauseating smell that put him in mind of a graveyard. Or a morgue—a place he'd had the misfortune of visiting far too often. Knowing he didn't have much time, he quickly looked around and snatched up the first book he saw: on the bedside table. It was too old to easily read the title on front or spine, so Mrs. Gutchinson would just have to take his word it was *Gray's Anatomy*.

Holding it protectively against his chest, he examined the rest of the small flat while listening for the landlady's return.

It wasn't particularly neat, but nor was Macey's living space cluttered. Her bed was made, and his attention lingered there for a heartbeat longer than strictly necessary, noting how inviting it looked with the white crewel-stitched coverlet and a variety of colorful pillows. Dresses of slinky, silky fabric were folded over the back of a chair. A few canned and boxed goods were on the kitchenette's counters along with a loaf of bread. Then he saw the broken broomstick. The broom part was on the floor near the fridge. The other half, with its wicked-looking point, was on her dresser next to perfume bottles, hair combs, a hand mirror, and several pairs of earrings.

Interesting.

He picked up the broken stick and sniffed it. The foul, musty smell was strong there. When he pulled his hand away, he felt and saw an ashy, gritty residue. It, too, smelled foul.

Damn. His suspicions were looking more and more probable.

A strand of beads glittered on the windowsill, and, replacing the broken broomstick next to a torn picture on her dresser, Grady went to take a closer look.

Good Catholic boy he was—or had been, anyway, in Dublin; he hadn't been in a church for years, thanks to the War—he knew a rosary when he saw one. The prayer loop was a circle of beads with a short extension that ended in a cross. The circular part consisted of five sections of ten beads each—for the Hail Marys—separated by a single, larger bead that represented the Our Father. The tail had three Hail Mary beads with an Our Father bead on each side. Then the cross, which was for the Apostle's Creed.

Usually.

But this rosary, made of silver links with blue-black beads, had an extra decoration on the extension. A bead that didn't match the others, linked in between the cross and the first Our Father nodule. It was a rosy pearl, set in ornate silver filigree, and dangling from the setting was a tiny silver cross. The size of his small fingernail.

Grady felt a tremor of something skitter up his arms…a sort of buzz, a pleasant warmth…and he sifted the beads through his hands again. *A rosary but not a rosary.*

Then he realized the stairs were creaking, and he quickly replaced the rosary, arranging it as it had been. He was walking out of Macey's apartment, book tucked under his arm, by the time a puffing Mrs. Gutchinson reached the top step. He squelched a niggle of guilt for inciting her to drag herself up and down the flight of stairs unnecessarily.

"I've got the book. Thank you so very much, ma'am," he said, giving her a tip of his fedora. "Macey will be very appreciative."

The landlady sniffed and looked at him, then into the apartment. She didn't seem worse for wear with the extra activity. "That young lady needs to learn how to keep house better. Instead of gallivanting off to the dance clubs and a *job* every day." She closed the door and locked it smartly, but by the time the bolt shot home, Grady was heading out the front door to his auto.

He had work to do. Research and investigation.

But it wasn't until some time later he actually looked at the book he'd taken from Macey's apartment.

Chas came awake abruptly when someone kicked him in the arm.

Groggy, he blinked and looked around. "What the hell?" he growled at Temple, who stood over him and appeared very riled up.

"I've been looking all over for you." She glowered down at him. "It's coming onto twilight, and Sebastian wants you guarding Macey."

Stifling a groan, Chas sat up. The world shifted and tilted a little and he took in the setting, remembering after a minute that he was in an abandoned warehouse. On the floor. His neck throbbed, still pulsing from a recent wound, and the dull scent of undead lingered. He felt Temple's attention shift from the oozing blood, to the stake still in his hand, to his shirtless chest where the *vis bulla* glinted, and onto the other bites decorating his bare shoulder.

She didn't say anything, but he could feel the shock and revulsion rolling off her. *Fuck her.*

He pulled upright easily and shrugged into his shirt, buttoning it with agile fingers. "Are you coming too?"

"How much bloody help do you think *I'd* be if a Guardian showed up?" she snapped. "I'm staying at the Chalice. Sebastian's going with you."

Chas nodded. He couldn't fault the plan. Despite the fact that he and Vioget had a different perspective on nearly everything, the two of them were a formidable team. That was why Wayren brought him here.

Macey Denton would be safe for another night at least.

"So, she didn't accept?" Temple asked, shoving his coat at him.

"Not yet. She's thinking about it."

"Will she?"

"I sure as hell hope so. Hate to see what Vioget will do if she doesn't. And it's only a matter of time till Alvisi or Iscariot dust him. Then they'll have the rings." He pulled on his coat, shoved the stake in his pocket, then adjusted his extra weapon in its hidden slot in a trouser leg and felt for his gun. "Will you be ready if she does accept?"

"Of course. I've been waiting five years for this chance."

"Good. Because she's going to need everything you can teach her. Any other news?"

"Iscariot's laying low. He's the one who makes me really nervous because he's so…insidious and quiet. Alvisi's busy with his business ventures, and The Blood Club is making him piles of money. Al Capone was at a Tutela meeting yesterday, and word is, it's only a matter of time before the count seduces him to the immortal, dark side. Man's like a greased pig, you ask me. All that slick pomade in his hair, pudgy fingers, full cheeks. Fat lips."

Chas grinned. One thing about Temple: she didn't mince words. Then he sobered. "An undead Capone would be catastrophic. I don't know if even Vioget and I could tip them if he joined forces with Alvisi."

"Then you'd better convince Macey Gardella to join your cause."

He snorted. "Right. She'd make all the difference when fighting a vampiric gangster and his thugs. *Vis bulla* or no, she'd blow away in a stiff breeze—not to mention be thrown through the air like a doll if the vamps get their hands on her. She's about as sturdy as rice paper." He shook his head. "Macey's here to help Vioget save his damned soul. That's about all we can hope for."

"I have a feeling the same sort of thing was said about Victoria Gardella, her aunt Eustacia, and the other female Venators like Catherine. And that would have been wrong."

He chucked Temple under the chin. "You've been studying your Venator history. My, my. Well, you just keep on hoping, lulu. Because I live in reality. The undead and their Tutela bitches didn't have fucking Tommy guns and a corrupt government protecting them back then. If Iscariot or Alvisi turn Capone and he joins the

undead, it's curtains—for all of us."

Seven

Of Long Promises and Heartbreak

MACEY DIDN'T KNOW WHAT possessed her to walk past Old St. Patrick's Church, but many hours after leaving The Silver Chalice, she found herself doing just that.

Perhaps it was because she was thinking of the old woman who, only last week, had pressed the rosary into her hand as Macey walked by. Such an odd thing for a stranger to do. Nevertheless, she'd accepted the string of prayer beads and tucked them into her handbag.

She hadn't thought any more of it until she read in *The Venators* that vampires were repelled by holy objects, particularly those of silver. Even then, she had no idea the rosary would be of such use to her.

What an amazing, unsettling coincidence.

Macey shivered as she stepped into the silent, shadowy church. Though it had a high ceiling, the space was compact and not terribly grand. The arch of the nave peaked high over her, and blue, red, and yellow stained glass images spilled colorful shadows over the rows of pews. A single aisle led from the interior doors to the dais and altar. To one side, she saw candles in red glass jars clustered in front of a statue of the Blessed Virgin Mary. Some of the wicks were lit, and their flames flickered randomly. Others were still and silent, waiting for someone to light them in honor of a prayer intention.

Macey dipped her fingers into the small bowl of holy water and rubbed them over the crusty wounds on her neck. It didn't sizzle and burn as violently as it had earlier, but she still felt a sting of awareness.

She wasn't Catholic, but something drew her to walk deeper into the small church. The silence. The peace. The underlying energy permeating the holy space.

It was a place for answers.

She hoped.

Only one other person was present when she walked down the aisle and slipped into a row of pews. She saw the figure huddled in prayer near the front, and, loathe to interrupt or even to reveal her presence, Macey moved as quietly as possible onto a kneeler far from the other occupant.

She closed her eyes and folded her hands prayerfully and thought about everything that had happened since yesterday. The violence at The Gyro…the invader in her apartment and his attack…her visit to The Silver Chalice…

Sebastian Vioget's intense, compelling eyes.

Chas's calm, matter-of-fact words: *"And then…you hunt vampires."*

Can it be true? Her head spun, and her mind was filled with questions, fears, disbelief. And pain.

Had Father really been some sort of soldier against the undead? Supposedly infamous? But it didn't matter, because he sent her away. He sent a grieving, devastated daughter away when she needed him most. Max Denton could have killed all the undead in the world, but he'd turned his back on her. He might be a hero to others…but he wasn't to Macey.

But if that was true…was it then her calling to be a Venator? To fight the immortal half-demon vampires—risking her life every day? Impossible to fully comprehend the change such a decision would make in her life—the violence, the danger, the reality of such a vocation. She was a simple library assistant. A woman. Young, sheltered, and hardly able to lift a fifteen-pound box of books. Heck…until less than a year ago, she'd lived in a rural village with the population of only a couple thousand.

And yet…the police—at least, the ones who weren't corrupt—put their lives in danger every day. There were women on the police force, too. Not many, but some.

And there'd been women who went to the battlefield as nurses during the War. Women voted, ran for office, had businesses, were doctors and scientists and inventors. Were librarians, even. She smiled tremulously in the dim light.

A woman can make a difference. Many women have.

But can I?

She shivered and a sudden vibration rushed through her in a warm, sizzling wave. It surged from the center of her being to her fingertips, to her toes, to the top of her head, like a sunburst exploding from her heart.

You can.

She heard the voice so loudly, so clearly, right in her ear, Macey's eyes flew open and she looked behind her.

No one was there.

The church was empty. Her heavy breathing echoed in the dim, silent space.

Heart ramrodding in her chest, she settled back onto the pew and tried to calm herself. Deep breaths, long and slow. But those words echoed in her mind as if someone spoke them again in her ear. *You can.*

Suddenly she caught sight of a movement out of the corner of her eye and whipped around.

"You," she whispered, clapping a hand to her thudding heart.

It was the old woman.

Macey couldn't even guess her age, she was so old. Eighty? Ninety? Older? Her skin was papery thin, and infinite wrinkles crisscrossed over cheeks covered by the fine down of hair that often grew on older people's skin. Over her head, she wore a crocheted shawl of pale pink. A few wisps of thick silver and white hair curled against her cheek and temples. Her mouth, curved in a soft smile, was framed by deep wrinkles. But her chin and jaw were surprisingly firm, and her unblemished skin hardly sagged anywhere.

Her dark eyes were set deep into their sockets, and as Macey looked at her, she was struck by the bright, lucid intelligence therein. For a moment, she was so arrested, she felt as if she were looking into her own eyes, in a mirror.

"You…thank you," she said. "Thank you for the rosary."

The old woman nodded, her smile widening and the corners of her eyes crinkling. "Yes. I knew you would make use of it."

A rush of air lifted tiny bumps on Macey's arms, as if someone had brushed a hand ever so lightly over her skin. "How did you know that? I'm not Catholic. I've never even met you before. I never come to this church. I haven't ever set foot in here until today."

A soft, wrinkled hand came out from beneath the enveloping shawl and settled over Macey's younger, smoother, smaller one. "Sometimes we just *know*. And when we do, it's important to listen to the message."

"Thank you." Macey's voice came out in little more than a whisper. Her eyes stung with unshed tears, and she didn't know why.

Ah, perhaps she did. There was just so much she didn't understand, didn't believe…didn't *want* to believe.

The woman squeezed her hand, then pulled away as she gave Macey another long look. This time, there was a layer of grief and torment in those large, dark eyes. "Be safe and strong. Your strength is needed."

Before Macey could think of a response, the woman turned and edged out of the pew. She walked slowly across the church toward the red candles, her movements measured and labored as if every step was a great challenge.

When Macey slipped out of the pew a few moments later, the woman was still there—kneeling on a *prie-dieu* in front of the glass-enclosed flames, the Blessed Virgin Mary looking down at her.

Macey stopped at the font of holy water near the entrance and swished her handkerchief in it, and then, without thinking too hard about why, sprinkled some of the water over herself.

Once outside, she was startled to find the sun setting. How long had she been in the church? A wave of nervousness had her walking faster. Fear settled in the pit of her stomach as she hurried along the street, around the block, and headed home. She was only three blocks away, but once the sun was gone, the vampires could safely move about. She'd intended to be home and safe before the undead came out.

How foolish she'd been, staying away for so long.

Or maybe she should have remained at The Silver Chalice until...well, until she made a decision. What to do?

But a sense of inevitability had settled over her. She knew what she had to do. She wasn't certain when she'd decided. Perhaps because there was no other decision to be made.

When Macey reached the sidewalk to her house, she breathed a sigh of relief. The sun was gone, but a last bit of light lingered. And not one glimpse of glowing red eyes, nor any shadowy figure lurking about.

Once inside her apartment, she'd be safe—now that she knew what to do. Rosary on the windowsill. The door barred and its threshold blocked by the handkerchief she'd dipped in holy water.

And she'd sleep with her makeshift stake.

No. No, she wouldn't sleep. Not a wink. Not until the sun came up.

To her surprise, Mrs. Gutchinson wasn't waiting for her. Either the woman had taken a break from spying out the front window, or she was still at her Saturday night mah jongg club. Macey didn't waste any time, dashing up the two flights of stairs as quietly as she could.

As she unlocked the door to her apartment, she glanced toward the window at the end of the hall. By now, the last bit of sunlight had drained away, and the remaining shadows disappeared into darkness. A shiver caught her by surprise—the subtle chill that seemed to settle over the back of her neck.

A fresh wave of nerves had her stumbling into the darkness of her flat, closing the door swiftly behind her. She bolted it, took out the holy-water-soaked handkerchief, and tucked it along the bottom of the door. She could also put some garlic bulbs along there too.

She stood—and just as she sensed she wasn't alone, a hand covered her mouth and an arm captured her, pulling her back against a strong body.

Macey was already fighting. She managed to jam an elbow into her captor's middle and stomp on a foot, twisting and bucking in his powerful grip.

"Shhh, lass. It's only me you're pounding on," grunted a voice in her ear as he struggled to hold her immobile.

"Let me go, you goon!" she hissed.

He released her or she broke free—she wasn't certain which—and Macey spun to face Grady, furious and frightened and relieved all at the same time. She wasn't certain her heart would ever return to normal. "What are you doing here?"

"Hush!" He looked at the door. "Tryin' to keep your landlady from barging in."

Her breathing was still out of sorts. She drew in a deep, ragged one. "An excellent idea. But, I repeat: What are you doing in my flat?"

"You're having the brash to ask me that after going off today with that gangster? How else was I to make sure you got back all right?" Grady loomed over her, dark and imposing, and clearly affronted by her question.

Macey set her handbag down and took off her hat, which had gone askew with her struggles. She turned on a lamp and faced him. "I'm all right. As you can see."

"Aye, and indeed I can," he said, making a point of rubbing his firm midriff at the approximate point her elbow had jabbed him. "A scrapper you are, Macey Denton."

"How did you get in here? Surely Mrs. G didn't let you in."

He gestured to the broken window—which she hadn't yet told Mrs. G about. It was now open and offered just enough of a nice breeze to stir the air in the stuffy third-story room. Even from across the way, she could see the rosary still in its place on the sill.

But there was no tree or trellis nearby, and the fire escape ladder had to be let down from the window. She knew he couldn't have sneaked past Mrs. Gutchinson. "We're three floors up. How on earth did you get up here?"

He grinned, his smile flashing wicked in the soft lamplight. "You've only begun to discover my many skills, lass." His voice dipped and she felt a shiver that was decidedly not chilly.

But the rosary reminded her of her new reality. The broken broomstick handle sat ready on her dresser, ironically, next to the framed, torn picture of her parents. "So now that you've assured yourself I'm safe…surely you can be going now." Then she realized it was dark, and the night held more dangers than merely gangsters and Tommy guns. An undead could be in wait below. "On second thought, maybe you'd better not leave."

"Oh?" His dark blue gaze flared with surprise, then turned warm and heavy. Her insides did a slow, pleasant flip as he moved closer. "You're invitin' me to stay, are you, Macey Denton? Whatever will Mrs. Gutchinson think?"

Her heart thudded, and for a moment she forgot about vampires and stakes and vocations. "I…"

Before she could formulate the rest of the sentence—which was somewhere along the lines of *I don't care*, Grady kissed her.

His lips were soft and warm. Mobile, but most certainly not sloppy.

No, they molded deliciously against her mouth, nibbling and caressing just long enough to make her knees wobbly and her pulse pick up speed. She closed her eyes, and one of her palms settled flat against his chest as she sagged into him. Leaning against his warmth, she parted her lips and his tongue slid past them, strong and bold and slick. He pulled her tighter against his solid chest, his hand sliding up over her bare neck to cup the back of her head. They tangled together, their tongues, sleek and slow and thorough.

When he pulled away, his hand sliding from beneath her curls, Macey realized she'd forgotten to breathe. She drew in an unsteady stream of air as he looked down at her with heavy-lidded, smoky blue eyes. His heart thudded erratically beneath her palm.

"That," he murmured, "was the best thing that's happened to me in a long while, Macey Denton." His grin was a little off-kilter and he reached out again, brushing a finger over her puffy, moist lips. "And I sure as hell hope it's not the last of it."

"I'm not making any promises," she said blithely, trying to regain her senses. She'd kissed boys before, but Grady was definitely not a boy, and this was definitely not the same. Her knees were *weak*. As she stepped back, she realized the window was uncovered—giving anyone, undead or mortal, a clear view into her apartment. She moved over to pull the curtains closed.

By the time she turned, he'd removed his coat and stood there in his vest and white shirt, tie loose and top button undone. And he was holding a book. She recognized it immediately. *The Venators.* Her last bit of muzziness from the kiss evaporated.

"Interesting reading. It explains a lot." He hefted the volume in his hand.

"Does it?" Macey made her voice light, and it was with great effort she kept from touching the bites on her neck.

"Are you going to tell me what's going on?"

Right. And have you think I'm completely looney? "I found the book at the library and started reading it," she said nonchalantly.

"And of course it's no coincidence that shortly thereafter, you're present during a vampire attack at The Gyro, and that your apartment smells like musty death. Oh, and that there's a wooden stake on your bureau and a bitemark on your neck." His eyes glinted with irritation and his tones matched. "A mark that seems to be healing quite quickly." His focus settled heavily on her wound.

"Musty death? I'm sorry you don't care for my choice of perfume," she said. "Maybe you should just leave."

He smiled, but it wasn't filled with humor. "Nice try. All evidence is that you encountered a vampire in this very room last night, and you—or someone else—staked him. I've never smelled undead ash before, but I suspect that's the awful scent lingering in here."

Macey turned away, busying herself by removing her shoes and hanging up her handbag and hat. She wished she had the nerve to unroll her stockings and slip them off too. They were hot and clingy, and it was warm in the apartment. Grady's presence and his avid gaze weren't helping matters either.

"Macey." His voice was low and gently urgent, and close. When she turned, he was standing there, looking down at her with intensity and concern. "Tell me about it. You can trust me."

She bit her lip and looked down. In many ways, she *wanted* to tell him. She wanted to tell *someone*, to find a friend she could talk to about this crazy, frightening, unbelievable turn her life had taken. But she'd only known him for a day!

And if she did tell, he'd either think she was crazy—or, perhaps worse, he'd get as far away from her as possible. What man— especially one who kissed like *that*—would want to be around a gal who attracted vampires? A woman who was the target of the undead? One who might have to spend her life *hunting* them?

"I…" Maybe there was a way to balance truth with evasion. "You're right. I was attacked by a vampire. Last night, in this room. He came in through the window. He bit me, as you know, but I was able to stake him. And he…went away."

"You fought him off? Yourself?" The light in Grady's eyes grew admiring and warm. "You're even more impressive than I realized, lass." Then the light dimmed and he sobered. "And today. You went off with that gangster. What was that about?"

"I told you. He was a friend." She smiled, spreading her hands nonchalantly. "I was in no danger being with him." *At least, not yet.* "He's not a gangster, anyway."

"He's not." Clearly Grady didn't believe her. She couldn't blame him. "What else, Macey? There must be something else going on. I can't believe you were randomly chosen by a vampire and attacked in your flat. Three stories off the ground. There are much easier pickings for the undead on the street by the clubs and bars."

Her heart thudded. He was too damn smart. "I didn't have a chance to ask him why he picked me. I was too busy trying to get his fangs out of my neck."

Grady's lips twisted in a wry smile. "Point taken. Still." He looked down at the book, then around the apartment. His attention landed on the windowsill. "That's the most unusual rosary I've ever seen."

"What do you mean?"

"The extra bead."

Macey shrugged, finally sitting on the edge of her bed. Between the sleepless night, unbelievable day, and that knee-wobbling kiss, she figured she'd earned it. "I've never had a rosary before—until this old woman gave it to me one day. About a week ago. Good thing she did, or I wouldn't have had it to put on the sill. Not that I know whether it did any good or not, but at least it made me feel better. What do you mean, there's an extra bead?"

He brought the chain to her. Macey felt a little spring inside her belly that matched the mattress's jolt as he sat next to her on its edge. His arm brushed hers and the mattress caused her to tip slightly toward him. For one crazy moment, all she wanted to do was lean against him…sink into his warmth, taste that warm mouth, and forget about vampires and stakes and Venators.

"See here? This bead…it's an extra one. With the small silver cross dangling from it. Usually, one big crucifix suffices for the rosary." Grady's smile was crooked and so very close to her, and the beaded chain appeared flimsy and delicate against his strong fingers. They were ink-stained again.

"I didn't realize it was an extra one." The truth was, she hadn't noticed. But now as she fingered the beads, she wondered about the fact that the extra bead and its tiny silver cross were very much like the Venator *vis bulla*. A little shiver of awareness took her by surprise…and for a moment she wasn't certain if it was because of the rosary or Grady's nearness.

"I was worried about you today. I was afraid…well, I didn't want you to meet the same fate as Jennie Fallon." He was so close and he smelled so good Macey found herself hardly able to breathe. His eyes were like Lake Michigan on an autumn day, dark blue and turbulent.

Then came the terrible thought that he might have known the woman after all, even though he'd denied it originally; that Jennie might have been a girlfriend. A guy this intelligent, good looking, and charming had to have a gal. "Did you know her?"

"No. But I told you, I'm a newshawk. And my uncle—Linwood, you met him the other day—keeps me up to date on important news so I can get the scoop."

"You could be the next Mulro or Goldstein." That made sense—Grady was out for the story, emulating the young, determined reporters who'd broken the infamous Leopold and Loeb murder case.

"I could. But there've been two other victims found in the same condition in the last month—the same mauled torso, left in a back alley. Another young woman and a young man. The story is one thing—and if it's a matter of public safety, then you're damn right I'll write it. But I'm more concerned about finding out what's happening and how to stop it so we can keep other pretty young lasses from meeting the same fate. Like yourself." He reached out, tracing his finger over the bite wounds on her neck. The soft touch over her warm, sensitive skin made her shiver pleasantly, and her belly did a delicious little dip. "You could easily have been another victim, Macey. I think it's miraculous—and no mere accident—that you weren't."

"I consider myself very lucky things worked out the way they did."

"And I also find it quite interesting that this morning, these little marks were oozing blood. They were still fresh and bleeding. And now…they're nearly gone. How can that be?" He withdrew his hand.

Nearly gone? Macey reached up to touch the injury and was surprised when she could hardly feel the bumps. "I don't know," she said honestly.

"I read in the book that Venators—surely you know they are vampire hunters—heal extremely quickly."

"I must not have gotten that far," Macey said, suddenly breathless. "I only read a few pages."

"Enough to know that silver and holy objects repel the undead. And that a wooden stake to the heart will kill them." He looked at her for a long moment. Then, his voice gentle, he asked, "What exactly happened when you stabbed him?"

She swallowed. "He…uhm…froze in place. And then all at once, he sort of exploded. The stuff went everywhere, and it smelled awful."

"His clothing too? His shoes? Everything just…went away?"

"*Wait*! Is this an interview? For the paper?" She was outraged, and gave him a shove. "Are you going to write a feature about me and my experience killing a vampire?"

"No!" He glanced toward the door, then turned back to her, lowering his voice and taking her hands in his. "No, this isn't for the paper. Even if I *wanted* to print this—which I don't—do you really think my editor would believe it? He'd have me certified insane and sent off to an asylum." He squeezed her hands. "It's *you*, Macey. You're not just a pretty lass with great legs. You've got a brain. That broomstick didn't break by coincidence. What else is going on?"

She didn't know what to say to that, so she tugged her hands away and stood. She put space between them. "I got lucky. That's all. There's nothing more to tell."

Grady merely looked at her with steady blue eyes. "If that's the way you want it."

That was how it had to be.

"Who the bloody hell is that with her?" Sebastian muttered, shifting his stake from one hand to the other.

"Probably that Irish bastard we had to ditch earlier today."

Sebastian gritted his teeth. Dammit—he hadn't even heard Chas come up behind him. Blasted sneaky bastard. What the devil? Was he getting too old to notice these things, now that he was over a century in age? Or was Chas that damned good?

More likely he was simply ready to pass the torch—to Macey or Chas or whoever the devil would take the responsibility from him. Where the hell was Wayren now that he needed her?

"Bastard's going to be a problem. I can already see it."

Sebastian frowned, looking up at the window of Macey's apartment just in time to see the two silhouettes merge into one. Something inside him shifted as he watched the two kiss—leaving him feeling empty and distant, in more ways than one.

Ah, Victoria.

By God, even in the short time he'd known her, Macey reminded him so much of Victoria...but Victoria, melded in with Giulia. The two women he'd loved beyond all reason, now represented in one being. A petite, stubborn one who held his fate in her hands.

And he'd thought he was damned before.

He choked on a bitter laugh.

Watching the two lovers from a distance created stirrings in Sebastian that had lain dormant, or been suppressed, for decades. He remembered now the pain, the renewed wave of emptiness when he finally realized Victoria didn't love him the way he loved her. That she'd chosen someone else.

As for Giulia...

The stab in his heart felt as pointed and real as if someone slammed an ash stake there. Giulia had never wavered in her deep feelings for him. It was Sebastian who'd destroyed their love, sending her away.

Sentenced her to eternal Hell by driving a stake into her heart.

"What's wrong?"

He turned to Chas, who was too damned nosy for his own good. Spying on him. "I'm going to walk around to the north side."

"I'll keep a close eye on things up there." Chas was looking up at the window. "Damn…peepshow's over."

Sebastian followed his gaze just in time to see Macey pull the curtains, swathing the light-filled rectangle with gauzy material. He was about to walk away when his companion spoke again. "You've been around for a long time. How much do you know about the feud between Alvisi and Iscariot?"

Sebastian's lips moved in a wry smile. "So have you. Longer than I, I think."

Chas shook his head wearily. "In age, perhaps. But not in years on this earth. You forget—I was brought here. You lived it."

It was rare Chas spoke in such a raw, heartfelt manner, and Sebastian blinked. "I cannot argue with you on that, Woodmore—and to be truthful, I'm not sure which of us has had the easier path getting here. Perhaps one day we can sit down over a bottle of excellent Bordeaux and hash it out. The losses, the sacrifices, the heartbreaks."

Chas gave a sharp, appreciative laugh. "That would be quite instructive. Perhaps when this is all over."

"When this is all over." Sebastian looked at him consideringly. "Interesting. I feel the same way. As if I'm on the brink, waiting for something to happen…some event, some culmination. Some truth."

"What was it the prophecy said? The one you mean to fulfill? Something about a 'long promise'?"

"'*And in the New World shall be a savior who carries the deepest taint. A long promise shall the savior make, and in the end those for whom he lives will be saved.*'" As if Sebastian could ever put those words from his mind. They'd been burned there, branded inside him, his holy mantra since the day he realized what he must do.

"We're most certainly in the New World," Chas said. "But you—a savior?"

"'A savior who carries the deepest taint,'" Sebastian reminded him, not at all put off by the other man's wry comment. He heard the acknowledgment buried deep in Chas's voice—the acknowledgment of sacrifice. And admiration and respect. "God knows the taint I carry."

"And you took it willingly. Allowing yourself to be turned undead, giving up your mortality and your soul. For a woman." Now there was the barest hint of a sneer in his voice. Or perhaps it was disbelief.

"For two women."

"Two? It was not merely to save Victoria Gardella?"

Sebastian's lips moved in a wry smile. "There was no need to save Victoria. In fact, in the end, it was she who saved me. But it was, indeed, for her that I…became the way I am."

"And the other woman?"

Giulia.

Before he could decide how—or whether—to respond, a sharp, unmistakable chill settled over the nape of his neck. He and Chas became silent and exchanged looks.

And then, stakes in hand, they went to work.

Macey opened her eyes to morning sunlight, and the first thing she saw was Grady. He was sitting in the chair by her bureau, head tilted against the wall, eyes closed.

Even in sleep, he gripped a wooden stake.

His unruly sable hair was mussed, and he had the dark shadow of stubble over his square chin and jaw. Tie, vest, and shoes had long been removed. He'd unbuttoned the top few buttons of his white shirt, and Macey couldn't help but notice the hint of more dark hair peeking from behind his tight undershirt. Something inside her quivered, hot and slow, and she swallowed hard. He looked rumpled and delicious and more than a little dangerous, especially with that stake in hand. Had he been holding it all night? Watching over and protecting her?

Then she realized—it wasn't the broken broomstick he was holding. It was a real carved and whittled wooden stake.

At that, her heart gave another little awkward bump. He'd brought it with him.

Just then someone knocked on the door. Grady's eyes flew open. He seemed instantly awake and aware, bolting silently from his seat, facing the door. Then he looked at her.

What should I do? he mouthed.

Damn. She was completely rolled. Mrs. Gutchinson would have a fit if she found Grady—or any guy—in here. The landlady might even evict her.

The pounding grew louder and more insistent. "Macey! Are you in there?"

"Flora!" A rush of joy and relief flooded her. Still fully clothed, she had nothing to hide from Grady except a flash of thigh beneath the flutter of her skirt as she flew from the bed. "Shhh," she warned him just before she grabbed the doorknob and turned.

"Thank God you're all right!" She and Flora said the same thing in the same breath as the door opened. Macey assured herself Mrs. G wasn't lurking on the landing, then flew into Flora's arms.

Her best friend was taller than Macey by more than a head, as well as slender and boyish-looking in build. She had the perfect flapper figure: narrow hips, small breasts, and long legs. Flora also had a head of curly orange-red hair cut in the same style as Macey, and freckles everywhere.

Macey knew exactly when Flora saw Grady over her shoulder, for the taller girl froze and then pushed her friend away. She barged fully into the room, her light blue eyes wide as saucers.

"Who is—"

Macey hushed her friend as she shut the door, then turned. "This is Grady."

Flora was looking back and forth between them as if they were batting a tennis ball, her wide mouth curving in an approving smile. "You are *rolled*, Mace! Mrs. G is going to blow her stack."

"Only if she finds out. Which she *won't*." Macey looked at Grady, who'd slipped his shoes on, at least. The stake was nowhere in sight. "Time for you to go. Where is Mrs. G anyway? I can't believe she didn't follow you up here to spy on me. Did she let you in?"

Flora flounced onto the edge of the bed, patting it with her hand as if to test its springs. She winked at Grady, who managed—barely—to look innocent. Which, as a matter of fact, he was.

But then Macey remembered that long, tonguing, sensual kiss and her stomach butterflied. Innocent...at least for now. Her cheeks warmed and she felt that little internal quiver again. She averted her gaze before he noticed her ogling him.

"Of course Mrs. G let me in," Flora said as Grady pulled on his coat. "But apparently my visiting you isn't newsworthy or unusual enough for her to walk me up here. She said her coffee would get cold."

"And it's Sunday. She's probably getting ready for church."

"That old bat goes to church?" Flora laughed. Her eyes danced, then slid to Grady, then back to Macey. Her smile became slightly wicked. "I assume your friend isn't just an early morning visitor."

"He was just leaving." Macey gave him a firm look. After all, kiss or no kiss, she'd never actually *invited* Grady to be here. He'd sneaked in—and laid in wait. With a stake.

"What—no breakfast?" he said, looking longingly at the kitchenette. "Not even a coffee?"

"Not even a coffee." Macey smiled sweetly at him. "And you can leave that—uh—broken broomstick here. I'll take care of it."

"Maybe I'll just stop by Mrs. G's and see if she has a cup to spare," Grady said with an arch smile—then slipped out the door before Macey could stop him.

Surely he wouldn't do that.

"Broken broomstick?" Flora appeared fascinated. "Jeepers—what were you two doing last night?"

Macey shook her head. "It's a long story. But enough about that—tell me what happened at The Gyro. I couldn't find you anywhere."

Flora's bright expression sobered. "It was a terror, wasn't it? I looked for you too, and Chelle and Dottie, but it was such a madness, I just got out of there."

"I did too. Did you—uh—see what was happening? Who was doing the raid?"

"Not really. It was all so scary, I just got outside, to safety. *But*," Flora said, her eyes shining, "it all worked out. Because one of the fellas who was bolting out with me—we got to talking after, you know, when we got far enough away and we were all standing around trying to figure out what happened. Not only is he really snorky, but he gave me a lead on a *job*!"

"That's great! What kind of job? Are you going to see him again?"

Flora made an offhand gesture. "Oh, I already did. See him again." Her grin was wide and infectious. "And I have the job interview tonight."

"Tonight? What kind of job is it?" Macey frowned.

"Don't get all worried over it. I know you wouldn't approve, but it's serving tables at a club. It's really good money, Mace."

"A club? A speakeasy kind of club?" Aside from the legality of the situation—not to mention the personal danger that could be involved if it was a place gangsters frequented—Macey couldn't imagine the fun, long-limbed, gawky Flora waiting tables, pushing her way between crowded tables while carrying a tray of drinks. She couldn't even do a job interview without knocking over a cup of coffee into the hiring person's lap…how could she wait tables? It was a disaster waiting to happen. *I've got to find something for her at the university.*

But not with antique books. Or in a lab, with all the beakers and burners…

"No, goof. It's a dance club like The Gyro. I'll tell you more later, after I go. But now you have to tell me about your Mr. Grady—or is that his first name?"

Macey realized with a start she didn't even know the answer. But she was saved from formulating a reasonable reply when someone knocked peremptorily on the door.

It could only be Mrs. G, and for once, she was glad for the interruption. Unless her landlady had seen Grady leaving and was coming to lecture her…

With no little trepidation, Macey looked out the peephole. Temple stood there, and even through the small view, her impatience was obvious. Macey glanced at Flora, but saw no choice but to open the door.

Temple flowed right in. "All right, sister, we've got to get—ah, hello. Who's this?" She looked from one to the other and paused, hands on hips.

Both women were taller and sturdier than Macey, and for a moment, the group of them was reflected in the mirror over her bureau. Flora, gangly and looking like fun and sunshine, was slightly more slender than the Negro woman. Temple was the picture of grace and elegance, with her café au lait skin and sleek cap of black hair. While Flora looked like a farmgirl, Macey thought Temple resembled a Nubian princess dressed in modern fashion.

"I'm Flora. And who are you?" There was no small note of surprise and suspicion in her voice. She looked at sharply at Macey.

"This is Temple. I met her the night of the raid at The Gyro. We ran out together—like you and your new guy. What did you say his name was?"

"Antony." She was still looking at Temple. "So, what are you doing here?"

Macey's cheeks heated. Flora, aside from being sunshine and fun, could also be painfully blunt. And her father was a member of the Ku Klux Klan. Not that Flora herself donned white hooded cloaks and burned crosses on the lawns of Negroes, Catholics or Jews, but she'd grown up in a family who spoke with open prejudice toward those minorities.

"Temple was going to take me to—"

"I promised Macey I'd show her my auntie's millinery shop. Would you like to come?" Temple's voice was cool and polite, yet the glint in her eyes acknowledged Flora's aversion to her presence.

"I haven't seen you for days, Mace. Can't you do that another time? Jimmy wanted to take us out tonight too. He was mad he wasn't at The Gyro with us the night of the raid—to take care of us."

"I thought you had a job interview tonight," Macey said weakly. Temple had walked over to her bureau and picked up the broken broomstick handle. Then her attention wandered to the torn picture of Macey's mother on her wedding day. "What about if I come over after we go to the milliner's shop—unless you want to go with us?"

"No. I'll just go home. You can come over to the boardinghouse when you're done." Flora gave her one last look, then flounced out the door.

No sooner had it closed behind her than Macey turned to Temple. "I suppose Sebastian sent you."

"You suppose correctly. I hope you've made the right decision."

"The right decision for whom?" She glared at Temple, then at the world in general.

She'd had more visitors in the last twenty-four hours than she'd had since moving into this flat, and more upheaval in her life since she finally arrived in Skittlesville.

"I'm talking about the right decision for mankind, sister."

"For mankind? Don't you think that sounds a little… dramatic?"

Temple shook her head, arms still crossed over her slender middle. "From what I hear, even Victoria Gardella wasn't as stubborn and narrow-sighted as you. When you're one of the Chosen few called—and given the skills—to fight to eradicate a demonic evil, your decision does, indeed, affect mankind. Now, are you coming with me or not?"

And then…you hunt vampires.

Macey looked at the broken broomstick, the *Venators* book, the rosary…the chair where Grady had sat guard all night. And then at the mutilated photo of her mother on her wedding day.

She nodded. "I'm coming."

And then she promptly felt sick to her stomach.

Eight

Of Trying and Thinking and Doing

"AND SO YOU ARE READY to take on the *vis bulla*," said Sebastian in his velvety voice. He smiled at her, his amber eyes warm and intimate.

Macey found it difficult to swallow. She was both nervous and a little intimidated by him—this unaccountably handsome man who looked like a golden angel.

A golden angel with an air of deviltry.

"I will try…" she began, but the words stuck in her throat.

"*Try?* One cannot *try* to be a Venator."

Macey spun at the sound of the condemning voice. Chas walked through the door, dark and slick and gloomy. He was dripping wet, for it had begun to pour rain just as Macey and Temple arrived at The Silver Chalice.

"If you are called as a born Venator, you must either give your life for the legacy, or you deny your Calling. If you do, your mind is erased of all knowledge. You live in ignorant oblivion."

Macey stared at Chas. "You said that before…but do you mean that literally?"

"Of course. I told you yesterday."

She turned to Sebastian, whose sensual, angelic appearance had turned black and furious. Chas sauntered past the table that had been set up in the center of the room and took a seat in a plump brown armchair, heedless of his soaked clothing. He crossed his legs and gave Sebastian an amiable smile.

"It *is* true?" she said to Sebastian, knowing this was her last chance to change her mind.

"It is." The words sounded as if they were wrung from his throat.

Silence hung, taut, in the room for a moment. Macey tried to steady her breathing, grab hold of her thoughts. Temple had taken her through Cookie's Smart Millinery and down into a hidden cellar, which led to a tunnel connected to Sebastian's quarters. Once she delivered Macey, Temple had taken herself off somewhere, leaving Macey with Sebastian—and now Chas.

She looked around, taking a moment to examine the space as a way to clear her mind. This was a chamber she'd not seen on her previous visit to the Chalice. Attached to Sebastian's private quarters, the rectangular area was more of a library or office than a living room.

There were two doors at opposite ends of the room—one through which they'd entered, passing through the parlor in which she'd originally met Sebastian. Filled bookshelves lined one wall. Two armchairs—where Chas currently left small puddles on the rug—were arranged in front of a desk, sporting stacks of books and papers, a lamp, and writing implements. A glass-doored cabinet on the shortest, far wall held a variety of curious objects—odd statues, unusual jewelry including a tarnished metal cuff. Even a large, shiny black splinter made of some material she couldn't identify. The items looked like artifacts, as if they belonged in a museum. A large book that appeared to be a Bible sat on a shelf in the center of the cabinet. Arranged on a bookstand, the tome was open to a page Macey would swear had been hand-lettered by a twelfth-century monk.

Her fingers itched to examine the book, and she could hardly keep her eyes away. She didn't work at a library for nothing.

The tension in the room was still high, and Macey hadn't formulated her response when the far door opened. Immediately, a sense of peace filled the place, as if a glass wall had shattered and allowed air to flow freely.

A woman glided through the door and Macey stared. She'd never seen anyone dressed like her: in a simple, undyed floor-length gown that reminded her of illustration plates of Lady Guinevere, with wrist-length sleeves that had cuffs long enough to drag on the ground. Her waist was cinched with a simple chain belt—silver—and her pale moonbeam hair reached well below the links. Two sets of three narrow braids at her temples were gathered back from her face and plaited together to hang down the back of her hip-length, loose hair. Despite her medieval garb, the woman carried a modern leather satchel.

She smiled at the three of them, and Macey felt another wave of unexpected warmth and comfort settle over her. She looked at Sebastian, who wore what could only be described as an expression of chagrin—as if he'd been caught with a hand in the candy jar. Chas stilled and seemed to sink deeper into the embrace of his armchair.

Neither of them spoke, and the woman turned calm gray-blue eyes toward her. Macey considered, but couldn't decide how old she thought the new arrival was. Certainly older than she, but not old at all. It was as if she were ageless.

The woman inclined her head. "Macey Denton. You are very nearly the image of your great-great-grandmother."

"But with her great-great-grandfather's eyes." Sebastian spoke at last, his voice low. Then he addressed the newcomer. "And what a sight for sore eyes you are, *madame*. I've been wondering when—or if—you might…er…*grace* us with your presence ever again." He gave a short, tight laugh.

She turned a bemused smile on him, and Macey watched in fascination as Sebastian's show of irritation eased. Once again she thought he resembled a shamefaced little boy, caught doing something wrong by someone he adored and yet feared. And Chas looked as if he wished to be anywhere but here, yet was afraid to get up and leave.

Macey, intrigued but not intimidated, spoke to her. "You seem to know me—and you're the only person so far to call me by my real name. But who are you?"

"I'm Wayren, of course." Her bemused smile widened as she glanced at Sebastian and Chas. "I'm not certain whether I should be pleased or offended neither of these two fine gentlemen have spoken to you of me."

"Since you haven't made an appearance in over a decade, I wasn't expecting to have to introduce you to Macey anyway," Sebastian said. "Aside from the fact that no mere words can do you justice, of course. Even I dared not attempt it." He gave her a genuine smile, clearly more at ease now. In fact, Macey thought she detected a definite sense of relief.

"It was time to return," Wayren said simply, then looked at Macey. Her gaze, though mild and warm, seemed to penetrate deep. "Your given name is certainly Denton, but more importantly, your legacy is Gardella. Have you made your decision?"

"I…think so."

"First it's *try*, and now it's *think*? For God's sake, there can be no hesitation for a Venator. You either take up the stake, wed it, and live with it, or you exist in ignorance!"

To Macey's surprise, Chas's outburst elicited nothing but a glance from Wayren. Not even a lifted brow for punctuation. She returned her attention to Macey. "Perhaps I should send them away so the two of us can speak without interruption."

At that, Macey smiled. "That's the most sense anyone's made since Temple dragged me out of The Gyro and tried to force me down the stairs to meet Sebastian."

"Indeed. I can imagine how that must have gone." Wayren laughed lightly and charming little crinkles appeared at the corners of her eyes, which had turned to a clear cerulean blue.

"I pushed him down the stairs."

"Of course you did."

She must have seen Macey's eyes flicker toward the ancient book in the cabinet, for the next thing she knew, Wayren was going over to it and then opening the doors. "This is the Gardella family Bible. The oldest pages have been in the family since the mystic Rosamunde recorded her prophecies in them at Lock Rose Abbey in the twelfth century."

Macey couldn't keep from reaching toward the aged, aged pages, then snatched back her hand before she touched them. She looked up at Wayren, who nodded permission. "The book belongs to you, Macey Gardella. If you choose to accept the call. Your name will be added on the frontispiece below that of your father's, where are listed all of the Gardella Venators who have descended in the direct line from—"

"Gardeleus," Macey whispered, remembering the story in *The Venators*. "The first Venator—a gladiator in first-century Rome."

Wayren nodded. "He was called on a quest to protect mankind and rid the earth of the immortal half-demon creatures descended from the betrayer Judas Iscariot. Those beings were given their immortality—and an unquenchable need for blood—by the fallen angel Lucifer." She turned to the back of the book, showing Macey the writing there. "See you here…the list of all the other Venators from far-flung branches of the family, or otherwise brought into the fold: Max, Sebastian, Michalas, Brim…and the list goes on to the present day. Martinus. David. Ranetti. Alphonsus. And Chas Woodmore."

When Macey touched the Bible at last, a shock of awareness, of vibrating, sizzling energy shuttled through her. *Yes.*

The word reverberated through her…not so much in her head or ringing in her ears, but within her. **Yes.**

Then she remembered the voice in the church: *You can.*

She looked up at Wayren, who was watching her with steady eyes. Macey was hardly aware Sebastian and Chas were still present; all of her attention was on the book and the serene blond woman next to her. She looked down at the aged tome once more. Something swelled in her, warm and full and peaceful. Certainty. Serenity.

"Yes. I'll do it."

At her words, it was as if the room itself gave a great sigh of relief.

Or perhaps it was something inside Macey, that part which had long been waiting for the chance to blossom and grow into what had long ago been planted.

"Very well then," Wayren said, her gaze still calm and warm. "Sebastian, do you have the *vis bulla*?"

He handed the blond woman an ornate glass bottle, hardly larger than his thumb. Its cork was fixed in place by a melted seal that glinted, as if the wax had been mixed with silvery dust. The small bottle was filled with clear liquid and inside was a delicate silver cross suspended from a hoop that wouldn't even fit over the tip of her small finger.

Macey's heart thumped harder as Sebastian broke the seal. She noticed for the first time he was missing half of the pinkie finger on his left hand, the hand on which he wore the red-stoned signet ring. But she was distracted from wondering how and when the accident occurred when he opened the bottle. As he poured the contents into his cupped palm, there was a small puff, followed by a bit of steam.

Sebastian glanced at her, the wince easing from his expression. "One of the many hazards of my condition."

He could easily have avoided touching the holy water, as well as the *vis bulla*. Macey didn't know whether he meant to show off for her—or Wayren, perhaps—or whether he had other reasons for exposing himself to the pain. It occurred to her then, also, that if he was a Venator, he too must wear a *vis bulla*. Did it cause him constant pain as well? The holy silver amulet against his undead flesh?

Sebastian handed the tiny cross to Wayren, who turned to Macey. "Steeped in holy water from beneath the Vatican from a font in the private quarters of the Venators—a place known as the Consilium—the *vis* is forged of silver. Every undead is repelled by this pure metal because it represents the thirty silver coins for which Judas sold Jesus. The amulet must be worn pierced through the skin in order to give the full benefit of its power. Only one who has been called to the Gardella Legacy, and who has also slain a vampire on his or her own, may wear and feel the effects of the holy amulet."

"But…" Macey frowned and looked at Chas, remembering the offer to show her his *vis bulla*. "I thought you weren't Called."

"I'm a special case. In more than one way." His tone was slightly less caustic than usual, due, she suspected, to the presence of the mysterious Wayren. "Perhaps someday I'll tell you how I came to be here, in the twentieth century, when I was originally from a much different time."

Wayren continued. "Chas is correct—there is that rare exception. If a mortal who is not born to the Gardella Legacy so chooses, he or she may attempt what is called a Trial. If he or she succeeds—and there have been many who tried and only six in all the centuries who have succeeded—then he or she is given a *vis bulla*."

"With all the same powers of a born Venator?"

"Indeed. There is no difference except the new Venator has actually sought the chance to become a chosen vampire hunter instead of being called to it. And he has accomplished a task that could only be completed with the help of divine intervention."

Macey hesitated. But she had to ask. "What about my father?"

"Max Denton was a born Venator and an incredible warrior. He and his father before him." Wayren gestured to the table in the center of the room. "Now, if you are ready, Macey Denton, I shall arm you with the *vis bulla*."

Her palms suddenly sprang damp, but Macey climbed onto the table, sitting on the edge with her legs dangling off. "Where do you put it?" She reached for her earlobe, where many women wore pierced earrings.

"You may wear it wherever you wish, but most Venators choose to have it pierced through the upper lip of the navel. In that way, not only is it out of sight and protected from any undead who might use it to identify you, or worse, disarm you by tearing it away, but it is also very near the center of your body. Its power can more easily flow through every limb and elsewhere."

"Yes. I agree. That would be the best." Then, realizing what she'd just agreed to, Macey swallowed. Not only would it be uncomfortable, she would also have to bare her midriff in front of Chas and Sebastian. Her cheeks grew hot and, without meaning to, she looked at Sebastian. He caught her doing so, and, his lips twitching into a devilish smile, he held her eyes for a beat too long. His gaze turned dark and warm, like rich golden velvet. He didn't even need the flare of his glowing thrall to capture her.

Macey tore her eyes away, her insides fluttering with winged creatures, heat rushing through her body as she imagined his elegant fingers sliding over her bared flesh.

"If you will recline." Wayren's direction was mild, but Macey dared not look at the imposing woman for fear she'd seen the interplay with Sebastian.

Instead, she hoisted her legs onto the table and lay flat on her back, taking care not to expose any more of her thighs than necessary. Fortunately, she'd worn a skirt and blouse today rather than a dress, so it was simple business to work the top free from the waistband into which it was tucked.

The air was cool on the uncovered skin of her belly, contrasting with the warmth of self-consciousness flooding her face and throat and Wayren's easy touch on her abdomen. The blond woman paused to retrieve a pair of spectacles with square lenses from her satchel and she put them on as Macey tried to relax.

She drew in a deep breath, arms flat at her sides. Her attention fell on Chas, who stood next to Sebastian on one side of the table. He wore an inscrutable expression, something between pain and hope. His hands were curled into tight fists, hanging at his sides. Was he remembering when he received his *vis bulla?* That thought had her wondering where he wore it, and the image of a bare torso rose in her mind.

Would you like to see my vis bulla, *Macey?*

She swallowed and then gasped at the sudden, sharp pain at her belly. But Wayren's movements were smooth and quick, and moments later, Macey felt the slight, cool weight of the tiny cross settling into the hollow of her navel.

At the same time, a sizzle of energy and light flooded her. She felt it. She truly *felt* it.

Before she could do it herself, strong hands helped her upright—it was Chas—and she nodded her thanks to him.

"It's done," he said simply, then stepped away. His hand settled on his own midriff.

Sebastian was looking at her too, his golden brown eyes soft and warm. "Thank you."

"Welcome." Wayren handed Macey the empty bottle, its cork stopper back in place. "You may keep this if you like."

"Thank you." She took it. Then, very conscious of the sharp throbbing at her belly mingled with a sizzle of awareness, Macey tucked the shirt tail back into her waistband. "Er...now what happens?"

"You hunt vampires," Chas said. And grinned.

There were speakeasies and gambling houses and brothels... and then there was The Blood Club.

Chas didn't think much of the establishment's name, but it wasn't as if it were emblazoned on a sign over the door. Ah, no. Access to this exclusive club was limited to those who knew where to find it and how to enter.

Thus, he knew to patronize a tailor shop named Rico's, and to ask for the trousers he'd dropped off a week ago. "To be double-stitch hemmed over the back of the heel," he told the man behind the counter.

It was a different person every day.

Nevertheless, the man gestured to the back as whoever was behind the counter always did. "Third dressing room. You gotta go try 'em on."

Chas went into the indicated dressing room. Once inside with the door closed behind him, he swung open the floor-length mirror to reveal a large, dimly lit room. The familiar scraping sensation deep in his belly confirmed there were many undead in the vicinity.

At first glance, the place looked like any other saloon or cabaret. Tables were scattered about, some in darker corners than others. Many were booths with high, rounded sides. Decorated with red-swathed lamps, the space was unusually warm in temperature as well as appearance. Smoke and the scent of stale whiskey mingled with a pungent, metallic aroma. Despite the freshness of the libation of choice, a long counter with bottled options lined the short end of the room and a sharp-faced, undead bartender moved behind it. As Chas entered, closing the mirror-door behind him, he heard the telltale clink of bottles amid low, rumbling conversation.

Outside, the sun was still up, but that didn't matter—the small, windowless place was crowded. Smoke stung Chas's eyes, which were still becoming used to the dim light, as he wound his way through the tables. While there were no waitresses per se, there were other club employees scattered throughout: beautiful young women in short, bright dresses with glittery headbands, high heels, and boas, and handsome men in spats and tailored suits with bloodred ties. Some stood near the counter, others leaned against the side of a shoulder-height stage, others wandered from table to table, greeting the patrons and then sliding into an offered seat.

"Welcome to The Blood Club," said a throaty voice.

Chas turned, the gnawing in his belly very strong now, and took in the woman's appearance. Slender, blond-haired, with the paper-white skin of an undead, she was nevertheless an attractive creature with generous curves and full lips. No surprise, for the Club's proprietor, Count Alvisi, offered only the best service—whether from an undead or a mortal, depending upon the patron's choice.

"What's your pleasure, handsome?" she asked, showing a hint of fang from behind dark red lips.

Too soon for that yet, so he jerked a thumb toward the bar. "For now." He did allow his attention to linger over her before pushing on past, just to keep the option open. Sliding onto a stool, he ordered a whiskey. When it came, he tossed it back in one motion, then ordered a second before the bartender even walked away.

Vioget would say it was a waste to slam a good Scotch down without savoring it, but Chas had his reasons. And though the drink was smooth, aged, and pure—unlike the vast majority of liquor served in Chicago—if he was going to have any success tonight, he had an impression to make.

A short time later, he fumbled into his pocket to withdraw a bill to pay for four whiskeys. Then he slurred his thanks to the bartender and made a show of being potted off his arse. Sliding off the stool, he staggered and clunked his hand clumsily against the bar as he turned.

The blond vampire who'd greeted him watched from across the way, despite the fact that she'd seated herself at a table with what appeared to be a less interesting mortal—older, rounder, and grayer than him. That was no surprise; Chas attracted women as easily as a stake slid into an undead heart—a benefit of which he took great advantage. The blonde's eyes narrowed into obvious invitation, and Chas knew she'd ditch her current "customer" if he gave her the slightest bit of encouragement.

But he didn't. Not yet. Not until he decided on his own target.

The whiskey warmed him, made him a little too aware of his needs and desires—particularly with a sensual woman giving him that hungry look. At least she was blond. Blond was easier. Yet, every time he stepped into this place, it reminded him of Rubey's establishment, of being with the raven-haired, incomparably beautiful Narcise, of memories he'd tried to leave behind—his troubled past, falling in love with a vampire.

Wayren had offered him a way out, but even she couldn't eradicate history.

He continued on his path, and despite the amount he'd imbibed, Chas found he was still horribly steady and clear-headed.

Fuck. Perhaps he should have had five shots.

No. He didn't have the luxury of being impaired…not yet. Nevertheless, he made a show of being deeply into his cups as he wandered among the tables. It was easy as breathing for him to differentiate the undead from the mortals who'd come to play dangerous vampire games.

Now it was just a matter of finding one who could give him the information he needed.

A change in the air had the hair at the back of his neck lifting a little, and the gouging sensation in his belly grew stronger. Chas pretended to trip, and as he righted himself by stumbling against a table, he looked over and saw Alvisi entering the room.

The count was well over a century old, having been turned a vampire during the time of Victoria Gardella. Despite being undead and cloistered from the sunlight, he remained olive-skinned. He had thin, lank brown hair and a dapper personality: slender, lithe, and bordering on effeminate.

Every bit as in control as Al Capone would be when he walked into the Four Deuces, Alvisi captured the attention of every patron and worker as he surveyed the saloon. Instead of being accompanied by gun-toting bodyguards, on his arms were two attractive women. Taller than he, both were slender with curling strawberry-blond hair and almond-shaped eyes. Other ladies surrounded him as well, each one a different shade of blond, wearing a blue frock and headdress, each one tall and willowy. From his distance, Chas couldn't tell for certain which of the escorts were mortal and which were undead...a fact it was imperative he rectify before making his move. But at least now he had more of a target.

He navigated his way toward the large curved booth where Alvisi and his entourage settled in. And he caught the eye of one of the blondes as he slipped, still clumsy, into a seat at a nearby table. He didn't want to appear too sauced. Just enough to look like easy pickings.

The blonde noticed him. They always did, especially if he gave any encouragement. He smiled and shot her a hot look, and when she flashed her fangs at him, he felt a repulsive shudder of attraction. But just as she was about to ease away from the group to join him, a passerby cut in between them, slicing through their gazes. Thus distracted, Chas allowed his attention to shift around once more. His eyes fastened on another woman with long, inky hair that hung sleekly past her shoulders. She had a delicate, oval face, indistinct because of the smoke and the distance, but it didn't matter.

A hitch seized him in the gut, and he met her stare. He felt a little clammy; the effects of the whiskey surging a little stronger now. When she flared her eyes and they glowed, he swallowed hard. And nodded at her, holding her gaze even as he felt the tug of the thrall.

As the brunette stood, their connection broke, giving him the opportunity to draw in a breath designed to clear his head. *Too late now.* His pulse pounded, and his insides sloshed with whiskey, revulsion…and, *goddam* him, anticipation.

"I've never seen you here before," she murmured as she slid into the chair next to his. Now she was close, and other than the long, straight fall of shining hair, she didn't look anything like Narcise.

"I've never been here before," he replied, easier now. It was always good when he wasn't recognized. "But I thought I'd… try something new." He smiled—a balance of seduction and hesitance.

She licked her lips, showing the tips of her fangs. "Something new? Well, you've come to the right place." She was nearly in his lap, her hand placed intimately on his thigh.

"Do you have a name?" Chas asked casually, then leaned in to cover her lips. One cold, one warm…but he was used to the odd sensation.

After a long, thrusting kiss, he eased back, keeping his eyelids heavy as he traced a finger over her exposed collarbone. Even as he played the seducer—or the seduced, depending upon how one looked at it—he had one ear fixed on the conversation coming from Alvisi's table. He could only hear bits and pieces, and hoped the woman in his lap would fill in the rest.

"Valia," she replied, sliding her hand over his chest then up to play with his long hair. Her other hand slipped over the growing bulge of his cock. "My…"

He nibbled on her neck, then murmured, "Another whiskey first?"

"Of course." She smiled with delight and signaled the bartender. "And then…would you prefer to stay here, or find somewhere more…private?"

Chas gave her a long, slow smile, making his expression surprised and delighted. "That's permitted?"

She laughed, low and husky, and unbuttoned the top button of his shirt, pulling the cloth away from his throat and shoulder. Blood surged in his veins, but Chas eased back slightly. *Not yet, darling.*

"The count allows us to do whatever our patrons wish. Whatever *we* wish," Valia told him, her attention focused on his throat. The drink appeared at his elbow, and when he made a show of digging out his money, she waved him off. "My treat."

"I certainly hope so."

She flashed a glow of ruby approval in her gaze and began to unbutton his cuff. Chas allowed her to do so, but he had to work quickly. His pulse was beginning to speed up, and she seemed determined.

"He…that man over there? Is that the owner?" he asked.

She began to roll up his sleeve, baring his wrist. The marks from previous bites had all but faded, and she wouldn't notice the faint scars in this dim light. "Count Alvisi. Yes, he is the owner."

"He looks as if he could give Al Capone a run for his money. Unless…is Capone like him?"

Valia gave a husky laugh, lifting his arm in her two hands as if it were a silver platter. "Capone? One of us? Not yet. But soon." She slanted a look up at him, her eyes at full glow, her fangs long and ready to plunge.

He licked his lips, his mouth dry. *Not yet, goddammit.* Curling his hand around the back of her neck, he dragged Valia up against him and covered her mouth with his. He didn't worry about being too rough. The undead were violent creatures.

She arched her breasts into his chest, releasing his arm in order to climb onto his lap even more, all the while matching his delving, thrusting tongue with her own. Then, giving a sharp twist, she nicked his lip with a fang. Chas tasted blood as their mouths smashed together, and felt the deep shudder trammel through her as she sucked brutally at the cut, drawing in a bit of his life.

He eased away when she began to unfasten his belt. "Let's go," he murmured, shifting his hips from her questing hands.

She was out of the booth before him, and when he stood, he remembered to stagger a little. "Follow me." Valia took his arm.

Chas didn't want to be seen leaving with her, but there was little he could do about it except keep his face averted and move quickly. The sooner they were out of sight, the less likely they'd be noticed.

By now, the whiskey had begun to soften his control and loop wickedly through his mind. Still, he was assured and confident as they slipped out of the saloon into a dark hall.

"This way," he said, tugging at her when she would have led him to one of the private rooms. He knew better.

Valia didn't resist; she would have no reason to. With superhuman strength and lethal fangs, she didn't fear a mere mortal man.

It was too bad she wasn't dealing with one. Chas hid his tight grin by backing her up against the wall for a long kiss and a serious grope between her legs. She moaned and hissed into his ear, and he felt the scrape of fangs against his bare throat. Ducking away just in time, he said, "Impatient, are we?" and directed her into the storage room behind the tailor shop.

He'd hardly closed the door when she was on him, kissing and tearing at his clothes. Her eyes were pink-red beacons in the darkness, and he stumbled back against a stack of crates under her onslaught.

They crashed into the wall, and even in the darkness, the room tilted and spun, and he had to close his eyes for a moment. Chas shuddered at the rush of arousal when Valia pressed against him, all her lush curves and warm skin, sliding her hand down his trousers and over his ready cock. She stroked, her fingers tight around him. Without warning, she slammed her fangs into his shoulder.

He couldn't hold back a groan of pain and release as the blood burst free and he tumbled into that dark place of pleasure and need. She writhed against him, moaning and stroking, sliding belly to belly as she fed on his blood. He responded, sagging against the brick behind him, filling his hands with her breasts, allowing himself to think only of the moment…of the heat and rising release pulsing through him with each of her gulps.

When she pulled away, covering his mouth with hers, he tasted metallic blood. Revulsion surged deep in his belly, but eroticism pushed it away as he devoured the vampire's mouth. Chas shifted, moving so she was pinned between him and the wall. Her skirt lifted, she gripped his cock and guided him into place, all the while panting in his ear, moaning and gasping against his throat.

As he slammed inside her, blind with arousal and pain, desperate to fight off the darkness and find relief, she bit him again, viciously and deep. Chas cried out as the orgasm flooded through him, shuddering and quaking a violent release.

Then he spun away, staggering from her. When he turned, he had his stake in hand and in one smooth movement, he plunged it into her chest.

Valia froze, her ruby eyes flaring wide, her fangs pale and white in the dim light. Then she was gone in a cloud of ash.

Chas leaned against the wall, breathing heavily. The whiskey surged sickeningly in his belly, loathing and remorse washing over him in a dark, vile wave.

And yet his body still hummed and twitched, still breathed of repletion, still wanted.

"Sebastian."

"Giulia," he breathed, reaching for her. But his hand swiped through air and fell uselessly to his side, among the twisted blankets and sheets of his bed.

The movement threatened to pull him out of sleep, out of his dream. Caught in that moment in between the two planes, he fought to stay deep in slumber, to remain in the nocturnal realm with her. It had been so long since he'd dreamed of his beloved. He stilled, willing himself to slip back into the embrace of Morpheus…

"Sebastian." Giulia smiled at him, her eyes soft and filled with love. She was still there. "You are relieved."

"She accepted the call," he replied from deep in his slumber. "Now to finish it. And then the long promise will be kept."

She shook her head sadly. "But your work is not finished. You still wear the rings. There is more to come, *mi adorate*. You must be strong." Her dark hair swirled around ivory shoulders, her expression rosy and alive as it hadn't been in life. She stood at the side of his bed, so close he swore he felt her push against the mattress. He reached for her again, desperate, and again his movement was ineffectual.

But this time, when his hand fell helplessly to the bed, he lurched out of the dream. Fully awake. Damp with perspiration and hard with need, his heart pounding, the blood surging through his veins.

Flinging the bedclothes away, he sat up and looked around the shadowy, windowless chamber. Heaved a long, heavy breath. Wiped his eyes.

A burst of fury and loathing shuttled through him. He snatched up a glass from the table and whipped it into the wall. The fact that it shattered beautifully, exploding in a glittering rage, did little to calm his own.

By God, when will this be done?

Wasn't a century of hell long enough of a punishment? A hundred years of uncertainty, of temptation and iron control and *loneliness*, held together by the gossamer threads of an occasional dream and his own damned blind hope.

Every day he felt his hold on sanity waver and falter. He was exhausted, stretched taut and terribly thin. He felt like a candle that had burned down to the last of its wick and was nothing more than a tiny blue dot of flame, struggling in a deadly pool of wax.

And now that Macey Gardella had come into the fold, so to speak, he felt even more strongly the tenuousness of his battered control. She was his hope, his salvation—or so he believed, so he *prayed*—and yet she could just as easily be his downfall.

You must be strong.

Yes, and Macey too. She had no idea what awaited her.

Wayren had returned. That alone meant something; *surely* it meant something. She was the one who'd led him on this path—or at least shown him the way. A century ago, Sebastian had made his choice freely and with a pure heart. He'd done it for love of Victoria, but most of all, for love of Giulia and the reclamation of her soul. Though Wayren had not yet spoken to him directly, her very presence was instrumental in acquiring Macey's agreement to take on the *vis*.

But now…what more must he accomplish before he could be released from this hell on earth?

Even in the dim bedchamber, he could see, of course. There was no need for a light, and so when his gaze happened to fall on his right hand, his attention was caught by the glint of the ever-present rings.

Five of them. One on each digit. Made from slender copper strands, each braided intricately and uniquely.

Forged by the malicious and magnificent Lilith the Dark, the Rings of Jubai had been acquired through a variety of means by Victoria Gardella, Max Pesaro, and Sebastian himself a century ago. And it was Sebastian who'd insisted on wearing the rings and plunging his hand into the enchanted pool at Muntii Fâgâras.

But when he was up to his elbow in the dangerous, mercurial pool, Giulia appeared to him as a reflection in the waters. Instead of the haunting, sensual dreams he usually had of her, this time she begged him to save her—something he'd never conceived as possible. And thus he'd embarked on the impossible task of redeeming the soul of a vampire. A vampire *he'd* slain. One *he'd* sent to hell.

The copper rings, which must be worn in order to immerse one's hand safely in the pool, had fused to his fingers. And there they had stayed for decades. Sebastian knew the only way they could be removed was upon his death, for copper was the only substance that remained after an undead was slain.

For all he cared, Chas Woodmore or Macey Gardella could pike him in the heart tomorrow and have the rings, if that was what was needed to fulfill his "long promise" and set both him and Giulia free.

In fact, he prayed for it. Daily. On his knees.

He'd long ago lost his sense of humor over being a vampire with a tainted soul, praying for divine intervention. He was done.

Release me. Please release me.

The whole idea of hunting vampires was so incomprehensible Macey could hardly wrap her mind around it. But the delicate dangle of her *vis bulla* against the sensitive skin of her belly was a constant reminder of how her life was to change.

And then there was the training.

"Temple isn't a Venator?" she asked Wayren, who seemed to be the only person willing to answer her questions without prevarication—and without some ulterior motive.

"No indeed. Temple is your Comitator. She'll train you in the hand-to-hand combat styles of *kalaripayattu, qinggong,* and *tae kwon do,* as well as how to handle a variety of blades. Each Venator is assigned one such person to act also as bodyguard and companion—especially for their early days when things are still new."

"Bodyguard?"

"A Venator can't always be awake and aware," Sebastian told her with a wry smile. "And though Chas and I will be here, it never hurts to have someone to help. Don't expect her to come with you on the hunt. Temple's an excellent fighter, but she's not equipped as you are. Interestingly enough, most born Venators would have received some training before facing their first undead and receiving the *vis.* You took matters into your own hands. I do hope that isn't going to be a portent of the future, *ma cherie.*"

Chas made a derisive sound, then lapsed into silence. Macey ignored him.

The same day she received her *vis bulla*, she began her training with Temple. They worked in a basement room beneath Cookie's Smart Millinery (apparently, Cookie really was Temple's aunt). The underground chamber was large, taking up what would be the same space as the back room of the millinery shop. But it was empty of furnishings other than a wall lined with cabinets. The walls were strung with electric lights, the floor covered with an unusual tile made from cork, and a stack of large cushions leaned against a corner. In the cabinets Macey saw an array of stakes, pikes, and knives—everything from scythe-like curved blades to finger-sized stilettos to daggers and swords of European and Asian influence. She wasn't surprised to note there were no guns to be seen, for a bullet would have no effect on a vampire.

But a sword, she learned, could be used to behead an undead, and was just as effective as stabbing one through the heart. Both actions resulted in the same explosion of undead dust.

Temple, her long, lean body covered by a pair of loose cotton trousers and a matching undyed tunic, looked fierce, elegant, and intimidating. Macey, dressed in similar clothing, barely reached to her trainer's chin, and the other woman had smooth muscles in her arms.

How am I ever going to do this? She's going to flatten *me.*

But when Temple lunged gracefully toward her, Macey reacted without thinking. She ducked, grabbed the other woman as she slipped beneath her arm, and on her upward thrust, fairly threw her across the chamber.

"Oh my God!" Macey gawked as Temple pulled to her feet. "Did I do that?"

Despite being dumped in a heap, the other woman was smiling broadly. "You certainly did." She dusted herself off and walked back, her almond eyes gleaming with challenge and anticipation. "This is going to be more fun than I thought."

⁜

Macey knew without being told she couldn't share any information about this new part of her life with the people Chas termed "civilians"—Flora, Jimmy, Mrs. Gutchinson, her boss, or her other friends. Even Grady, if she could count him as a friend. After all, she'd only known him for a few days.

Macey was also aware she had much to learn about the undead and how to combat them. But when Sebastian suggested she didn't need to report to her job at the Harper Library on Monday morning, she immediately disabused him of that notion.

"Of course I have to go to work," she said, adjusting her left stocking so the line up the back of her calf was straight. She was going to be late if she didn't leave in five minutes. "How else am I going to pay for my rent, or my food and clothes?"

"Rent? *Cherie*, you know you could live here, free of rent, and have everything you need." His voice dropped low and suggestive at the last bit, and Macey felt a flush of heat swarm over her throat and cheeks.

"Absolutely not." But her heart pounded, and her gaze slid automatically to Sebastian's torso. It was covered properly by a fine tailored shirt. But she knew somewhere beneath it was a tiny silver cross…and she had a difficult time keeping herself from imagining how it would look against his golden, muscled skin. A flush moved up along her throat.

"But was my hospitality that poor last night?" He smiled and his gaze warmed. "Surely you found the bed comfortable, and you need not fear any unwelcome visitors while here."

She had stayed in a guest room attached to The Silver Chalice last night and was wearing clean clothing Temple had somehow located for her, but Macey wasn't about to make that a habit. For though Sebastian had been nothing but gentlemanly, she wasn't certain she trusted him…or herself. Not yet, anyway.

"I'm going to my job. Dr. Morgan is expecting me. After work, I'll meet Temple for more training. Then I'll return to my own flat, where I'll stay tonight." Her calling as a Venator might be important, but she had no intention of letting it take over her life. She'd worked long and hard to move from rinky-dink

Skittlesville to the excitement of Chicago, to find her dream job and get her own place. She wasn't giving that up now.

Besides. A gal could only spend so much time fighting and learning how to use the curve-bladed *kadhara*. "Now I know how to protect myself from any undead entering my apartment."

"Yes." Sebastian's eyes narrowed. "And besides—since you killed the Guardian vampire who broke into your room, you have no need to fear him coming back. Presumably he gained permission to enter your house from that silly landlady of yours, who invited him in."

"Yes. He must have come to warn her and the other residents about the so-called gas main leak on Friday. That's how he was able to enter, and that's why no one was there when he attacked me." She settled her saucy new hat—courtesy of Cookie—in place and picked up her pocketbook. "When I get home tonight, I'll put some more precautions in place and try to find a way to tell Mrs. G not to let anyone in the house she doesn't know." Although that was going to be a challenge. "I'll tell her there's been a rash of robberies or something, and that the thieves have been scoping out the houses first."

And before Sebastian could attempt to dissuade her further, Macey left and went to work. Then she went to Cookie's to train, eventually made her way home, and collapsed in bed. She didn't remember anything until her alarm clock rang the next morning.

After this routine, by Friday morning she was slightly less exhausted but definitely sore from all her unfamiliar activity. And she had blisters on the inside of her thumb from handling knives and swords, not to mention stakes.

And so her life went for the next three weeks: working during the day and training with Temple in the evenings and on the weekends. Most of the time, she ended up sleeping in a small room above Cookie's instead of taking the time to go back to her flat. She didn't see any of her friends—although Chelle and Dottie called and left messages through Mrs. Gutchinson.

When she got to work one Friday morning after a particularly exhausting week, Macey found two boxes of books sitting on her desk. They'd been donated by one of the university's benefactors, and though the volumes had been classified, they still needed to be catalogued. She spent the first few hours of her morning typing up a card with the Dewey code for each volume, plus ten copies of each. Truth be told, it might have taken her less time if she hadn't gotten sidetracked by a chapter on Greco-Roman bricklaying (fascinating!), a diagram of the interior of Tutankhamon's tomb compared to that of Rameses II, a description of how absinthe was traditionally fermented, and the bound collection of love letters between Dolley and James Madison.

When she finally finished typing the cards, Macey inserted the appropriate bookplates announcing the donation and then imprinted the raised library seal on each title page. Then she took the books, as many as she could carry and by classification, into the depths of the stacks. As the director's assistant, she could have sent them down for one of the pages to put on the shelf, but Macey loved books, and loved roaming the stacks. She never knew what she'd find among the rows and rows of shelves.

The scent of old and new books mingled—dusty, musty, and with the sharp tinge of glue and fresh paper. On the main floors near the reading rooms, the shelves were comfortably spaced and loomed high over her head. She needed a step stool to reach the top three rows. But in the basement stacks, the ceiling was very low and the metal shelves were close. Some enterprising person had painted floor and stacks numbers and arrows on the floor and walls so as to ensure none of the students would get lost in the labyrinth and be wandering therein for hours—or days. (That was, according to Dr. Morgan, an old joke among the library staff—where to look for the medical students if they didn't show up for their final exams.)

Macey went to the basement level with her last group of books, making her way through the Philosophy and Religion section. With no natural light down there and random lamps studding the ceiling, the space was dim and shadowy in areas. The pages were at lunch, and it was empty and quiet among the rows of books.

But as she bent to slide a book into its new home, she heard the soft scuff of someone's shoe. The sound was so faint she almost thought she imagined it. But the air gave a subtle shift and the hair on her arms lifted, prickling uncomfortably. She shoved the book in place on a lower shelf and rose, looking around. It was a library, and students and faculty visited constantly. Even with the pages gone to eat, someone else among the stacks wasn't a surprise. But Macey's heart was pounding hard, and she found herself vibrating with awareness as she listened and waited. Someone was there, and he or she was trying to be abnormally quiet.

Then she heard it again…the faintest sound, the breath of a shoe against the concrete floor, the shift in the air accompanied by a subtle new scent—crisp and a little smoky. Absent was the sound of books being taken off the shelves or papers crinkling—the normal noise of a student or professor in search of a research volume.

All at once, a book fell from the shelf next to her. It landed flat on the floor at her feet, the sound as loud and sharp as a whipcrack. Macey stifled a startled gasp and looked where the book had been.

A dark eye peered at her through the empty slot on the shelf, and she felt a rush of relief when she recognized it. Though her knees were still a little wobbly, her breathing steadied as she snatched up the fallen book and shoved it back into place.

"Steady nerves you have there," said Chas as he sauntered into view from around the corner. "Definitely the making of a good Venator."

"You take great delight in sneaking around and popping up on people, don't you?" She collected the rest of the books she needed to shelve and held them against her like a shield.

"One must find amusement where one can." He skimmed his dark hand over a row of book spines and casually plucked out a selection.

"What do you want?" Macey saw no reason Chas should distract her from work, so she started walking toward the TA-TE row, leaving him to follow if he chose.

"Temple says you're doing extremely well with your training." He was right behind her as she turned down the main aisle, her heels thudding purposefully on concrete until she found the section she needed.

"That's not what she told me." Macey shoved her pile of books into Chas's chest then turned to make room on the shelf for a new addition. In fact, Temple had been ominously silent about her progress, or lack thereof. So much so that Macey was planning on skipping her session tonight.

It was Friday, after all. She hadn't done anything but work, train, and sleep for three weeks, and Chelle had left a message that she and Dottie were planning on going to the grand re-opening gala at The Palmer Hotel. It was open to the public, if you could get a ticket—or, in Dottie's case, if you were dating the hotel's assistant manager. She'd wrangled four tickets through him, and Macey and Flora were invited too.

The message reminded Macey she hadn't heard from Flora since that morning she showed up at her flat, when Grady was there. More than three weeks ago. Macey had a feeling her friend wasn't very happy with her.

And then there was Grady.

Yes, the handsome Irishman had certainly popped into her mind more often than he should have. Especially whenever she noticed the broken broomstick that still sat on her bureau. He'd actually stopped by the library last week, wanting to take her for a cup of coffee. But she'd been in the middle of a project and had to decline. Besides, he was probably mostly interested in grilling her about the vampire situation.

Chas watched her as she shifted the books and aligned them on the shelf. "Temple says she can tell you are quite gifted, even at this early stage. So, we're going out tonight, you and I. Bring a stake. And wear something that shows off your legs." When she spun to glare at him, he merely smiled and handed her a book—surprisingly, the one for which she'd just made space on the shelf. "See you tonight, Macey. Be ready to spill some dust."

He set the remainder of the books on an empty spot next to the TAs and slipped away. By the time she realized he hadn't told her where to go or what time to meet—and, more importantly, that she didn't want to go anywhere with him anyway—Chas was gone.

"Wear something that shows off my legs my *eye*," she muttered, already considering what she could wear that *didn't*. Because pretty much everything she owned did.

Then she smiled. What was she worried about? She wasn't going anywhere with Chas. She had other plans.

"That is an adorable *chapeau*." Chelle reached to finger the velvet roses adorning Macey's headband-like scarf. "I love the detail. Where did you get it?"

"It's a new place I found called Cookie's." Macey gave her companions directions to the shop, figuring Temple's aunt could always use the business, then looked up and down the street again. "Have you heard from Flora? Is she coming?"

Macey, Chelle, and Dottie were standing outside the front of the Palmer, which rose twenty-five stories above them in an elegant brick structure. Although the entire hotel had been renovated and expanded over the last three years, it had remained open during the entire time. But now that the work was finished, there was to be a gala to celebrate the largest hotel in the world being completely redone.

Flora, if she was coming—for no one knew for certain— was late, and they'd been waiting for nearly thirty minutes. Automobiles and taxis bogged down the street, pulling up to the curb and stopping traffic. The bellmen were non-stop, assisting jewel-and-fur-clad women and fashionable men from their vehicles and beckoning them into the hotel. The sounds of loud, excited conversation and jazzy music spilled into the evening air every time one of the doors opened.

The sun had just sunk below the city skyline, and the last bit of pink-orange in the sky was fading. Streetlights were already on and the bright lights from Joony's Vaudeville and the uptown B&K motion picture theater blinked enthusiastically from opposite ends of the block. On nights like this, Chicago was colorful, well lit, and boisterous—a far cry from one-cross-street Skittlesville. Macey loved the vivacity and the activity. She felt as if she belonged here.

"I want that lady's boa," Chelle murmured into her ear as a woman climbed out of a dark red Cadillac. "The pink feather one? With the sparkles?"

"Darling. And it would look so snappy with your coffee-colored frock."

"Right. The one with the seed pearls. Yes." Chelle smoothed her perfectly straight brown hair, tucking the short strands back so they flipped forward in a perfect curl around her ear. "And look at her *shoes*."

Chelle was a little taller than Macey, and rounder in the hips and bosom, but she knew how to dress fashionably to suit her body type. She worked at Field's Department Store and got great discounts on the best clothing, which she, in turn, passed on to her friends. She was the one who'd introduced the Simington Side-Lacer to them as an alternative to binding the breasts, as the most trendy flapper dresses required, and for that, Macey was eternally grateful.

"It's chilly out here." Macey pulled the smoky gray velvet wrap closer around her shoulders and throat. She was wearing a calf-length slip of sheer pink material over a short opaque under-dress with slim shoulder straps, and the ensemble—though very fashionable—was little protection against the cooling April air. Her shoes were a soft dove color, and she'd clipped a black bow with jet beads onto each one, and wore gathered gray gloves. The outfit had cost an entire paycheck, but she'd been saving it for a special occasion. And this was definitely one.

"Here comes Al," someone said behind them, and Macey looked up.

"Oh my God…that's Al Capone!" hissed Dottie needlessly as she grabbed at her two friends' arms.

Sure enough, the infamous gangster had just stepped out of a sleek black automobile. Rumor had it the vehicle was armored, which wasn't a surprise since his colleague and former boss, Jimmy Colosimo, had been gunned down only a few months ago.

Capone was dressed in a white suit with a black shirt. A red tie and red and black spotted handkerchief added color. His hair was slicked back, and he didn't wear a hat, so his jowly face and heavy brows were fully evident. He was a solid man, stocky and yet surprisingly graceful. A cadre of men in dark suits surrounded him and kept the rapidly gathering bystanders at a distance as their boss laughed jovially with one of his companions. He paused on the sidewalk to jest with three other men who'd alighted from the same vehicle. Macey vaguely recognized them from pictures in the paper, but she didn't know their names.

"Mr. Capone!" A flashbulb popped. "Is Johnny Torrio ever coming back?"

"Hey, Snorky! Are you going to meet with the new mayor?" called another voice. Laughter spattered through the audience, for everyone knew Capone and Mayor Thompson were already very cozy.

"Mr. Capone! What do you think of the city council meeting about banning smoking on the street?"

The gangster gestured to the crowd at random, his cigar clamped between two thick, powerful fingers. "Now you don't want to get me talking about business tonight, boys. I'm here to have a good time—and check out the competition." He laughed and breezed on into the hotel.

Macey shivered, a chill lifting the hair on her arms. She couldn't believe she'd been less than ten feet away from one of the most dangerous men in Chicago.

"How much longer should we wait for Flora?" Dottie was standing on tiptoes, presumably hoping that would allow her to see their taller friend's approach. But the block was even more crowded now with people who were trying to catch sight of Capone, as well as those who didn't have tickets for the gala but were hoping for a glimpse of the partygoers.

"I left another message at her boarding house earlier today," Chelle said. "Said we were going to meet here at seven. Her landlady said something about her being at work, though. It's quarter till eight. She must not be coming. Let's go in! I wonder if that lady will tell me where she bought her shoes."

"Yes. Even though we have tickets, Ben warned me it could get too crowded with crashers, and they might have to stop letting ticket-holders in." Dottie took one last look up the street, frowning. "That's too bad for Flora. I hope she at least got the message. That landlady of hers is a real bitch, and always drunk to boot."

Macey felt more than a little guilty as she followed her friends inside, but they couldn't wait on the sidewalk all night. Then a spur of excitement nicked her as she stepped into the hotel lobby.

Crowded with people, the space nevertheless didn't feel close because the ceiling was so high. Graceful arches painted gold with art deco designs rose three stories above them. Red upholstered chairs and sofas were arranged in clusters throughout the lobby, the tables between them laden with massive vases of flowers.

"Ben said to go toward the north-side dining area and find the powder room. There's a cabaret in there, if you know the password to get in. We do." Dottie's eyes gleamed and her smile was bright. With her light blue eyes and shiny blond hair, she was an interesting mixture of sass and innocence.

"We do?" Chelle asked, dragging her attention away from a woman in a red dress with gaudy makeup and a feathered turban. "Wait. There's a cabaret in the powder room?" She giggled and tucked her hair behind her ear.

Macey rolled her eyes and gave her a nudge. "Silly. Not *in* the powder room. Let's go before it gets too crowded." She adjusted her wrap, still a little chilled even though they'd come inside.

Dottie was already leading the way. "Come on."

They found the powder room, which was a work of art unto itself. It was a Z shape with a row of private stalls to the left and the counter to the right. Past the sinks was another small wing with two large stalls, presumably for those who needed more room.

The lounge was decorated in black enamel with gold and dark red trim. Vases of red roses sat on the gold and white marbled counters. The attendant sat in a chair offering hand towels, lotions, and perfume to each woman as she finished washing.

To Macey's surprise and interest, Dottie walked past the sinks and turned into the row of the larger stalls. She went into the farthest one, situated in the far corner of the small alcove. When Macey and Chelle hesitated, Dottie poked her head back out and beckoned.

They exchanged amused glances and ducked in after her. The door, which, unlike most stall doors, went from floor to ceiling and swung closed behind them. Inside the small space was a sink with a mirror over it, and a commode.

Dottie looked in the mirror and Macey was just about to poke her to get the show on the road when she raised both hands next to her ears and gave the mirror a pair of thumbs up.

All at once, the empty wall in the stall moved, swinging back into nothingness.

Dottie stepped through, and Macey and Chelle were right behind her. Only a week ago, Macey might have been more hesitant to walk through a secret door into darkness, but she was very conscious of how things had changed. Despite the lingering soreness of her muscles, she knew she had the power of the *vis bulla* with her—as well as having learned some potent self-defense moves from Temple. They would be just as effective on mortals as they would be on the undead.

And so it was with confidence and a thrill of excitement that Macey walked into the dark space. She realized immediately that someone was there, sitting on a stool in the dark. The door closed behind her. At the same time, a light blazed in the darkness, revealing a set of spiral stairs descending behind a sturdy railing.

"You ladies enjoy yourselves now." The man sitting on the stool waved them on, flashing a gold tooth as he grinned. Macey was relieved to see that the way his two-way mirror was positioned, it would not give a view of the inside of the stall. Just in case.

At the bottom of the stairs was another door, and behind it the sounds of music and activity. Dottie opened it.

The cabaret was a large, windowless room with low lighting. A cloud of smoke had already formed near the ceiling and would likely get deeper and thicker before the end of the evening. The entrance through which Macey and her friends stepped was at the rear on a narrow balcony. Stretched out below and across the way was a low stage with a piano. A woman in a tight blue dress stood in front of a microphone and sang Irving Berlin's "All Alone."

Around the perimeter of the stage and on several wide steppe-like strips of floor were tables and booths. Most were filled by well-dressed ladies and gentlemen, many of them smoking, and their conversation and laughter muted the entertainment. Servers rushed about with trays of food and drink.

"Are you cold? Don't tell me you're nervous, Macey!" Chelle must have felt her shiver next to her.

"No, I'm not nervous." But all at once, Macey realized something she should have done much earlier. "Or cold," she added faintly as an uncomfortable recognition settled over her.

She'd felt that odd, uncomfortable chill over the back of her neck—which had caused the little shiver her friend noticed. She'd experienced the same strange sensation several times in the last week—in fact, every time she'd come into Sebastian's presence. As well as the night of the raid at the The Gyro. And, most importantly, when the vampire broke into her flat last Friday night.

Chas's comment just before they went into The Silver Chalice for the first time—*So you feel that, do you? Not bad for a novice*—now made complete sense.

What it meant, what that eerie, nauseating, finger-like chill over the back of her neck told her, was that there was an undead nearby.

But as Macey looked out over the crowded, boisterous room, she wondered how on earth she was ever going to figure out where or who the vampire was. And what she was going to do about it.

Nine

The Difference Between Hawks and Hounds

MACEY FOLLOWED CHELLE AND DOTTIE down the steps from the balcony, all the while staring out over the crowded room. She held tightly to the railing so she wouldn't trip, for her attention was not on her descent. Despite her intense observation, it would be impossible for her to tell who was a vampire, unless she was standing next to them.

Which meant, she realized with a sudden unpleasant quiver in her belly, that she should probably figure out what to do if she did find one.

Had she brought a stake?

No. She didn't have room for one in her tiny pocketbook, and frankly, she hadn't thought about it. She didn't plan on seeing any vampires tonight. It was her day off. Her evening out.

Heart pounding, lips pressed together tightly, Macey wove her way through the crowd in Dottie and Chelle's wake. There wasn't anything she could do at the moment. She'd have to play it by ear.

The woman in the blue dress had finished her song and, after accepting an enthusiastic but random smatter of applause, left the stage. Moments later, a group of seven young women in shocking, skintight outfits that showed most of their legs and a deep vee of cleavage on each one, took the singer's place. Around the crown of the head each of them wore a headband with tall, graceful feathers and a great number of sequins. A small band to the side began to play loudly, with an emphasis on brass and percussion, and the ensemble launched into their act: a singing and dancing routine that seemed to capture the full attention of every male in the place.

Including Al Capone.

Macey couldn't help but notice the gangster, who'd taken a seat at a round, high-walled booth next to the stage. He seemed to be enjoying the performance, along with the others in his group.

Just after receiving her *vis bulla*, she'd heard Sebastian and Chas talking about Capone and Count Alvisi, who was a powerful and dangerous vampire. From what she'd gleaned, they were concerned Alvisi would get to Capone—who was his mortal equal when it came to violence and power—and turn him into a vampire.

Being turned undead required some participation on the part of the victim. After being drained of most of his blood, the mortal must then drink the blood of the siring vampire. Then he or she would slip into a state of unconsciousness, and upon awakening, would be turned.

The other fear expressed by Sebastian was if Capone wasn't made undead, then he might be enticed into becoming involved with the Tutela.

"What's the Tutela?" She figured she had the right to know what they knew, being a new Venator and heir to *Il Gardella*—whatever that meant. She'd read a little about the secret group in *The Venators*, but Macey had already learned there was much information missing or misconstrued in Mr. Starcasset's book. Thus she took none of it at face value.

"The Tutela is a secret society of mortals—men and women—who like to be around vampires. They are usually interested in becoming immortal undead themselves—or at least think they are," Sebastian added with a grim smile. "They have a particular fondness for being fed upon by the undead, and are often obsessed with the lifestyle they crave for themselves. The vampires use them as servants or associates, for, of course, the undead can't move about in direct sunlight. Having a loyal group of mortal followers who can do so, thus affording protection and conducting any business during the daylight hours, is a benefit to the vampires. And the mortals are lured by the benefits of power, protection, and—once having proven themselves—immortality, by pledging their service to the Tutela."

"There are people who actually enjoy being fed upon? Being mutilated like that?" Macey couldn't comprehend that concept. She still remembered with revulsion the violation of her own flesh and blood when the vampire bit into her neck. "One would have to be *insane* to enjoy such a horrible thing. It's no wonder feeding on a mortal is the point of no return for an undead."

"It's not your place to judge. The same has been said for those who shoot their veins with heroin or smoke opium," said Chas flatly. "Or even imbibe in spirits. Hence the Temperance movement, imposing its own morality on an entire nation."

Sebastian looked as if he were about to say something, then merely shook his head.

Macey got the impression she was missing some undercurrent, but before she could probe further, Sebastian continued on a different topic. "Your ancestor Victoria attended a Tutela meeting in Venice as Count Alvisi's guest. Back in 1819, I believe it was. Or thereabouts. He wasn't undead at the time, but he was already wearing that abominable lavender after-shave cologne. It left a bloody damn cloud behind him everywhere he went. At least one always knew when he was in the vicinity."

"And so he is a vampire now?"

"One of the most powerful ones. He and Nicholas Iscariot are particularly close minions of Lucifer. And both of them are here in Chicago. I'm certain it can't be a coincidence." Chas looked from Macey to Sebastian.

"Iscariot. A relation of Judas, I suppose."

"Of course. The son of the Betrayer and brother of Lilith the Dark. Nicholas was imprisoned by his sister, and only upon her death did he gain release. He's been wreaking havoc in Romania, Turkey, and Moscow for the last century. But what on earth has brought him here, I cannot fathom. He and Alvisi are fierce rivals and mortal enemies." Chas looked pointedly at Sebastian. "Unless he's realized the rings are here."

That was when Macey learned about the Rings of Jubai, the five copper bands fused to Sebastian's fingers. "There is a magical pool in Romania to which these rings will give access. Inside the pool is, according to legend, a pyramid-shaped object that can yield great power to mortal and immortal alike. One can only suspect Iscariot has tried every manner of dipping his hand safely into the pool, and has finally decided to attempt the one sure way of breaching the magic shield." He brandished his ringed hand.

"That puts you in danger, then," Macey said.

Sebastian's eyes glowed with humor, and his beautiful lips twitched. "Indeed it does. As it has done for decades. But I thank you for your concern."

Now, as Macey watched Al Capone and felt the telltale iciness at the back of her neck, it occurred to her that perhaps Count Alvisi had already accomplished his goal of turning the gangster into a vampire. Her mouth went dry and her organs turned into blocks of ice.

I can't stake Al Capone. I wouldn't get within a foot of him before those goons shot me. But then again, that could be the reason no one had been able to kill him yet. He was impervious to bullets.

"I thought you didn't go into speakeasies."

Macey nearly jumped out of her skin at the low voice in her ear. She stifled her surprise, however, and turned to find Grady at her elbow. The ice inside her melted into something much warmer and friendlier.

"What are you doing here? Covering the cabaret's entertainment for the *Tribune*, I presume?" She looked up at him—all blue eyes, unruly dark hair, and broad shoulders. His square jaw and cleft chin were clean-shaven, and he smelled like something masculine and fresh. Her heart stuttered. *He sure cleans up nice.*

"Something like that." Grady stood close enough she could feel his warmth against her bare arm. "What are you doing here? Hoping to find a vampire?"

Macey nearly choked. "What?" Her heart thudded harshly, the last vestiges of warmth frittering away.

He took her arm, leaning in closer. "Don't tell me you have a stake in that pocketbook of yours."

"Hey, Macey! Who's this?" All of a sudden, Dottie and Chelle were standing there expectantly. Chelle's eyes danced as she looked from one to the other, and she wagged her brows at Macey. Fortunately, Grady wasn't looking.

Macey made introductions, reminded again she didn't know his full name. She felt odd about it, but her friends didn't seem to notice. She was relieved when they launched into an animated conversation with Grady, who responded to their nosy questions (how do you know Macey, what do you do for a living, do you come to these places often) with charming aplomb.

It gave Macey time to collect herself. Grady's questions weren't jokes; he'd been completely serious. But what did that mean? And how should she respond? *Yes, as a matter of fact, I am a vampire hunter. But I forgot to bring a stake tonight. And I'm stalking Al Capone because I think he's an undead. Call me crazy.*

Macey came back into the conversation just in time to hear Grady say, "Now, ladies—a word of warning. Don't be drinking the whiskey here. Or anywhere cheap. The beer is usually all right if you really must imbibe, but anything stronger than that— whiskey, rum, or gin—is too dangerous."

"You mean illegal." Was Chelle actually fluttering her eyelashes at him?

"That too. But unless you're about knowing where it came from, lass—where and how it was distilled—don't drink it." He turned sober eyes on Macey. "Too many poisoning deaths from liquor distilled from methyl and wood alcohol. Even a small amount can be lethal. But it's easy and cheap, and it's what the low-level bootleggers are using all too often. I've seen the results."

"Surely the Palmer would pay for good booze," Dottie said.

Grady lifted a brow. "Surely the Palmer wouldn't admit to paying for *any* booze."

"Oh. Right." She blinked and smiled.

"Thank you for the warning," Macey replied. "Although I wasn't intending to partake tonight."

"Want to keep your mind clear because you're on the job, lass?" he murmured, his voice rumbling just below the cacophony around them and somehow going straight to her ears.

She merely lifted her brows and tried what she hoped was a mysterious smile. "Speaking of jobs…don't you have a story to investigate? People to interview? I'm going to visit the powder room and…powder my nose."

Before he could respond, she ducked away into the crowd.

In the powder room, she found a place between two other gals in front of the mirror and checked her reflection. Her cheeks were flushed and her eyes bright, but her hair still looked good. The wide headband with the velvet roses on it kept her wild mass of curls under some control, and they tumbled pleasantly around her jaw and the nape of her neck. Her velvet wrap was a little warm now that she was in a crowded space, but there was nothing else she could do with it. And her pocketbook…

She glared at it, and at the memory of Grady's interrogation. The bag wasn't large enough to hold a damned stake and he knew it. And what was he thinking, asking her something like that anyway?

Surely he couldn't know. Surely he was just trying to figure out what he could. And she supposed she couldn't blame him. After all, he knew she'd staked a vampire. And…hell. He'd spent the night in her flat. Stake in hand. A little quiver of pleasure reminded her how he'd looked that morning, all rumpled and fierce, with his weapon in hand.

Macey refreshed her rose-tinted lipstick and, last of all, powdered her nose. And then, figuring she'd wasted enough time and hoping Grady was involved with something else, she left the mirror to return to the cabaret. On the way out, she noticed an umbrella stand by the door. There were two umbrellas and a walking stick in it. All had wooden handles.

Glancing behind her to make sure no one was watching, Macey filched the only one with a straight handle. Then, in a trice, she broke the umbrella about four inches from the end. Thanks to her *vis*, doing so was like snapping a toothpick. And now she had a makeshift stake that would actually fit—diagonally, at least—in her pocketbook.

Relieved and filled with purpose, as well as a renewed spike of nerves, she walked out of the powder room.

Grady was waiting outside the door.

"You again. Just like a bad penny."

He smiled and offered her his arm. "Have I mentioned how bloody sensational you look tonight, lass?"

"No."

"If you'd care to take a stroll over to one of those tables, where I can be sitting you next to me and drownin' myself in your deep brown eyes, I'll be more than happy to tell you how keen I am on you." His crinkly-eyed smile had her insides warm and fluttery again, and reminded her about that luscious kiss in her flat.

"I suppose I could agree to that." *Though* I'll *be the one drowning in someone's eyes.*

As they walked to the table he'd somehow procured, Macey noticed the chill on the back of her neck had eased. She looked around. Capone's booth was empty, and she didn't see him anywhere.

She couldn't deny it—a wave of relief washed over her. *I'm not in the mood to face a vampire tonight. And I'm certainly not ready to face* Al Capone *as a vampire.*

"Looking for your friends?" Grady asked as he gestured to a small round booth. Just big enough for two, the seat enabled them to face the cabaret stage where a jazz trio was now performing. A candle burned on the center of the small table, and goblets with seltzer water were already poured. Paper-thin wedges of orange, lemon, and lime were arranged on a small gold-edged plate.

"No. I was wondering if Al Capone had left." Macey slid in and adjusted the silky fabric of her slip-dress so it didn't show too much thigh. "I don't see him anywhere anymore."

Grady's expression hardened. "I didn't take you for being one of those gangster-celebrity watchers."

"No, not at all. It's just…I've never seen him before tonight, and to be honest, being in the same room as a gangster is a little unsettling. I just wanted to know where he was."

"So he doesn't sneak up on you, you mean?" Now he was smiling, and his eyes had gone warmer. "Don't worry, lass. I'll protect you."

"Do you see them often? Gangsters? You must, if you're a newshound."

"I prefer newshawk. Hound—the word, not the animal—has such unpleasant connotations. And a hawk is strong and graceful, as well as being a fierce fighter."

"Thank you for that clarification." Macey's tone was nonchalant, but inside she was turning to mush. Smart, literate, charming, and someone she could actually imagine being a strong, fierce protector….Grady was definitely more hawk than hound.

"And in answering your question: Yes, I see and interact with the gangsters a lot. It's an odd thing. Everyone knows they're violent criminals, yet they walk the streets without fear of repercussion." His tight mouth and fierce eyes told her exactly how he felt about that.

"Except they fear one another."

He looked at her and nodded, his eyes sober. "Those men are repulsive—for what do they stand for but violence, greed, and pure hedonism? And yet, damn it, even though it nearly kills me to say it, I can't deny the bootleggers do provide a useful service."

Macey was fascinated by his honesty—and his integrity. "What useful service? Breaking the law?"

"By *organizing* and *regulating* the breaking of the law. That warning I gave you and your friends tonight about drinking the whiskey here? I was serious. If you don't know where it comes from, you could drink something fatal. Saloons serve up poison drinks made from industrial alcohol all the time because it's cheap and relatively easy to come by. At least we know that the beer Capone's saloons serve comes from proper breweries. And his whiskey is the same. From a real distillery. You're not going to get watered down methyl alcohol from one of his places. And that, at least, is one benefit. Despite Prohibition, people are going to drink spirits. At least if they drink Capone's, there's less of a chance they'll die."

"You almost sound like you admire Capone."

Grady stiffened, his eyes going flinty again. "Don't think that for a minute, Macey. I have no respect for that murderer. Nor for any of them—the Gennas, the Torrios, the Weisses. Any of them. They've spilled enough blood in this city—both innocent and otherwise. All in the name of greed. I'd be more than happy to see them behind bars, which is one of the reasons I do what I do. Some day, somehow, each of them will be caught out, and justice will be served. If I'm a part of taking them down, I'll die a happy man."

"What about your uncle?"

"Since my aunt was killed in gangster crossfire, you can be sure he feels the same way, to the bottom of his heart—and that'll never change. And let me tell you, lass, he and I—we're in the minority. But that's why those bastards still walk the streets and carry their automatics and run this city—because the cops and the mayor and even the governor are in their pocket. They like the money and power too much to come down on them, so they offer protection instead."

Macey shivered and realized how uncannily similar the description of the corrupt authorities was to that of the Tutela. And how the vampires were very much like the gangsters, wielding underlying power as they controlled their turf. They were invincible. Untouchable.

It was no wonder Sebastian and Chas were worried Capone would be turned undead. That combination of power and influence along with immortality and strength would be lethal.

"Did you know Big Al goes to confession once a week? As if that'd save his soul. I'll be damned, but I'd like to be a fly sitting on that priest's shoulder." His intensity eased a little, the laugh-lines at his eyes appearing once again.

Macey laughed at the mental image, which somehow included a fly wearing a priest's collar, and her shoulder bumped against his.

"By God, you're *it*." Grady touched her cheek with a gentle finger as he looked down into her eyes. "I've had a hard time keeping my mind off you, Macey Denton."

"Why would you want to do that?" she replied cheekily, even as her heart thudded harder.

"I don't know," he murmured. "I must be a damned fool." He leaned in, gently gathering her near, and settled his lips on hers.

Macey shivered lightly and pressed closer, then slipped her tongue out, teasing it over the seam of his mouth. He inhaled sharply against her and curved a hand over the back of her neck. Gently nibbling on the edge of her mouth, Grady shifted her so she was nearly sitting in his lap. The kiss grew deeper and Macey felt hot and cold at the same time. She forgot to breathe, forgot they were in the middle of a semi-public place, forgot everything but the hot, sensual stroke of his tongue and the full, erotic brush of his lips.

The heat bubbled up from her middle, flushing over her torso and along her throat as the kiss went deeper and hotter. She felt damp and moist, and the insistent twinge between her legs grew stronger, turning into a delicate little throbbing.

Then a brush of cold air whisked over the back of her neck, beneath his warm hand, raising the hair along her sensitive nape and tiny little bumps on her skin. A faint hint of nausea accompanied the chill and had the effect of yanking Macey from the depths of a hot, languid place she didn't want to leave—and back abruptly into the secret cabaret beneath the Palmer Hotel.

Where an undead was present.

She pulled away, more sharply than she intended, and had Grady smiling with chagrin. He glanced around as if to see if anyone was watching, then looked back at her. "I lost my head for a minute." His Irish was heavy and thick, and sounded rich and musical on his tongue.

Macey was trying to steady her breathing and look around for Capone—or whoever the undead was—at the same time. She couldn't see well enough from their table, however, and much as she was enjoying herself—really, *really* enjoying herself—she knew she had to at least try to investigate. "Tell me again why you're here, if it's not for the booze?"

"I didn't say it wasn't for the booze. I'm Irish. I can tell a fine whiskey when I taste one." His smile turned slow and warm, and Macey got the distinct impression he wasn't talking about spirits any longer.

She couldn't control a warm shiver. *Damn, but I've got to ditch him.*

"Now don't be doing that sort of thing, biting your lip like that, lass, because you're going to make me lose my head again."

She smiled and covertly scanned the room again. "Don't you have to interview people? Or take notes for the story you're writing?"

"I have the distinct impression you're trying to get rid of me, Macey." The warmth in his eyes eased, and he looked at her intently. "What's going on?"

"I just feel bad I ditched my friends. Dottie got us in here, and it's supposed to be the three—well, the four of us, but Flora couldn't make it. I should probably find them."

He looked at her a moment longer, then, with a tilt of his head, nodded reluctantly. "I'd forgotten the female species tends to travel in packs."

"Most of the time." Then she allowed a spark of mischief into her gaze. "And then there are other times when three is definitely a crowd."

His eyes widened just enough to let her know she'd hit the mark. "You're about killing me, lass." But he sighed and slid out of the booth, then offered her a hand to help her do the same. "And I suppose you're about right—I'd best be getting to work. Editor got me a press pass, and he'll expect me to get at least a few good quotes and do a good write-up. But don't leave without saying good night."

"Hmmm," was all she said, but with a smile and laughter in her eyes.

Macey strolled through the crowd, keeping to the perimeter of the room while trying to appear nonchalant. In reality she was trying to "read" the chilly sensation that indicated a vampirical presence and determine who was causing it.

When she saw Al Capone standing nearby, surrounded by a cluster of dark-suited men, she veered in that direction. To her chagrin, the chill didn't ease as she made her way toward the group, and Macey was certain the temperature was becoming even cooler.

In a moment of nervous absurdity, she remembered a game she played when she was young. An object was hidden, and as she tried to find it, the hider would tell her whether she was "hot" or "cold." This was almost the same thing, except the closer she got to the hidden object, the colder she got.

If only she could get Capone alone. But that would not only be impossible, it would be suicidal. What would Chas do if he were here?

Macey submerged another wave of discomfort. She'd ditched him too, tonight. Of course, he deserved it—the way he announced they were "going out" and to bring a stake. And to wear something that showed off her legs. The jerk.

She wondered if he'd come to her flat to pick her up, or if he expected her to meet him at The Silver Chalice. Or Cookie's. That was a good excuse, come to think of it. He hadn't told her where or when to meet him, and so she'd made other plans.

And if she could come back to The Silver Chalice and tell him and Sebastian she'd staked Al Capone…

For the first time, excitement spurred her. She *was* a Gardella, after all. A descendant of Victoria. She could do this. According to Sebastian and Chas, and even the intriguing Wayren, she was *born* to hunt vampires.

Macey slipped her hand inside the flap of her pocketbook and curled her fingers around the makeshift stake. She hovered near the wall, in a corner-like indentation behind a cluster of tables. A tall potted plant strung with tiny lights obscured her from the rest of the room. Unless someone was looking closely, she doubted they'd notice her.

She considered several options that might put her in close proximity to Capone, or, better yet, alone with him (well, maybe not *better*), but before she could decide on one, he turned his head from a conversation and looked up sharply.

At first, she thought he'd noticed her—but even if he did, why would Big Al be the least bit concerned about a young woman standing in a corner?

But he wasn't looking in her direction. And though he continued speaking with his companions, Macey thought he seemed distracted. Capone kept glancing toward his left, and she noticed he used his conversational gestures to subtly manipulate himself and the entire group so he was eventually facing that direction.

Something had definitely caught his attention—or something was going to happen. Oh no. Not a shootout. Not here, in this confined, subterranean room. Nerves exploded in her belly.

Macey looked over but saw nothing that seemed threatening or worrisome to her. More people. Men and women, smoking, laughing, drinking, flirting. But a subtle change in the prickling at the back of her neck shivered over her shoulders and along her arms, giving Macey the impression her instincts were right.

Something was up.

Capone broke away from his companions with a jovial gesture and one last obviously firm statement, then began what looked like a random ambling around the room. But Macey was watching, and it was clear to her that he had a purpose as he made his way quite rapidly in the direction he'd been watching.

She began to skirt the room in his wake, keeping a distance between them. Then Capone paused near a large floor-to-ceiling painting of Bacchus. Oddly enough, it was obscured by a trio of potted trees, and the lights were low in that area of the room.

She blinked, and Capone disappeared.

Macey hurried toward the painting as quickly as she could without drawing attention to herself. It had to be a hidden door. Her palm felt slick as she gripped the stake, and she dumped her pocketbook in the pot of one of the three plants and draped her wrap over a nearby chair. Hopefully they'd be there when she returned.

If she returned.

Her throat was stone dry and her pulse ramrodded so strongly she felt as if her heart was going to explode from behind her ribcage. She approached the painting, wondering how she was going to figure out the way to open the door…but when she got close enough she saw it was slightly ajar.

Before she went through, she paused…and still felt the chill of the undead.

Taking a deep breath, Macey pulled the Bacchus painting open and slipped in behind it.

Ten

Macey Bluffs

MACEY FOUND HERSELF IN A PLAIN, well-lit passageway no more than fifty feet long that ended in a T. One direction probably led to the outside. Thankfully, no one was in sight…although she could hear the sound of voices in the near distance. Two, perhaps three or even four—it was hard to tell, for they were low and intense.

Her heart was so high in her throat, she thought she might choke. But she started along the corridor silently, trying to figure out exactly what she was going to do when and if she encountered Capone.

Suddenly, up ahead, she saw the shadows of several figures reflected on the wall at the end of the hall. They were moving violently and there was the accompanying sound of an altercation. Bodies thudded and slammed against the wall, and one of the figures tumbled into sight ahead of her. She tensed, easing back—but there was nowhere for her to go. Aware of the ever-present chill at the back of her neck, she remained still, prepared to duck and run if she heard gunshots.

Before she could react, suddenly there were three men stalking down the corridor toward her. One was Capone. Another had blood all over his shirt and he was staggering a bit, held up by the third one—who was carrying a pistol.

She couldn't move and froze like a rabbit caught in the garden

"Hey! Who da hell are you?"

Macey was paralyzed. Then inspiration struck. She sagged and loosened her limbs, doing her best to appear drunk. Still holding the stake, hiding it behind her skirt, she tipped her head awkwardly and then stood unsteadily as if she needed to push herself away from the supporting wall.

"Heyyyy…youse…ain't sh-posed to be in the ladiesh room," she told them. And pointed with a very unsteady finger that made large, wavery circles in the air.

"This ain't da ladies room, ya dumb broad," said the man holding the gun. He looked terrifying. "Git outta here. We got biz-ness in here."

Macey stumbled away from the wall and tried again. "Sho where ish the pow…der room? I thought…" She looked around, swinging one arm broadly, making herself stagger as if she'd thrown herself off balance, all the while keeping the stake behind her back. She did her best to keep her eyes wide and glassy, and her mouth hanging slightly open. But when she noticed the bloodstains on the injured man's shirt were from a wound on his neck, she nearly lost her act.

"The goddamned powder room's not here," said Capone, his dark eyes piercing her. Violence and power exuded from him. "So I suggest you take your sweet ass out of here sooner rather than later."

"Okey…doke…y," Macey said. But she couldn't leave. The man was bleeding to death. Something—or someone—had interrupted Capone's feeding, and she was the only chance to save the victim. She could pretend to leave, then spin around and launch herself in their direction. She'd have a good shot if she took them by surprise.

She'd taken two staggering steps toward the painting-door when a strong hand clamped around her arm and plucked her backward so hard she nearly flew through the air.

"What the hell is this?" It was Capone, and he yanked her arm up by the wrist—the hand holding the stake. His gaze speared her, black and frightening, and for a minute, Macey lost her inebriated facade. Their eyes clashed, and then she sagged back into her act, stumbling against him.

"Wha…?" she said, tilting her head in confusion while looking up at the stake as if she'd never seen it. "'S broken. Sheeeeshhh… how'd it get bro-ken?" It took every bit of strength she had to keep herself loose-limbed and wide-eyed, as she looked from the stake to her captor and back again. His grip was painfully strong. A little harder and he'd break her wrist.

"Who the hell are you?" Capone demanded, thrusting his face close to hers.

Her heart was in her throat now, and her insides a jumble of nausea and nerves. But she kept a tight grip on the stake, knowing if she had one chance, this would be it. This would be the chance to kill Al Capone. She was close enough.

She gritted her teeth, struggling to keep focused while finding a way to aim the stake for his vulnerable spot, even as he gripped her wrist in a death-hold. All of a sudden, he flung her away from him. "Get the fuck outta here."

She slammed against the wall, her head cracking hard as it whipped back into it. By the time she pulled groggily to her feet, Capone and his goon with the gun had pushed past her and were gone—back out the painting-door and into the cabaret. The injured man lay at her feet, eyes glassy and wide as blood oozed from his wounds.

Macey knelt next to him and checked the bite. He'd live, but the man needed help. And if she went for help, people would panic, wouldn't they? Seeing bite wounds on a man's neck? Heck, seeing any blood would probably turn things upside-down. Maybe she could…yes, she could wrap them up so it wasn't obvious.

Then…*Grady*.

Damn it. It would just make him ask more questions, demand more answers. But she knew he'd help.

Grady was shooting the bull with motion picture theater mogul Sam Katz and the *Tribune*'s managing editor, Rob

McCormick, when he caught sight of Macey. Immediately he knew something was wrong—her face was pale, her expression tight, and her pocketbook and wrap were missing.

He set down a glass of the excellent, grain-distilled whiskey Katz had smuggled in via his chauffeur and wove his way through the ever-growing, increasingly inebriated crowd.

"What happened?"

She spun at his demand, displaying obvious relief at his appearance. "Thank God. Grady. I need your help. There's a man…he's injured. He needs help."

He didn't give a damn about an injured man. Not at the moment. "What happened to *you?*"

Her hair was out of control and her head-thing with the roses was askew. The silky, transparent dress she wore was torn at the shoulder seam, and one of her long necklaces was missing. And her wrist was red and chafed. "Are you all right? Who did this?" He controlled the need to grab her and demand answers.

"I'm not hurt. But there's a man who is. Will you help me? Grady, please. Before someone else finds him."

She didn't even wait for him to respond; she just turned and started off across the room. Of course he followed, and when she pulled him through a secret door courtesy of Bacchus and he saw the man…and the wounds. He looked at her.

"What the hell is going on, Macey? Dammit, you better tell me what the hell you've gotten yourself involved in."

She shook her head, her eyes cool and steady. "It's a whole lot of bad luck. Being in the wrong place at the wrong time. There's nothing more to—"

"Jesus Christ, Macey, do you really think I'm that stupid? Would you believe it if you were me?" But he was already kneeling at the man's side. Battling anger and disbelief at her continued equivocation, he put that aside for the time being to attend to the man.

Fortunately, the victim was conscious and strong enough to be helped to his feet, but he couldn't walk on his own and there was blood every-damn-where. The sight of it would send people into hysterics. "Where's your wrap?" Grady demanded. "Or a scarf."

She understood immediately and darted off, returning more quickly than he expected. She had the wrap and her pocketbook back in her possession—which led him to believe she'd put them aside herself and they hadn't been taken from her or knocked away during the assault. A woman didn't just leave her pocketbook. He filed this information away for future contemplation.

Arranging the heavy velvet throw around the injured man's neck, Grady helped him out of the secret room. With no sign of blood, everyone would merely assume the man was drunk.

Macey came along with them, also pretending to be inebriated, announcing to anyone who'd listen that her "man" had so much to drink that he'd decided to wear her shawl, and wasn't he *adorable*?

If Grady hadn't been so furious, so deeply confused and concerned, he might have been filled with admiration for her play-acting. She was convincing and entertaining at the same time, petting the soft velvet, stumbling about, batting her eyelashes.

And he was completely besotted with her.

Between the two of them, they got the "drunken" man out of the cabaret, up through a staff elevator, and out a side door of the Palmer. For a variety of reasons, Grady thought it best not to alert security, but to take the man directly to the hospital.

He had one of the bellmen hail a cab, and when the taxi pulled up, Grady eased the injured man into the backseat. "Get in," he said, turning to Macey.

But she was gone.

After she ditched Grady (again), Macey didn't want to go back into the secret cabaret again, for fear of encountering Capone. She wasn't quite ready to face the man with lethal black eyes and power exuding from him.

But if she went home, there was the chance she'd be accosted by everyone from Mrs. Gutchinson to Chas to Grady.

There was always Cookie's, for she knew where a key to the back door was hidden. But then she might have to answer questions about why she wasn't out with Chas, hunting vampires.

So Macey sat in a corner of the lobby of the Palmer for a while, listening to the jazz trio in the corner, watching the people go by. If Chelle or Dottie would appear, maybe she could go home with one of them and sleep at their house, thus avoiding Chas and Grady that much longer.

While she waited, Macey had nothing to do but think. Which wasn't a particularly good thing, considering the fact that she'd just had a very unsettling encounter with the kingpin of all gangsters.

But she couldn't help mentally reviewing everything that had happened in that secret hallway, and all at once it struck her—the chill. The chill at the back of her neck…had been *gone*.

Macey frowned and thought very hard, dragging back into her mind every part of the memory from that moment when he had her by the wrist, his dark, cold eyes boring into hers. She felt terrified, and adrenalin rushed through her…but she hadn't been *cold*.

Which meant…Capone hadn't yet been turned undead.

She drew in a deep breath. Exhaled. *So I was wrong. I guess that's good; he hasn't been turned yet.*

Then a little shiver caught her by surprise. *Good grief. I almost tried to stab him.*

What would he have done if she had? Macey shivered and felt a little nauseated at the thought. Lordy, she hoped he didn't realize what she'd been up to. Hopefully, he believed her drunken act and wouldn't think twice of it.

Why would a guy like Al Capone be worried about a gal like her bothering him, anyway? Surely he wouldn't even remember the incident.

But what was he doing with a man who had a vampire bite if he wasn't a vampire? Saving him? Perhaps. Or…

Macey mentally snapped her fingers. Right. Alvisi was trying to get Capone on his side. What better way to do that than to bring him into the Tutela first? Even remaining mortal, Capone would be a great asset to the vampires, with his network of power, people, and funds. Perhaps even more valuable than if he were turned undead. Chas and Sebastian were wrong.

The vampires didn't want Capone turned. They just wanted him on their side. A full member of the Tutela.

Macey subdued a shudder at the thought of those people who craved the attention of the undead. Likely the man she and Grady had helped was a member himself—or maybe someone Capone had brought as a guest to the undead, just as Alvisi had done to Victoria Gardella a century ago.

Having come to that conclusion, and uncertain what to do about it, Macey turned her thoughts to something less unpleasant. Flora. What was up with Flora?

While Macey wasn't overly worried their friend hadn't shown up tonight, it was still unusual for her not to have heard from her for such an extended time. She and Flora had been best friends for more than a decade. They'd even moved to Chicago within a month of each other. And since none of their group of friends had telephones in their apartments, they had to rely on using those of others—and rely on any messages being delivered. If something had come up at the last minute, Flora had no way of letting anyone know. And with Flora, things like that happened all the time. So her absence wasn't terribly worrisome.

But since Temple showed up at Macey's flat and Flora left in a little bit of a huff, Macey realized her friend might even be sulking a little, and waiting for her to contact her. And she hadn't. Generally, Flora was too happy and upbeat to hold a grudge against anyone, though, so maybe she was just busy with her new job—and her new guy.

Macey would go visit her tomorrow. Unfortunately, Dr. Morgan insisted she come in for a few hours, even though it was Saturday, because of preparations for the upcoming fundraiser. But she'd go over later, drag Flora out dancing. They'd have a great time.

She looked at the huge clock on the lobby wall. Nearly midnight. No sign of Dottie or Chelle, or even the helpful manager Ben. The gals might have already left. Macey sighed. Might as well go home herself. She did have to work tomorrow.

Outside, the chilly April night made her wish she hadn't donated away her wrap. The breeze seemed to blow right through her gauzy frock. Unwilling to draw attention to herself (in case Capone had his men watching for her—but would he even do that?) and ask a bellman to flag her a taxi, she walked down the block away from the hotel toward the motion picture theater.

Though it was late, people clogged the sidewalks everywhere, coming from the vaudeville show, the theater, the hotel—or on their way to one of them. Cars trundled along, beeping and honking if a pedestrian dared set foot in the road nearby.

A car slowed next to her, and Macey looked over just as the back door opened.

"Get in," said a thick male voice. "My boss would like to speak to you."

At the same time, a man emerged from the front of the car. As Macey stepped back, she caught sight of a black metal object in his hand. She didn't need to see anything else.

She dodged the hand that lunged for her and took off down the sidewalk, weaving between people, bumping into them, causing outcries in her wake. Back at the Palmer, standing by the doormen, she finally felt safe enough to turn and look back.

Her pursuers—if indeed they'd even pursued her—were nowhere in sight.

Now what?

She went back into the hotel, and, luck of luck, Dottie and Chelle were standing in the lobby, looking around. When they caught sight of her, they rushed over.

"Where have you been?"

"We've been searching everywhere."

"Oh, I got caught in a tangle—had to help a man who got hurt, uh, in a fight. We called him a cab. Hey, Dot, mind if I sleep at your house tonight? Mrs. G's going to be waiting at the door for me, wanting to grill me about the gala." Macey was looking around the lobby even as she spoke, watching for anyone who appeared to be looking for her.

"Sure, Mace. A pajama party sounds great. Haven't done that in months."

Still leery, Macey insisted they leave through the exit at the far end of the hotel, opposite the main entrance. They hailed a cab and rode off.

As she watched for anyone who might be following them, Macey realized she'd opened one hell of a can of worms.

Al Capone was definitely looking for her.

Whenever he could manage it, Sebastian conducted his private vigil at Old St. Patrick's just before the sun rose. Not only was the church always empty at that time, still as a tomb, it was also the least likely time of day for him to be found and ambushed by Iscariot or Alvisi—or any of their goons.

And it required him to leave the church after or during the breaking of dawn, which only added to the experience.

So to speak.

The first few times he'd walked into a church after being turned undead, Sebastian thought he'd self-combust as soon as he stepped over the threshold. But when he brushed his fingers over the *vis bulla* at his belly and rubbed the red signet ring from Wayren into his other palm, the blaze of pain ebbed and he was able to continue inside. That was how he knew he still had some humanity, some bit of his soul, buried deep inside.

Not to say it was pain-free, those moments inside a holy space. Not in the least. But Sebastian bore it, as he'd borne his "long promise" all these years.

Tonight—or, rather, this morning—though it was approaching four-thirty, Sebastian found he wasn't alone in the nave. The single other occupant was a woman, kneeling in front of the Blessed Virgin Mary on the left side of the church. A collection of red candles, many of them twinkling with tiny flames, cast a soft, pinkish glow in the dim space. He could tell she was a woman simply because of the shawl over her head and shoulders. A tingle of awareness shuttled through him as it did when Wayren was present, and he frowned, his attention settling on the veiled figure.

It wasn't Wayren. But there was something in the air, some energy, some prickling, that sizzled between or around them.

He must have made a scuff on the floor, for she turned slightly as he forced himself to continue on, stopping where he always did: at the fourth row from the back. He caught a glimpse of her face and got the impression she was frail and elderly—though not as old as he himself was. Gritting his teeth against the incessant pain, he knelt in the pew, and the old woman returned to her prayers.

As he settled in place, Sebastian noticed the five rings on his mutilated left hand. He'd lost half his baby finger in 1821, thanks to a bloodthirsty young woman named Sara Regalado, but it was the ever-present copper bands that captured his attention.

Even though it had been so long, he still occasionally tried to dislodge them. But while his skin hadn't grown around them during the last century, thank fortune, the circles would neither twist nor turn. It was as if they were affixed to his flesh. Part of him.

And there they would remain until someone drove a stake through his heart.

There was always the possibility of decapitation, or even frying to a crisp in direct sunlight, but when he thought about his death—which was absurdly often, considering the fact that he was immortal—Sebastian pictured the fast, painless pike to the heart. *Poof.* He'd be gone.

And whoever killed him would take possession of the rings.

That's why you're here.

The voice was in his head, firm and clear, as if someone was sitting next to him, speaking in his ear.

The rings. The pool. The prism. To keep them safe.

He opened his eyes and turned. Wayren was there, smiling serenely at him as she tended to do. Merely looking at her eased the throb of incessant pain.

Sebastian looked over. The old woman was still kneeling in front of a bank of candles.

"She's quite devoted." Wayren glanced toward the veiled figure. "As are you."

"How delightful to see you again so soon," Sebastian murmured. "You disappear for more than a decade, and then you appear twice in less than a month."

She shook her head, still smiling. "Now, Sebastian, sarcasm is not one of your best attributes. Best to leave that to someone who wields it better."

"Like Chas?"

Her eyes twinkled. "You said it. I didn't."

His irritation deflated, but he couldn't quite bring himself to a full smile. Besides the physical pain, there was still the despair and weariness that had cloaked him so heavily as of late. He felt finished.

"It's because of Macey."

He looked at Wayren. "Reading my mind again?"

She shrugged. "It was upon your face, Sebastian. You're weary and ready to pass the torch—and now that Macey Gardella is here, you believe it's time."

"It *should* be time."

"I cannot speak to whether it should or shouldn't, whether it is or isn't. I can't even say whether she will measure up and fully take on the mantle of her calling. All I can do is bid you be strong, for the challenges you face—all of you—will be great. And there will always be the easy way out."

"I haven't taken the easy way out for a hundred damned years," he hissed, fully aware that he'd just cursed in a holy place. And at Wayren.

But again, she merely looked at him with those steady blue-gray eyes. "And you thought Victoria Gardella was strong. She cannot hold a candle to you, Sebastian. Never forget it."

With those words wrapping around his mind, settling over him like a cloak, he pulled heavily to his feet. Casting a brief glance toward the praying woman, he gave a nod to Wayren. "I hope to see you again soon."

"As do I."

Sebastian walked out of the church and allowed a splash of the burgeoning dawn to touch his bare skin. Then, the searing pain still throbbing on his face and hand, he pulled his coat and hat closely around himself.

He'd walked no more than half a block, huddled under his protection, when two pairs of black shoes and legs appeared in his vision. They straddled the walkway in front of him.

Sebastian looked up and then over to see an automobile, its door open, and two more pairs of black shoes and trousers standing next to it. He gripped his coat tighter, knowing the moment his clothing fell or was pulled away, he'd fry—which left him limited options for defending himself.

"Sebastian Vioget." A vaguely familiar voice drew his attention to the vehicle, and Al Capone emerged. "I believe it's time you and I had a talk."

Despite the fact that she and her friends were up past three o'clock, talking and giggling, Macey didn't sleep well at Dottie's. She had too many things to worry about, too many things on her mind.

So though dawn was barely breaking at five-thirty, she left and went back to her flat, secure in the knowledge that at least she wouldn't encounter any vampires. And most likely, if Grady or Chas had been waiting for her, they'd've given up by now.

She tried not to think about the possibility of Capone's thugs waiting for her too.

But there was no one threatening lurking about, and Macey slipped up the stairs to her flat. She tumbled to bed and slept for a short time, then got up and went to work—all without seeing anyone, even Mrs. G. (Although she heard her talking loudly on the telephone when she passed by her door.) When she was finished at the library, she stopped by Cookie's. Temple wasn't there, but there was an adorable new hat Macey commandeered. Then she went home and got changed to go to Flora's.

But when she arrived at her friend's boardinghouse, Macey hit a dead end.

"That Flora's not here," said her bad-tempered landlady. She reeked of spirits, and Macey had to step back off the stoop to keep from being overcome by the fumes. "She's got that job now."

"What kind of job? On a Saturday night?" Macey glanced up the street, hoping against hope she'd see her best friend loping home on her long, freckled legs. She smothered a pang of guilt. If she'd been around instead of being so busy with Temple for the last few weeks, she'd know all about Flora's job. They would have gone out to have a celebratory cup of coffee or, better yet, a chocolate sundae at Frank's.

"Saturday? Is it Saturday?" The woman looked around as if to see the day of the week written in the twilit sky.

Macey gritted her teeth. "What job? Where is she working?" Maybe she got a position at a department store. Chelle worked on Saturdays sometimes.

"Some place…I don't know." The landlady—whose name Macey could never remember—shook her head as if trying to sort out her memory.

"When does she usually get home?" Maybe if she waited long enough, she'd catch Flora coming back. It was nearly seven o'clock. And if there was one rule her best friend had, it was Fridays and Saturdays were for fun. Since she'd missed the gala at the Palmer last night, surely Flora had social plans for tonight.

In anticipation of this, Macey had already dressed to go out in a loose, silky frock with a dropped waist, perfect for vigorous dancing. Two strands of fake pearls hung to the wide sash at the bottom of her hips and another of Cookie's hats—this one a crocheted cloche—sat on her head. As she stood on the stoop, the handkerchief-style dress hem fluttered pleasingly against her calves in the gentle spring breeze.

Macey looked up the road again. Surely Flora would be coming home soon, getting ready to go out—even if she wasn't going with

Macey. But…if she was working for one of the garment factories, she might not get off the clock until seven, or even later. Those girls worked long hours for low pay, and in such cramped spaces.

The landlady blinked, then refocused. Macey could almost hear the slosh of moonshine in the woman's brain. "She just left! I tell you that girl just left for her job. She don't come home till all hours of the morning now. Wakes the whole house, she does, slamming the door."

Macey felt an uncomfortable squiggle of concern and guilt. Working at night, coming home in the darkness—such a habit was more dangerous a prospect than she'd realized even a month ago. Now she knew the undead lurked and lingered along with the more common threats of thieves, rapists, and gangsters.

The April evening was getting cooler now that the sun had gone down and Macey pulled her wrap closer around her shoulders, wishing she hadn't given away her heavier velvet one last night. "I need to find her. Do you remember anything about where she's working? Anything at all? A restaurant or theater maybe? You must remember something."

The landlady scratched her red-veined nose. "Nah. Nothing. Maybe a blue circle, though." Her bleary eyes became focused. "Yes, that's right. She wore a blue circle to work."

She wore a blue circle? Whatever that meant, Macey didn't know how she'd find out, for the landlady was clearly finished with the conversation and slammed the door without warning. *Probably needs to get back to her hooch.*

Slowly, she turned to leave. Her insides were in turmoil, laden with guilt and worry. She had no idea her friend had been working at night. Macey *had* to help find Flora a new job—a normal one. She would put aside her training for a while, even loan her friend money to pay the rent if necessary until she did. But Flora simply had to get a better job. A day job.

The sun was low in the sky when Macey walked back down the steps from the boarding house. Grass grew wildly in the front yard and in the cracks of the sidewalk, and one of the upper shutters hung haphazardly from its moorings. One basement window was missing, the opening covered by a warped board. Not the most well-kept place. Not in the best neighborhood.

Flora could do better. And Macey could help her. She should have helped her months ago.

She wore a blue circle. What did that mean? Some sort of uniform? Maybe Jimmy would know.

The problem with Jimmy was, it wasn't easy to contact him either. He moved around from job to job and place to place himself. He often acted as a bouncer in some of the saloons or dance clubs, living with friends or even an occasional girl, then finding another as needed. He was always sweet and protective of his sister and her friends, but neither Macey nor Flora wanted to know too much about what he did for his employment, and he didn't like to share.

She walked briskly along the uneven sidewalk, holding her pocketbook close so its clasp wouldn't snag on her silky dress. The street wasn't deserted, for autos drove by regularly, but there wasn't a taxi in sight.

Now what? She could stop by Dottie's and see if she and Chelle were home, or if they'd gone dancing again. The last thing Macey wanted was to spend Saturday alone or practicing spins and leaps and mid-air kicks with Temple. And she definitely didn't want to be with the bad-tempered Chas Woodmore—who, by the way, hadn't even come to her flat last night, according to Mrs. G.

A car pulled up along the street next to her just as the wind picked up, bringing a chilly breeze over the back of her bare neck.

No, that wasn't a chilly breeze. That was—

Everything happened very quickly. The car stopped, its door opened, Macey spun away and ran two steps before she slammed into someone who'd emerged from behind a tree. She had the breath knocked out of her, and the back of her neck was freezing as a powerful, claw-like hand clamped over her nape.

Before she could gather in a scream, a great shove sent her crashing into a mailbox, knocking the breath out of her. Then strong hands grabbed her, manhandling her toward the auto as she kicked and struggled while trying to catch her breath. Her necklace broke, sending beads scattering on the sidewalk. She landed a good blow in someone's gut, and jabbed someone else in a glowing eye with her elbow, but she was overpowered.

Macey's hat tumbled to the ground, and she lost her grip on the pocketbook as she was shoved into the back of the open car.

Eleven

Wherein Our Heroine is Taken for a Ride

MACEY LANDED IN THE BACKSEAT on her hands and knees, and before she could recover, another rough shove sent her sprawling face-first onto the floor amid several pairs of shoe-clad feet. The floor was gritty and spattered with oil, and a heavy, cloying scent filled the air.

She noticed one female and two male pairs of shoes just as the auto door closed. "Keep her down," someone growled.

A hand twisted a fistful of her hair and whipped her to the floor again. Pain streaked over her scalp, her knees were scraped and bruised, and she was out of breath, taken utterly by surprise. She hadn't managed a squeak, let alone a scream. The vehicle started off with a gentle lurch, and she kept her head lowered for the moment, panting, as she looked around from her vantage point among her abductors' feet.

The back of her neck felt as if a block of ice was pressing there, which told her she was in the presence of more than one undead. And the backseat of this auto was unlike anything she had ever seen. It was roomy, and there were two bench seats, facing each other, like on a train. A covert look told her there was a third seat facing forward, where the driver sat. Surrounding her were three pairs of male shoes and one pair of Mary Janes. But something was wrong with the Mary Janes—and the feet they were on. Even in the dim light, she saw one high-heeled shoe dangling awkwardly from an unmoving foot, its strap catty-wonker and the button loose. The legs attached to the shoes sagged open.

A shiver streaked up Macey's spine, this one having nothing to do with the presence of an undead. She looked up the woman's body and saw the blood. Everywhere. It stained the front of her clothing, running in long rivulets from multiple wounds on her neck, shoulders, and wrists. She couldn't see if she was conscious, for the woman's head was tilted back into the shadows.

By now she recognized the dull, heavy smell in the air. Macey drew in a deep breath and realized the oil on the floor was not oil but blood. She closed her eyes, fighting back nausea and terror. *This is not good.*

And it wasn't Al Capone…unless he'd sent some vampires after her.

She was trapped in an auto with three undead. No one knew where she was. And her stake—the one stake she'd added to her pocketbook at the very last minute tonight—was *in* her pocketbook, which she'd dropped as she was shoved into the auto.

"Macey Gardella. Thank you for joining us."

The speaker wore the cleanest, newest, most fashionable pair of men's spats in the group. She lifted her face to look at him and her body went even colder. "*You.*"

It was the lean, dangerous-looking man who'd visited the library several weeks ago, asking for Miss Gardella. His eyes glowed faintly red, but he said nothing more; merely smiled at her, showing a hint of fang. Then he looked across at his companions and gave a slight nod.

Before she could prepare herself, Macey was dragged up onto the opposite seat by the other two men. Four hands, large and rough, imprisoned her as she tried to twist free. She bucked and twisted with all her might, using the chunky heels of her Mary Janes like billy clubs.

But, strong as she was with her *vis bulla*, she was no match for the two undead in the small confines. Already shocked and out of sorts, not to mention aching from the violent blow to the head, she was murky and slow. Her heart pounded and she couldn't catch her breath as the two held her immobile, sprawled between them on the seat. One wrapped an arm around her head, holding it at an awkward angle as he gripped her left wrist.

The other grabbed her right arm, then slid his free hand up over her thigh and along her hips, dragging up her skirt and baring her garters and the bottom of her knickers. Macey twisted sharply before he got to the juncture of her thighs and managed to free one foot, whipping it into her captor's cheek. He grunted when the heel slammed hard, then scraped along his cheek. This caused him to loosen his grip, giving her the opportunity to jam an elbow into the groin of her other captor. He cried out and backhanded her so hard her ears rang, and she tumbled to the floor again. Her knee landed on something sharp and with a start, she realized it was the clasp of her pocketbook. *How did my bag get in here?*

But she didn't have time to wonder, or even try to open it and fumble for the stake. They forced her back up onto the seat, this time holding her arms and legs even more tightly, stretching her at full length across the car so she had no ability to coil and buck.

Her chest heaving, internal organs turned to ice, Macey realized she was in serious trouble. Her one hope was to get the stake out of her bag. Which meant she had to get back on the floor again.

"Who are you?" she demanded, looking at the presumed leader. If she distracted them, got them talking, maybe she could take them by surprise and free herself. "What do you want?"

"Hold her." Something flashed in the leader's hand, and Macey stiffened when she discerned a knife blade.

She tried to wring herself free once more, but the four hands binding her were so strong and tight they might have been manacles.

The dagger gleamed in the bare streetlight that stole through the auto's window, and Macey realized the vehicle was no longer moving. They were going to kill her in this dark alley and dump her among the garbage. The man from the library reached for her, and with a sharp, swift movement, raked the knife straight down the front of her.

Her dress split and fresh air spilled over her torso as impersonal hands yanked the material away, uncovering her from breast to hip. Her head swam and her temple throbbed; something trickled from her eyes, and she realized it was a trail of tears.

Most of her breasts and belly were bare. Macey could see the growing stripe of blood all along her sternum to her stomach. And there, gleaming in the low light, was the silver *vis bulla*, settled in her navel.

"So you have taken the amulet." He looked up at her, his eyes burning red-pink, his fangs bared. "You are the Gardella." The tip of his tongue slipped out, caressing his thin lips. His eyes turned brighter.

"Did Capone send you?"

"Capone?" His eyes narrowed. "No, he did not. But I'm fascinated that you should think he might have done."

"Who are you, then? You know who I am, but you're too cowardly to tell me who you are." Macey forced every bit of strength and bravado into her voice she could. "And you need two goons plus yourself to capture me. What does that say about you?"

He laughed and reached toward her with the dagger again. She stiffened, preparing herself for pain. But he used the metal tip to flip the tiny silver cross as if it were a plaything. "Nicholas. Nicholas Iscariot at your service, Macey Gardella."

She tried to steady her breathing and calm her heartbeat to keep her torso from shuddering with every pulse and every breath. Iscariot continued to play with the knife, tracing it over the white, trembling skin of her belly, drawing an occasional line of blood, then returning to slide the blade's tip into the circle of the *vis* and jiggle it almost gently.

She tensed, waiting for him to slice it free, knowing the moment he did that, she'd lose what little strength she had left. Then it would be all over.

And no one knows where I am.

Fighting despair, knowing her only chance was to get her hands on the stake, Macey glanced at the woman who sagged next to Nicholas in the corner of the auto. She hadn't moved, and although she was mostly in shadow, Macey was certain she wasn't going to be moving any time ever again. She swallowed hard, knowing that was to be her fate unless she did something. Very soon.

"Oh, did I not introduce you?" Nicholas followed her attention to the victimized woman. He smiled coldly, and the knife moved away as he pulled on the bloodstained arm next to him. Macey caught sight of ribbons of flesh where the chin, neck, and shoulders had once been, mingled with the torn fabric of her clothing, dark and congealed and smelling of iron. The woman had not merely been fed on; she'd been destroyed. Mutilated. Bile rose in the back of her throat, and she swallowed hard.

Nicholas paused, his smile widening. "Ah, but wait...I believe you already are acquainted with this evening's entertainment, aren't you?"

The woman's head lolled forward, then back sharply as he yanked her upright, but not before Macey saw her face clearly in the low light.

She barely held back a scream. *Chelle. It was Chelle.*

"No," she breathed, hysteria rising from deep inside. She couldn't hold it back, it bubbled into her throat and threatened to explode in a horrified cry. "You didn't...you..." She choked and tears swam in her eyes. A band of horror wrapped around her chest, tightening, tightening, and she fought and twisted and bucked wildly against her captors.

"Now, now," Nicholas said, shoving Chelle back into the corner of the auto as if she were a rag doll. "Let's not overset ourselves. It could have been much worse, you know." Then he cocked his head to one side and smiled. His gaze burned like a glowing ruby as it skimmed along her bared skin, which appeared silvery white in the unsteady light. Macey could hear the deep, guttural breathing of the vampire nearest her head, and he gripped her wrists even tighter. She had no feeling in her hands and felt her bones grinding against each other.

The scent of blood was heavy in the air, and now some of it was hers. Her heart pounded harder and deeper. Like a death knell.

Nicholas adjusted her dress, pulling it apart enough that one breast was fully exposed and her undergarments fell away completely. As her heart pounded violently, visible in the vibration of her breast, reverberating through her limbs like a stampede, he used the knife tip to draw a light circle around her areola. A tiny bead of blood dripped down one side, merging into the first slice he'd made down her torso. It burned and stung, but she hardly noticed the pain. She feared it was nothing compared to what was to come.

"There was once a very powerful woman of my kind," her tormentor said conversationally, "who was fond of the combined ecstasy and pain she would experience from touching something so powerful" —he indicated the holy strength amulet by lifting it from her skin with the tip of the knife, pulling the upper lip of her navel taut— "while taking her pleasure. Feasting and feeding and whatnot. I've always wondered what that might be like. If I would enjoy it myself."

Then he lunged. His hand planted heavily on her belly, covering her *vis bulla* as he plunged his fangs roughly into the juncture of neck and shoulder. Macey jolted and screamed as he punctured her skin, felt the exploding release of blood surging from her veins.

His mouth was horrible: one lip hot and the other cold, each sensation revoltingly distinct. They fastened on her skin as he sucked deeply from her. The *m-kuh, m-kuh, m-kuh* sound of him drawing in and swallowing filled her ears in a horrible rhythm, like the heartbeat of death.

Macey could feel the life draining from her, her strength ebbing, the smell of her own blood, the fainter scent of burning flesh. His weight forced her into the seat, into the foulness of the other vampires who held her, his hand pressing, *burning* into her belly as the *vis* seared his palm.

The sound of shattering glass filled the air, and pieces rained down inside the auto. Everything turned to chaos, and in the midst of it Macey tumbled to the floor.

She landed on her pocketbook again, which shocked her into action, but by then a dark arm had jackknifed in and slammed into one of her captors. The vampire who'd held her feet burst into foul-smelling ash, and just as she grappled her stake out of the bag, that same strong hand grabbed her and she was plucked from the auto.

She caught a glimpse of Chas's face—dark, livid, and intense— as he yanked her past him and fairly tossed her to the ground. He dove back into the car, smooth and dark and powerful, extracting another figure. His new combatant fought with sharp punches and a head-butt. But Chas took the head-butt on his temple and flung the undead against the side of the auto. With one low, upward thrust, he held the vamp by the neck and rammed a stake up through shirt and vest, driving it into his heart. Just as the vampire poofed into nothing, the vehicle leapt forward, its door slamming closed from the sudden velocity. Chas jumped back as the tires squealed, and the auto blazed into the night.

By the time Chas turned to her, Macey had pulled to her feet. Panting and trembling, she held her unused stake. Her knees wobbled and she wasn't certain she could even form the words to thank him.

"I…" She swallowed, realized her dress was literally hanging off her, and pulled the fragments closed.

"Good God." He whipped off his coat and wrapped it around her shoulders far more gently than she'd anticipated.

"Chelle. Oh my God, they have *Chelle*," she managed to choke. She swayed and grabbed at a tree, but nevertheless managed a few desperate, staggering steps after the auto.

Chas looked at her, his mouth curving down as he caught her arm to steady her—and pull her back from the chase. "There's nothing to be done now." He hesitated, then said, "Let's go. You need…hell, you need everything."

Chas had no choice but to take Macey back to his rooms. He didn't even consider bringing her to The Silver Chalice. Vioget certainly couldn't see her like this, half naked and with blood everywhere.

Hell, Chas shouldn't even see her like this—at least the half-naked part. At least, not yet. He smiled grimly to himself.

His small flat was conveniently situated on the top floor of a carriage house right next to St. Anselm's Church. What better place for a vampire hunter to live than in the shadow of a holy place?

Chas unlocked the door and Macey stumbled in, still clutching his coat around her shoulders. He had given it to her for modesty just as much as his own self-preservation. The flash of breast and belly, even covered with blood as they were, had been burned into his mind's eye.

This is probably not your best decision ever, Woodmore.

But when he closed the door and turned on a lamp, getting his first good look at her, whatever lewd thoughts he might have harbored disintegrated.

He'd seen worse. On the dead.

"I…" She swayed and allowed her knees to buckle. Fortunately, the sofa was behind her and she sank into it. And, by God, she was still holding her stake. Despite everything else, he had to give her kudos for that.

First things first. "Let me see what they did to you."

She peeled the coat away from the blood congealing on her neck and shoulders while keeping it modestly over the rest of her torso. Her glossy black hair was crusted with blood and wild with curls that made her look as if she'd just been well fucked. And the way the coat bared her slender white shoulders was more than a little tempting.

But Chas wasn't thinking about that—he was looking at the four ugly gouges in her throat. Larger than a normal bite, they were angled and deep, already turning black and crusty around the edges. On anyone other than a Venator, those types of wounds would have been fatal—or worse. Fortunately, he'd arrived in time, or Nicholas Iscariot would have marked her for good.

But unfortunately, Nicholas had been the one vampire Chas hadn't had the chance to slay before the auto careened off down the street, narrowly missing his foot. *Damn and blast.*

"This is going to sting." He felt her brace herself, and he poured a generous helping of holy water in one fast deluge. It was best to get it over with quickly.

When the water hit her wounds, Macey arched and hissed sharply, biting her lip as she turned away to hide her face. Her breathing turned into panting, but there was nothing to be done to alleviate the pain until the blessed water did its work.

So Chas stood and set some water to warming over the stove, then located a cloth and one of his few shirts without bloodstains. His fury simmered well beneath the surface, where he intended to keep it—at least for a while longer. "Are you hurt anywhere else?"

She looked up at him, those velvety brown eyes even larger than usual, and shook her head. "Not…like that." At least some life had come back into her expression.

Good. He gave her a bowl of warm water sprinkled with more holy essence. The small silver cross he kept for such purposes soaked in the bottom of it. She smiled her thanks, but wariness lingered in her eyes, and she still clutched the coat like a fur stole around her bare shoulders. The blood had been mostly washed away by the rush of holy water, and a bolt of heat roared through him as he noticed the curve of her collarbones. With her head of full, unruly hair baring a long, elegant neck and those full lips, she suddenly had him thinking all sorts of untenable thoughts.

Putting the cloth and shirt on the table next to her, he turned to give her privacy, himself a breather—and to find something for them to eat.

And drink.

He wondered if Macey would deign to sip a whiskey if he poured one for her, after her ordeal. She sure as hell earned it.

"I know you're a young Venator, but you did a very stupid thing. " He cracked an egg forcefully into a bowl. Then followed four more, and, after consideration, a fifth and sixth. He was damn hungry—he'd anticipated eating dinner before having to slay vampires.

"No, I didn't."

Her cool, steady response made him furious for a variety of reasons, and the anger he'd managed to contain beneath concern and efficiency burst forth harshly. "What the hell do you—"

"I did *several*—no, *many* stupid things in the last two days." She raised her voice even louder.

He couldn't argue with that. From evading him last night and trying the same again tonight—fortunately, unsuccessfully— to letting herself get *dragged into a damn limousine by Nicholas Iscariot.* What the hell had she been thinking?

Chas drew in a deep breath and gritted his teeth.

She'd turned away on the sofa, but the coat was gone and so were the remnants of her clothing. He could see the titillating shape of her white back, the curve of her shoulders and flare of her hips, and the delicate bumps of her spine and scapulae. From the rear, you'd never know she'd been assaulted by one of the most powerful vampires in the world…except for the single dark wound that showed just over the back of her shoulder. And unfortunately, he had a very good idea what the front of her looked like. Watching Wayren insert the *vis bulla* in the intimate area of her belly had only been the beginning.

"You're damn right." He added milk, salt, and pepper to the bowl. "I was being kind when I said *a* stupid thing." He whisked with more violence than necessary.

Chas actually heard her snort at that. So unladylike from such a feminine creature—who was, he reminded himself, a warrior in training. "Kind is not a word that comes to mind when I think of you."

He grinned in spite of himself. "You and everyone else, lulu." He poured the eggs into the pan he'd heated and slipped a couple of pieces of bread in the oven to toast. "I didn't realize you'd left the library yesterday until it was much too late—you made certain not to leave via your normal route, which I hadn't expected. Because why the hell would you avoid me when you knew we had work to do?" His jaw cracked as he ground his teeth.

"Because you commanded me to wear something that showed off my legs, you…you *goon*. I'm not your damn *moll*."

"You have excellent gams, and they're a good distraction—"

She made a furious sound and turned. Fortunately, she was buttoning up the shirt she'd just pulled on and there was nothing to see except a disappearing shadowy vee. "I have no desire to distract you—"

"Not me, lulu. The undead. Gangsters. A bouncer at a club or the doorman at a speakeasy. Whoever needed to be distracted." He bared his teeth at her in a knowing smile. She made an angry sound and flattened her lips into a hard line.

And just as quickly, the last bit of levity evaporated from his mood. Anger blazed through him when he was reminded of her folly, her brazen stupidity. "And then you made a point of trying to do it again tonight. Good God, Macey. I thought you had more sense than that. And I had a hell of a time tracking you down. You're damn lucky I had the skills and desire to do so." He hoped like hell she'd learned her lesson.

She rose from the sofa and came over, showing those shapely legs and nothing else beneath his loose shirt. "You irritated me when you made the assumption I was going to be at your beck and call last night—or ever—and you made it even worse when you told me what to wear. As if I was nothing more than a showpiece to be on your arm."

"I told you to bring a stake." He plopped a spoonful of eggs onto a plate with more force than necessary.

"I did. Tonight, anyway."

What the hell did that mean? He made no effort to hide his anger. "You nearly got yourself marked, Macey. Your pride and stubbornness almost removed you from the picture completely. You're a damned *Venator*. There is no fucking room for pride or bruised feelings or willfulness." He shoved the plate with the smaller portion across the counter toward her. "Eat."

She glared up at him, her expression mutinous. "I worked hard all week. And for the last month! I wanted a night out with my friends last night, and tonight—well, yes, I should have been more prepared, I should have had my stake in a more handy place than the bottom of my pocketbook—and I've learned my lesson about that. I just wanted a break. A night out for some fun after three weeks of training. Is that too much to ask?"

He gave her a cold, flat smile. "Your only nights out now are going to be with me and a stake. You've got a job to do. *We've* got a job to do. And every night you stay home, every night you shirk that duty, Macey, someone else will die. *Many* someones. Do you understand that? We don't get fucking nights *off.* We don't have the luxury of sleeping in a comfortable bed, resting after a long day, or going *dancing* with friends…because when you're sleeping at night, or when you're flirting and giggling and gossiping, someone in this city is being mauled and torn apart and *fed upon.*"

That shut her up.

She drew in a breath that shook visibly, turned her eyes downward, and let her fork clatter gently to the counter.

He took a bite of eggs, and they tasted like dust. *Dammit to hell.* He clenched his jaw and kept his mouth shut and chewed. Took another tasteless bite. There was no sense in sugarcoating the truth. She needed to know what she'd signed up for, that people relied on her, that her calling was a vocation.

"Look—"

"They took Chelle. My friend. I'm pretty certain she was… she's…" Macey shook her head and looked up at him. Ferocity mingled with grief and shame in her expressive eyes. "He *knew* she was my friend. It wasn't an accident. It wasn't *random.*"

"Of course it wasn't. Haven't you been listening to anything we've told you? You're a Venator, and not just any Venator, but the daughter of Max Denton. Your lineage is not simply impressive, but stellar. The moment you were identified as a Venator, you became the most dangerous person in the world to Nicholas and Count Alvisi. You're the heir to *Il Gardella*. They want you dead—or, worse, they want you under their control."

The wounds in Macey's neck still throbbed, but that discomfort was nothing compared to the awful, ugly sensation growing inside her.

What have I done?

"What did you mean I was almost marked by Nicholas Iscariot?" she asked, half curious, half wanting to change the subject. She needed to grieve for Chelle. She *would* grieve for her; she would cry and rage for her…but not here, not with Chas. Not now.

She glanced down at the meal he'd made. He had been amazingly kind and considerate—such a contrast to his normal self, and so surprising in light of his barely concealed anger with her. Oh, yes, she could see how livid he was.

"Like Lilith the Dark did to Max Pesaro." When she looked blankly at him, his expression turned to irritation. "You need to bone up on your history. Suffice to say, the few vampires closest to Lucifer are more powerful than that of the minions they control. Nicholas Iscariot, whom you met tonight, and Count Alvisi are two of the fewer than half a dozen of that inner circle of Lucifer's—and they're both in Chicago, for some damned reason. Probably because of you as much as Vioget, now that I think about it. They might want his rings, but they're also most certainly interested in you."

Macey blanched and her insides swished ominously, but Chas didn't seem to notice. He continued his history lecture. "Iscariot in particular is close to Luce because of his relation to Judas. If they should mark you—which is an intentional process that is reserved for only select victims—it happens when they're in the process of feeding on you. The way I understand it, there is a special something—some essence, some intoxicant—released from their saliva that seeps into your blood and, for lack of a better term, it *hooks* or connects you to them. You remain mortal, but tied to them irrevocably. Your wounds never fully heal—unlike normal vampire bites."

Macey felt lightheaded and reached to touch the four raised marks on her neck. "Am I marked?"

"I'm certain I interrupted in time. But Wayren will be able to tell for sure—and perhaps Vioget. But I warn you—don't allow him to see you like that."

"Like what?"

"Bloody." His unfriendly eyes pierced her. "He'd be on you in a moment. The blood, and the fact that you're the spitting image of your great-great-grandmother."

A deep, hot shiver caught her by surprise. *He'd be on you in a moment.* That golden, bronzy body, those elegant hands and sensual mouth—then she went cold. And nauseated. "You mean…he'd…*feed* on me?"

Chas gave a sharp, bitter laugh as if he'd followed her train of thought. "Yes. And then his soul would be lost forever."

Macey might still be missing large chunks of information about the undead, but this she understood. Or thought she did. "He's been a vampire for over a hundred years, and he's never fed?"

"Not on a mortal. He drinks of course, but with the stockyards here, there's an ample supply of fresh blood." Chas's expression focused pointedly on her. "Which is why it was so vital that you accepted your calling. He needs you—or believes he does—to save his soul. Or something of that nature. Vioget isn't known for sharing information."

"So because he's never fed on a mortal, his soul can still be saved."

"Or so we believe. Once an undead feeds on a person, violating their very life, the vampire is damned to belong to Lucifer for eternity."

All that wasn't in *The Venators*, at least as far as she'd read. Macey drew in a long, deep, ragged breath. *What have I done? What am I going to do?*

Chas pulled a dark bottle from beneath the sink. It was labeled "vinegar," but as soon as he opened it, she smelled spirits. Without commentary, he set two finger-high glasses on the counter between them and filled both—one nearly to the top and the other halfway.

"Take your pick."

Instead of reaching for either, Macey pulled her hand back. "I don't think so."

The bottle replaced in its spot beneath the sink, Chas leaned on his elbows and faced her across the counter. His gaze fastened on her, steady and dark. "It won't hurt you and it'll take the edge off your pain. I still see shock lingering in your eyes." He slid the fuller glass toward her. "People have been drinking spirits for thousands of years. Do you think the United States government really has the right—or ability—to stop us from imbibing if we wish? Volstead is a farce and everyone knows it."

Macey eyed the amber-colored whiskey. She'd been just over fifteen when Prohibition went into effect, and, yes, she'd had her share of sips of moonshine and beer at the swimming hole back home, both before and after the passing of the Eighteenth Amendment. There wasn't much else to do in Skittlesville besides drink, swim, or sled (depending on the season), and attend petting parties with the boys. And she'd done them all.

"It may be a farce, the law," she said, closing her fingers around the drink, "but the Temperance people have a point. Spirits are evil to families where the fathers spend all the money on liquor or hit their wives and children when they're in their cups. Or drink themselves to death."

She thought of the last two years before her foster father, Hank, died, when he was in so much pain from the knot of cancer growing in his abdomen. He drank steadily all day, so he had to do his watch repair work early in the morning before his hands became too trembly. The drink gave him some relief, but in the end, his dependence on spirits cost Melissa, his wife, and Macey most of their livelihood and more than a few bruises.

"Anything when taken to the extreme can be a vice." Chas's voice was low and gritty. "And there are worse vices than spirits." He slung back the entire contents of his glass in one big gulp then set the vessel on the counter.

"You sound as if you speak from experience."

"Too much whiskey isn't my weakness, no matter how it might seem." He pinned her with his gaze.

Macey's heart bumped hard and for a moment she couldn't breathe. There was something there, dark and tortured, in his Gypsy eyes. Heat, too. Definite heat. She felt tight and warm all over and she hadn't even taken a drink.

Sure she'd come to regret it, she lifted the glass and sipped cautiously. Her eyes widened in surprise. Unlike the hooch she'd tried in the past, the whiskey was smooth and tasted just like it looked—like a warm, golden river flowing down her throat. She took another, larger sip and closed her eyes as the heat filled her belly, rolling gently through her limbs.

When she opened her eyes, Chas was watching her, his lips curved in a pained smile. And when their gazes met, he held hers boldly, allowing her to see the glitter of desire therein.

"It's a damned lonely life being a Venator."

Macey lifted her chin. "If that's an offer, I'm afraid I must refuse." But her insides were shifting and fluttering, and all at once, she'd become acutely aware of him—his fine mouth, his gleaming eyes, the memory of his smooth, lethal attack on the vampires tonight.

Chas responded by stepping back. "That wasn't an offer, lulu. But when and if there is one, you won't have to ask."

Twelve

A Dark Spiral

THE STALE SCENT OF DEATH mingled with an unfamiliar, pungent aroma that smelled like a chemical lab. Bare bulbs cast cold white light in an already sterile room.

Macey held her breath then looked down at the still, gray-faced figure on the table. The glimmer of hope she'd held onto since waking this morning in Chas's flat burst like a soap bubble. Grief stabbed her hard in the belly.

"Yes," she said more steadily than she'd thought possible. "I can identify her. That's Chelle—Michelle Chautier."

"Thank you, Miss Denton." The morgue attendant swiftly pulled the white sheet back up to cover Chelle's face. He had been kind enough to keep the rest of the ravaged body hidden, but it didn't matter. Macey had already seen the horror. "I'm sorry you had to do this, but we thank you for your assistance."

She turned away, filled with nausea and emptiness. It had been a small hope, but there had been a chance that she'd only *thought* it was Chelle in the back seat of Nicholas Iscariot's auto. A trick of the light, a reasonable mistake due to the shock and uncertainty of the environment.

Or maybe Chelle wasn't actually dead, just…wounded. Perhaps there was hope for her.

But no.

The body had been dumped, discovered, and was waiting in the morgue to be identified by the time Macey arrived.

She hadn't even gone home after leaving Chas's flat and was still wearing his shirt and a long button-down coat over it like a dress. Her shoes and stockings had made it through her ordeal unscathed except for a few spatters of blood that, in the daylight, looked like mud. No one seemed to give her attire a second look when she made an inquiry at the police headquarters. Instead, the attendant had sent her to this unpleasant subterranean room two blocks away.

"I'm glad I could help." She turned to leave, reaching for the door with a listless hand. Before she could turn the knob, the door swung open, and there was Grady.

He came to an abrupt halt, as startled to see her as she was to see him, and they both stared at each other for a moment. A blossom of warmth pushed away a little of her numbness, and she managed a weary smile at the unexpected but welcome meeting. He appeared exhausted and rumpled, as if he'd not slept for days. Dark shadows curved under his bloodshot eyes, and the expanse of dark stubble indicated he hadn't shaved either. His tie sagged and the bottom button on his vest was undone.

"Macey." Obvious relief showed in his face. "I…" He shook his head and drew in a deep breath. His blue eyes were sober but growing calmer by the moment. "I heard there was another… victim. I came to see if I recognized her."

She understood. He'd feared she was the victim, and had come to see for himself. She wanted to touch his arm to comfort him as much as herself, but stopped herself.

"Miss Denton has already identified the young woman," the attendant interjected, seemingly oblivious to the undercurrent. "Thanks anyway."

Grady's attention returned to Macey, his face grim. "You knew her? Damn. It's not your friend, the redhead."

"It was Chelle," she managed to say. "You met her at the Palmer."

"*Jesus.*" His voice was a low, tight hiss. He took her arm. "Let's go. There's no reason to stay here then." He glanced over her shoulder. "Thanks for sending word, Rob."

"Any time. Nasty business. Stay out of Capone's crossfire, boyo."

"Always."

Macey didn't mind when Grady kept her arm pressed against his side as they walked down the hall. She needed someone to touch, to lean on, even that little bit.

Grady led her up the stairs from the dreary basement morgue, then, blessedly, out into a brilliant and sunny spring day. At least there was one thing in the world that was right. Her eyes stung.

"I've been trying to find you since Friday night." His voice was taut, very near anger, as he gestured for her to sit on a park bench. He jammed a hand through his unruly hair, making it stand up even more wildly. "I thought I was going to walk into that morgue and find you on a goddamned slab! Why did you take off like that?"

That blossoming warmth warred with guilt and irritation as she looked up at him, forced to shade her eyes against the sun. "I'm sorry you were worried."

"Of course I was worried, for God's sake. You dump a vampire victim on me, then damned if you don't disappear. What the hell am I supposed to think?" Grady stood over her, looking exhausted and disreputable but oh, so attractive.

"As you can see, I'm alive."

His ire faded. "And just barely from the looks of you."

"What does that mean?"

"Have you looked in a mirror?"

"Have you?"

They glared at each other, then Macey turned away with a short laugh that threatened to turn into tears. She didn't have the energy to match wits or barbs with him. She didn't know what to even think about this man who broke into her flat and expected to be able to find her whenever he wanted, who kissed her in a cabaret booth in front of everyone, who asked too many questions about things he shouldn't—and who, oddly enough, made her feel warm and safe just by taking her arm.

She pulled to her feet, suddenly mind-bogglingly exhausted. "I'm going to go home. I'm tired." *I need time to myself. Time to think.* The nausea that hadn't seemed to leave the pit of her belly since last night churned roughly.

"Macey." His voice stopped her. "I'll drive you home. If you'll let me."

"It's better than taking the bus."

Despite her fatigue, her mind raced, spinning in circles during the drive through the busy Saturday streets to Hyde Park. Though she'd lived through it all, she could hardly fathom how much things had changed in less than a month. Just three weeks ago, she'd been on her way in this very vehicle with Grady for lunch—the morning after staking a vampire. And now…

She secretly touched the *vis bulla* beneath Chas's coat and felt the pleasant sting of energy bolt through her. Now she'd embarked on a completely different path.

And, oh God…Chelle was dead.

Was she to blame?

The nausea in the pit of her stomach surged into full-blown illness. Macey swallowed hard and used a shaky hand to push a mess of hair behind one of her ears. She wasn't ready to think about that quite yet, but she suspected she already knew the answer.

"Macey." Grady had taken his eyes off the road to look at her. "I'm sorry about your friend. Seeing her like that must have been awful."

You have no idea.

They were on her street now, and he pulled the auto expertly into a parking space across from the house. Resting his wrist on the steering wheel, he faced her without turning off the engine. "I'd like to walk you up if you don't mind."

"Yes. I can get you some…coffee." She managed a shaky smile, suddenly relieved she wasn't going to be alone. "It's early enough in the day that Mrs. Gutchinson won't blow a can."

But he didn't turn off the vehicle. "Is there anyone else who might?"

"What do you mean?"

His mouth was a thin line. "You're wearing a man's coat. And, as far as I can tell, not a whole lot under it."

Oh. Right. "It's a long story."

"I'll bet," he muttered, but turned off the auto anyway.

Macey walked quickly up the walk, and he was right on her heels. All she wanted was to get inside and up to her flat without her landlady seeing her. There was no flutter of curtain at Mrs. G's favorite spying window, and Macey breathed a sigh of relief when they made it all the way up the first flight of stairs without being noticed. The old woman must still be at church.

Macey had the key in her hand by the time they reached her landing, and as she fumbled it into the lock, she heard Grady sniff.

Just as she got the door open, he said, "Wait—!"

But it was too late.

Macey took one step into her flat, then froze.

Blood. Everywhere. The scent was heavy and full and awful.

And on the bed, soaking in a pool of it, her wrists and ankles tied to the bedposts, was Mrs. Gutchinson.

Thirteen

The Point of No Return

OH JESUS.

Grady tried to stop Macey, but she was already across the room and at the bed. He watched her stark white face as she tore at the bindings on the elderly woman's wrists.

"Mrs. G!" The wrought iron bedframe rattled and clunked as she struggled with the ropes. The heavy, sickening scent of too much blood and other bodily fluids filled his nose. "Oh, God, Mrs. *G.*"

"Macey." He pulled her away, looked into her wide, shocked eyes. "Go down and call the police. Have them send Detective Linwood. And Officer Bailey."

To his relief, she went, still dazed but moving purposefully. "Linwood. And Bailey."

Grady turned back to the carnage on the bed. He'd seen a lot of senseless violence in his life. But the brutality visited on a weak, elderly woman was one of the worst sights he'd ever beheld. Her throat and arms, even one of her thighs, had been mutilated, torn and fed upon in the same way Jennie Fallon and the victims from The Gyro had been. Blood still dripped off the edge of the bed in ominous plops, telling him the attackers hadn't been gone for more than a few hours.

And why the blazing hell did they need to tie her down like that? The poor woman hadn't had the strength of a gnat. He hoped like hell she'd died quickly. But the way the ropes dug into her wrists and ankles, along with the raw chafing of her paper-thin flesh, told him that was a futile hope. Jaw tight, he used his knife to cut her free. When he heard footsteps on the stairs, he grabbed a robe off the chair and flung it over the body.

"I called from…her telephone." Macey stood on the threshold of her flat, looking forlorn and exhausted. But the dazed expression had eased from her eyes, replaced by grief—and something else, cold and flat. "They're coming."

Grady wanted to wrap her in his arms, drag her close to him and hold her tightly, bury his face in her soft hair, make her forget, remind himself how easily it could have been her…but there was the matter of that coat she was wearing. He'd seen enough bare thigh through its bottom flap to know she was missing more than one article of clothing. And there were the marks on her neck, faint but unmistakable. He didn't care for any of the explanations that came to mind. Nevertheless…

"You can't stay here. I'll help you get some things together, all right?"

"I'll do it."

She dug through her bureau and closet, then went into the small bathroom while Grady took the opportunity to look around the flat for clues. Not that it mattered—by now he had no doubt the perpetrators were vampires.

At this thought, a chilly string of alarm trailed down his spine. If what he'd read in *The Venators* was even half accurate, these undead beings were evil beyond anything he'd encountered, even during the War.

The undead could leave bloodstained fingerprints or even a trail to their lair and it wouldn't matter. The police—even those few who were actually still interested in carrying out justice—would be ineffectual in tracking down a vampire. Attempting to arrest or incarcerate one would be absurd.

The sound of sirens announced the arrival of the fuzz, and Grady went to the window to look down. That was when he noticed the rosary, still on the sill. He stuffed it in his pocket.

The door to the bathroom opened and Macey came out, fully attired at last. She wore a soft pink blouse with a high collar over a taupe skirt that went just past her knees, and a wide swatch of floral fabric tied around her hair. Blue-black curls winged out around the nape of her neck and jaw. Despite her subdued attire, she still looked pale and the tip of her nose was tinged red. She didn't look toward the bed.

Grady met his uncle and colleagues at the bottom of the stairs and gave them a brief overview as they climbed up. As a homicide detective, and one of the few honest ones on the force—along with Gern Bailey, who'd accompanied him as requested—Linwood was already sadly familiar with this particular type of crime. Although Grady hadn't told him everything he'd learned from reading *The Venators*, or even about Macey and the stake and vampire ash in her flat, he and his uncle had discussed the unsettling possibility that something unnatural was causing these murders.

When Linwood was introduced to Macey, he flickered a glance at Grady and lifted a brow. Obviously, he remembered meeting her on the street a few weeks ago. Grady gave him a brief nod of acknowledgment and remained silent while his uncle took her statement.

"I came home early yesterday morning after spending the night at my girlfriend's house, and then I had to go into work around noon. I didn't speak to Mrs. G, but I heard her on the phone when I left. I was back briefly last night, around six-thirty. I didn't see or hear Mrs. G at that time. I haven't been back since." She didn't look at Grady.

He had just missed seeing her last night, then. He'd arrived a little after seven and spoken to Mrs. Gutchinson at that time—who told him she hadn't seen Macey for days. That was when the cold fingers of fear began to tighten around his middle. If the nosy landlady hadn't seen her on a Saturday, that was unusual. And his suspicions were correct: she hadn't slept in her own bed last night either.

"I don't need any further information from you at this time, Miss Denton." Linwood, a stocky, straight-speaking man, was businesslike but empathetic. He nodded a dismissal to his nephew, then turned to join Officer Bailey and the coroner in examining the scene.

"Let's go." Grady looked at Macey. She didn't hesitate, but as she picked up a valise with her things in it, she glanced toward the bed. Then, her jaw shifting visibly, she led the way from her flat.

He wondered if she'd ever return.

Grady debated all the way to the ground floor what to do next. He knew what he *wanted* to do…but there were a lot of unknown factors involved. Including the man's coat she'd slung over her bag and was obviously intending to return.

But when he settled behind the steering wheel and pushed the ignition, he finally had to ask. "Where to, Macey? Something to eat? A place to rest?"

"I'm not the least bit hungry. I…don't know." She looked down at her hands. "I'm not thinking very straight right now."

And obviously she wasn't intending to return that damned coat any time soon. Grady felt a little more optimistic with that realization. "All right then."

He took her to his place. It was, he told himself, reasonable. She wanted to rest, she likely didn't want to be around anyone who wanted to talk, but if she did, he'd be there. And she hadn't offered any other option—no other friends or family. No sense in checking into a hotel.

And maybe, just maybe, she'd finally tell him what was happening.

Macey didn't let on, but she was relieved when Grady took her home. She didn't feel comfortable making the suggestion herself, but it was exactly where she wanted to go.

Why, she wasn't completely certain. She kept having to remind herself she'd only known him for less than a month, and had only been in his company a few times. She had no claim on him or his time and attention. Nor could she expend any energy mulling over why she had such a connection to him. She had enough problems and questions tearing at her mind like angry claws.

Unlike Macey and Chas, Grady didn't live in an upper flat, but a small, two-story brick twin that took up half a narrow building on a neighborhood street corner. By the names on some of the establishments—O'Brien's, McFeaster's, Garrick's—she figured they were in the heart of some Irish enclave.

Desperate to give herself something to focus on besides the horror of the last twenty hours, Macey looked around his home with interest. At first glance she guessed it was about three times as large as her flat.

Bookshelves lined one wall in the living room, which was furnished with two sofas and an armchair. The shelves were filled with books on a variety of topics, and bibliophile that she was, Macey walked over to examine the selection. It was an amazing library, broad in subject and yet filled with depth. Biographies, atlases, mechanical instruction manuals, and books on mathematics, biology, chemistry, and physics—not to mention two shelves of fiction. Including *Dracula* and Polidori's short, *The Vampyre*.

On the kitchen table was a typewriter and sheaves of paper, which Grady tidied into a neat stack as she looked around. Notebooks and pencils littered the counter and coffee table. A stack of newspapers sat on the floor next to the armchair. A camera with its strap looped around it was on a side table next to the chair, along with a telephone. There was mail addressed to "Mr. J. Grady" (well, that answered the question about his name). On a compact table in the corner was a jumble of mechanical objects and tools: padlocks, keys, handcuffs, timepieces, and wires of all shapes and sizes.

"I wasn't expecting company," he said, picking up a mug and then a pair of shoes. "But I'm glad you're here."

"It looks comfortable. And cozy." She lingered at the shelf over a fireplace, examining the array of photographs, suddenly feeling awkward.

The pictures were a welcome distraction. Many were city streets that definitely weren't Chicago. There was one of Grady with his Uncle Linwood and a pleasant-looking woman she assumed was the aunt who'd been killed in gangster crossfire. Then Grady with two other men sitting at a restaurant table, toasting each other with beer mugs. Another of Grady, tall and straight, dressed in an Army uniform and standing next to a broad-shouldered, muscular man who looked familiar. It took her a minute, and then she recognized him as the great Harry Houdini. Next to it was the photo of a bride and groom along with Grady, and what looked like a wedding party. Most of the images were framed, but there were some loose ones with curling edges, stuck behind others.

So different from the stark, austere flat in which she'd slept last night. By contrast, Chas had nothing in his living space except furnishings, food, and whiskey. He'd offered her his bed, but she opted for the sofa, and once she was settled, he told her he was going out.

"There are a lot of hours left of the night," he told her, yanking a hat down low over his forehead and hefting a stake.

This morning, she awoke to find a note advising of his return, suggesting toast for breakfast, and informing her he'd be awake by noon. To Macey's surprise, her half-drunk glass of whiskey was still on the counter next to the message.

She had no idea when Chas came back; he must have been incredibly stealthy. And she had no desire to wait for him to wake at noon, even though she hadn't told him about her encounter with Big Al, for, in a blast of desperate hope, it had occurred to her she might have been mistaken about Chelle. So she'd scrawled her intention on the bottom of his note and left.

Grady spoke, breaking into her thoughts. "Do you want anything?"

You.

The thought popped into her head so unexpectedly and with such ferocity Macey blinked. She realized it was true on many different levels, and the certainty of it baffled her.

"No." She went to the window and looked out, wondering how the group of children in the courtyard could be playing tag so innocently when there was so much evil surrounding them.

Couldn't they feel it? Couldn't they sense it?

"You're involved in something serious—and dangerous. After what happened Friday night, you can't deny it anymore. Tell me, Macey."

She shook her head. There was simply no way to explain it and not sound looney. She didn't want to talk about it. She wasn't even ready to think about it. Chelle was dead. Mrs. G was dead. Not just dead, but tortured. In Macey's bed, which had been a clear and obvious warning. And Flora—

She spun from the window. "*Grady.* My friend, Flora…oh, God, what if she's next? What if they got to her?" She started for the door, but he moved swiftly and intercepted her.

"Tell me her name. Her address. I'll have Linwood check, make sure she's all right." He took her shoulders, his long-fingered hands steady and warm.

"She's working at a place at night. I don't know where. I haven't heard from her in days. If they get her too…" She pressed her lips together. "Or Dottie." It was all she could do to keep from shrieking and wailing.

What was happening to her? To her life?

"Where is she working?" Grady's voice was calm. He took her by the hand and brought her to the sofa, then picked up the telephone receiver.

"I don't know."

He handed her a paper and pencil. "Write down her name and address. I'll call the station and have Linwood or someone go to her house. If she works nights, she should be home sleeping now, right?"

Macey took the paper and wrote Flora's information on it with a shaky hand, and then Dottie's as well. "Will you have your uncle check both of them?"

Grady nodded, his face grave. "Sit down. There isn't anything you can do right now."

But that wasn't true. Not at all.

Macey was a Venator. The person who *could* make a difference, who *could* hunt down the bastards who'd killed her friend. Wasn't that her *calling*? Her responsibility?

According to Sebastian and Wayren and Chas it was. But, despite the *vis bulla*, the training, her encounter with Iscariot, the concept was still unfathomable.

Utterly exhausted—physically, mentally, emotionally— Macey wandered around Grady's home while he called the police station. A glance out the window told her it was many hours until dark. Until the evil ones would come out. She had time.

She had a reprieve before she had to act. Her fingers trembled.

Standing at the window, looking down again at the young boys playing outside, Macey noticed something that made her go still. The windowsill beneath her fingers was made of wood. And it had a trio of silver crosses embedded in it. She looked more closely and saw that someone had gouged the three plus-shaped figures in the wood…and it looked as if silver had been poured into the indentations.

Startled, she spun and found Grady watching her, just as he settled the telephone receiver back into place. "I did that two weeks ago. On every window and the threshold of the doors. There's the flathead screwdriver I used, right there." He pointed to the table with the tools. "I melted down some old silver that belonged to my aunt. Had it blessed at the church, too."

Macey could only nod.

"I'm not about to take any chances. *The Venators* claims an undead can't enter your home uninvited, but I'm fairly certain you didn't invite in the vampire who climbed through your window." His smile was crooked, but his eyes were still grave.

"No. But Mrs. Gutchinson…did." She choked a little as she was assailed by the memory of the frail woman spread-eagled on the bed, drowning in her own blood. Despair settled heavily over her, weighting her insides like a stone in the pit of her belly. "I tried to warn her, to explain not to let anyone she didn't know into the house…"

"But you can't really explain that to just anyone. Can you? *Macey.* You know I know. You know you can tell me. I have my suspicions, but I'd rather hear it from you."

She looked away. The desire to tell him, to unload everything in her heart and mind on this man with the elegant hands and sharp mind and steady, empathetic gaze, was so strong she could taste it. But the truth was bitter and unpleasant, and she knew it would change everything between them. Somehow.

"At least tell me what happened last night." His voice was taut.

That she could do. "All right."

He relaxed visibly and gestured to the sofa. "Sit?"

Macey shook her head. "I went to see Flora and she wasn't home. That's part of why I'm so worried about her. But her landlady said she was at work, so I left. As I was walking away, an automobile pulled up, and before I realized what was happening, the door opened and someone jumped out from behind a bush. They shoved me inside. There were three vampires in there."

Her stomach pitched and roiled at the memory of the heavy scent of blood, the sight of Chelle's torn body, and the feel of the vampires' iron-like hands, holding her immobile.

"They attacked me. One of them bit me." She gestured to her neck, thankful the malicious-looking wounds were already healing. "But fortunately, the auto had parked in an alley, and someone must have heard what was happening. He got me out of there."

"Someone?"

"Chas. The…uh…"

"Right. I know. The man from the diner." Grady's voice was cool. "The gangster."

"He's not a gangster. He's a…vampire hunter." Her voice dropped to a whisper.

A blip of surprise widened his eyes. Not what he'd expected. "You're telling me he's a Venator? Or is he some sort of Van Helsing?"

The lump in her throat made it impossible to speak, so she gave a sort of ambiguous nod. "Whatever you want to call it." She hoped she wasn't breaking some great Venatorial rule by telling him this.

"So he rescued you, and let me guess—that was his coat you were wearing today."

"My clothing was destroyed. By the vampires."

"Jesus." Grady hissed a low breath. His face was so grim, so stony. "That could have been you, this morning. On that slab."

"Very nearly was." Macey couldn't hold back the horrible memories. They rushed over her in a deluge of evil black sensations and images. The hand burning into her bare skin, the knife tip etching around her nipple, the raking of the same blade down her torso…the brutal fangs gouging her throat and neck. The repugnant smell of heavy blood, of undead flesh, of lust wrapped with malice.

"Macey."

Grady was there and, hardly thinking, she walked into his arms. They wrapped around her, strong and comforting, and she sank into him. Sagged, rested her head against his chest, allowed herself to let it go. She closed her eyes.

He smelled good. Like man and soap and pine. Something fresh, yet warm and alluring. His heart thudded beneath her ear, solid and steady. "You're safe now. Safe here," he murmured into the top of her head.

Safe? Never.

No. Oh no. She would never be safe again. A tremor of realization shocked her, and her eyes bolted open. Never again.

Was this to be her life, then? Forever, until she herself was shredded into a bloody mess?

Did she truly have the strength to live like that? To fight this evil, night after night, as Chas had so bluntly described?

It's a damned lonely life being a Venator.

Her heart thudded hard like a bell tolling a sober announcement. Realization—unpleasant and yet calming—

settled over her. She closed her eyes, rested her temple against his chest, inhaled him.

She might be lonely tomorrow, next week, in a year. But she wasn't lonely now. She could think about the future later. And she would.

But for now…

Macey smoothed her hands over Grady's torso, up and over his shoulders. He tensed, sensing the difference in her touch, and pulled back to look down at her.

Her hand cupped the back of his neck, fingers touching the short, crisp hair there. She pulled his head down, covering his mouth with hers. His lips parted slightly in surprise, then he responded hesitantly with a tentative brush against her mouth. After a moment of reserve, he made a soft sound in the back of his throat then, as if freed from some bondage, began to devour her, pulling her up close along the length of his body. His tongue plunged deep, strong and sleek, delving and stroking. Macey sagged against him with her own low moan and kissed him back just as fiercely.

Oh yes. She wanted this…wanted not to think. Wanted him.

Abruptly Grady pulled away, setting her back from him. He shoved a hand through his impossibly thick, rich hair. "I don't think this is a good idea." But his eyes told a completely different story. His breathing was rough and unsteady, and his gaze was hot and brilliantly blue. His lips were parted—not soft and puffy but chiseled and sensual.

Macey stepped closer, her hands returning to his warm chest. She could feel the outline of muscle beneath her palms, the thundering of his heart, the heat of his skin. "Why not?"

"I wasn't about bringing you here for this sort of thing." The brogue came out so thick and lilting, Macey's knees trembled. It was a beautiful cadence, deep and musical and rough with desire.

"I know."

"And you're upset. You're not thinking so clearly. I'm not about to be taking advantage of that, lass. It's not my way."

"You're not taking advantage, Grady. I kissed you, remember?" She smiled up at him, her heart swelling large and warm, certainty flooding her. His hesitance was only making her want him more, making her want to experience this with *him*. And no one else.

"And Macey." He stepped back, breaking all contact with her. His gaze changed from avid to icy blue. "I'm not the sort of bloke who's fond of followin' in another's steps. That's not my way either."

It took her a moment to pull out of her haze of desire to realize what he meant. "Chas? Oh, no. Not him. Not…not *anyone*, Grady. I'm…I haven't done this before." She felt a prickle of hurt that he'd think that of her, but immediately discarded it. After all, she *had* been wearing an overcoat—and nothing else— this morning.

"No?" He still appeared wary, still kept space between them. "Then I'm sure as hell it's not a good idea."

"Is that so?" A sudden, wild combination of boldness and affection for him coursed through her, and she swiftly unbuttoned the top button of her blouse. She felt his attention settle at the widening vee of her shirt, and he stilled. The second button came undone beneath her nimble fingers, then a third. Now a good portion of her Simington's corset showed, along with a hint of cleavage.

"Macey." Grady sounded strangled.

She merely slanted a hot, meaningful look up at him. Holding his gaze, she slipped out of her shoes. Then bent slowly and carefully to roll the flesh-colored stocking down over her left leg, then tossed it away.

"Wait." His voice lashed out. She looked up at him in surprise. But his eyes were a glittering midnight blue again. "Let me do the other."

Heart pounding, Macey rested her right foot on the seat of a chair, her knee bent. Grady's elegant fingers were steady and sure as they slid up along the length of transparent silk. Then, curving his hands around her thigh, just beneath the hem of her skirt, he flipped loose the garter and began to ease the stocking over her knee.

Macey's breathing was unsteady, and her whole body had been shocked alive. His touch was warm and erotic in the simplicity of sliding the whispery silk down her calf. She couldn't control a shiver that started in her belly and made its way down her limbs, mirroring his touch.

When he reached her foot, Grady looked up and caught her eyes as he stripped off the stocking and tossed it aside. "I've been about wanting to do that ever since you climbed into my Ford." His voice was deep and husky.

She smiled and he curved his hand over her lifted thigh, sliding his fingers beneath the silk of her skirt, and pulled her into another kiss. This one had neither tentativeness nor wild lust. But it was very thorough and filled with promise, leaving her breathless and hot.

Without warning, he lifted her into his arms and carried her effortlessly up the stairs to the second floor. Macey vaguely noticed wood paneling on the flight up, but she was more interested in unfastening as many buttons of his shirt as she could get to, and tasting the warm skin of his neck and jaw. His hair smelled as good as the rest of him, and it was silky and soft against her cheek and beneath her fingers. The opening of his shirt revealed smooth skin several shades darker than her own, and the hint of dark hair and sleek muscles.

In the bedroom, Grady released her, and she slid down his long body then stepped back. The bed was just behind him, sunshine spilling over the wrinkled but pulled-up bedclothes.

He looked down at her, question in his eyes. Macey's response was to reach for his vest and begin unfastening the three buttons there. He sank obligingly onto the edge of the bed, settling his hands over her hips. She wasted no time and flung the vest away, then his shirt. Beneath was that sleeveless white undershirt which fit like a second skin, showing smooth biceps, square shoulders, and the outline of his solid, flat pectorals.

Macey swallowed hard, her insides hot and fluttery at the thought of touching and kissing this powerful male body. She couldn't keep from running her hands up and over his chest, exploring the warm slabs beneath her palms and the firm shape of his broad shoulders.

Grady tugged her close, and she stepped between his thighs as he set to unbuttoning the rest of her blouse. She looked down, watching his nimble fingers, golden brown against the soft pink silk, pulling it away to reveal her white undergarment. The blouse wafted to the floor, but before he attended to the corset, he readjusted and shifted so she was sitting on him, straddling his thighs with her skirt and knickers hiked up nearly to her hips.

"Much better." His voice was a dusky murmur as he slid his hands up her bare arms and along her shoulders. He paused when his fingers reached the marks at the junction of her throat and looked at her. "Does it hurt?"

She shook her head and leaned into him, her confined breasts brushing his t-shirt. He seemed to understand and rained gentle kisses along the sensitive skin of her unmarked shoulder, his tongue making hot, sensual strokes over the ridge of her neck and throat. Macey shivered, delicious, liquid heat rolling through her body. He nibbled more, gently sucking and licking the delicate spot beneath her earlobe. A dart of pleasure stabbed her in the belly, and down to the hot center between her legs. She shifted insistently in his lap.

Grady made a soft sound, then eased away and began to tug on the side lacings of her corset. It loosened easily, and he had the complicated garment undone and was soon pulling it away with surprising efficiency.

"I can never be understanding," he murmured, tugging the bust-to-hip side-lacer up over her head, "why you women are about binding yourselves flat nowadays." The Simington's landed with a splat on the floor. "Especially when you look like this." His voice was rough and unsteady, and he looked down at her bare torso…then stilled.

It wasn't until that moment Macey realized what she'd done. Grady's darker hand moved, not to touch her tight, apple-sized breasts, nor her upthrust nipples…but over her pearl-white skin, along the faint red line down the center of her sternum…to the tiny silver cross dangling from her navel.

He looked up at her.

She met his gaze, heart thudding harshly, the moment of arousal slipping away.

With gentle fingers, he touched the *vis bulla*, lifting and sifting it between two of them so it glinted in the sunshine. The light brush of his hand against her belly was sensual and sure, in such contrast to Iscariot's horrific fondling last night. Little bursts of warmth spread over her skin where he brushed against it.

"I've never seen anything so incredibly erotic in my life." Grady let the cross fall back into her navel, then turned his eyes to hers again. "And yet it's for much more than sex appeal. Isn't it?"

Macey swallowed and nodded. She couldn't quite read the emotion in his eyes, but there was no sense in equivocating. And maybe…maybe it would be all right after all. At least, for today.

"Is it truly a strength amulet? It makes you stronger, faster— and that's why your bites are nearly healed." There was wonder, curiosity, and awe in his tones. To her surprise, his lips moved into a half-grin. "How strong?"

She shifted on his lap, suddenly relieved. Her secret had been revealed; he seemed to be accepting it in stride. She gave her bobbed hair a little toss. "I could throw you across the room if I wanted. Flip you onto your back."

"Is that so? A delicate woman like you?" His attention was on her torso again as his fingers slid up her ribcage, raising little prickles of skin along the way.

"Want to try me?" A delicious shiver caught her by surprise as he caressed her.

His palms settled beneath her breasts, thumbs curving beneath each one. "Not at the moment. I've other things on my mind, Macey, lass. You're damned beautiful, and even your secrets don't matter too much to me right about now." He covered her nipples with his hands, brushing gently against their taut, sensitive tips as he circled his palms lightly over them, round and round and round. Pinpricks of pleasure tingled through her like tiny licks of electric shock, and Macey arched closer, wanting more than just a delicate tease.

He obliged, grasping her hips to pull her sharply up against him. Her legs were bent, calves on the bed, and he ducked to kiss one of her breasts. Macey gasped at the unexpected sensation of his hot mouth over the tight bud of her nipple, the slick stroke of his tongue as he sucked and licked and circled around her until she was shifting and moaning on his lap.

She pressed into him, the hard length of his erection evident behind the fastening of his trousers, separated from her own hot, throbbing quim by a few layers of fabric. Grady groaned against her throat, then collapsed back onto the bed, dragging her with him.

She sprawled on top of his hard, warm body. Before she could pull away, he dragged her mouth back for another kiss while loosening her skirt from behind. Then his hands covered her bare back, sliding up the curve of her spine, burying in the short curls at her neck.

Macey pulled away, hoisting herself on her elbows to look down at him. His eyes were heavy-lidded and hot with desire. "Take off your shirt," she told him.

"With pleasure." He shifted and suddenly she was on her back on the bed, Grady next to her. He eased back and stripped off his undershirt.

Macey sucked in her breath at the sight of his bare torso—golden, muscled, and sprinkled with dark hair that narrowed into a trail over his ridged belly.

But before she could touch him, slide her hands over the warm, firm skin, he eased away and off the bed. His expression could only be described as resolute. "I'll be right back."

Macey hauled herself up onto her elbows and stared after him as he left the bedroom. She heard him go quickly down the hall, then what sounded like a cabinet opening and closing. When he returned, he held a small, flat packet and wore a sheepish smile.

That smile, however, gave way into a more sober, intense expression as he looked down at her bare breasts and adorned belly. "You are beautiful."

He slid back onto the bed next to her and bent to kiss her breasts, one after the other, teasing and fondling them as she shivered and sighed. The burn of pleasure grew, filling and swelling the tiny nub between her legs.

Grady shifted, trailing kisses along the slender red scar over the sensitive, quivering skin of her belly, to her navel. Slowing, almost reverent, he paused there to gently nuzzle and tease the delicate amulet. The soft click of it against his teeth and the warmth of his lips made her arch up in demand. She wanted more…and she wanted no more of this teasing.

As if he received the message, he moved on, sliding her skirt and knickers down over her hips, thighs, knees…and then he climbed off the bed to strip her last bits of clothing away. Macey realized she was fully nude, sprawled on the dark bedcovers, and a wave of shyness had her biting her lip, turning away to avoid his eyes. She'd thrown herself at him, insisted on this… But there was that little niggle of doubt worming its way into her mind.

"Lovely. You're lovelier than I was even imagining." The lilting rhythm in his voice was heavy and thick, like a sensual caress. Before she could respond, he gently parted her legs and began to kiss a hot, moist trail up the inside of her thigh.

Macey jolted at the unexpected sensation on such an intimate area of skin, but he didn't stop there. Nuzzling and licking, he moved north to the wet, throbbing center between her legs. And when he settled there, covering her with his dangerous mouth, she couldn't control a gasp at the sharp, intense sensation of his lips and tongue tasting her…stroking and licking and teasing.

She was panting now, as the pleasure built, tightening and rising inside her like a coil ready to spring free. She could hardly breathe, was *afraid* to breathe, for fear she'd miss this…whatever it was…this hot, liquid sensation building inside her beneath the rhythm of his mouth.

Then suddenly, she got there—she reached the peak and tipped over into a maelstrom of pleasure. Shuddering and trembling, she closed her eyes as the orgasm undulated through her, shocking her from head to toe and bursting over her in a delicious wave.

Grady finished with a gentle kiss on the top of her mound. When she opened her eyes, she found him looking at her with a hot blue gaze. "Okay?" His mouth was tight and yet quirked up at the corner as if he was attempting to smile but found it much too difficult.

"I'll…say." The syllables came out in little more than a breath, but he must have heard, for that tense smile became a little more relaxed. "But…" She gestured to him, to the room, unsure what to think.

He stood and looked down at her, his blue eyes very dark. Nearly black. "Are you truly certain, Macey?"

Still quivering and throbbing and twitching, she nodded. "Most definitely. Please."

"You needn't be asking twice, then." He unfastened his trousers, skimming the last of his clothing down and off. And before she could fully admire the beauty of his nakedness, he joined her back on the bed, gathering her up for a long, deep kiss. He tasted of her—of musk and heat, and she sighed against him, pressing into his bare chest, easing her leg along his muscular thigh. Their bodies slid against the other, warm skin to warm skin, rough hair and sleek muscle pressing into soft curves and silky skin.

He kissed her neck, eased his fingers down between her legs and slid them around, stroking her back into arousal. She was vaguely aware of the sound of paper tearing and then the gentle jerking motion of his arm, and opened her eyes to see him rolling on a condom. She'd never seen one before, but now was not the time to care.

When he finished, he looked up to find her watching him. His mouth was tight and controlled and when she smiled, pulling at his shoulder to bring him closer, his tension eased. Then, carefully, he eased between her legs, and after a little more attention down there with his nimble fingers—riling her up into a panting, needy mess—he settled into place and pushed home.

Macey's eyes flew open and he paused, fairly vibrating with tension, but he felt so good inside her, she couldn't wait for whatever he needed. The fleeting stab of pain was over so quickly she hardly accounted for it, and so she shifted her hips experimentally. Grady blew out his breath in a gust and began to move in long, slow strokes. The muscles of his arms bulged and shifted as he propped himself over her.

"Faster," she breathed, jerking her hips impatiently. She was ready; he'd made her ready and now she knew what she wanted.

She didn't have to urge twice. He complied, thrusting harder and faster, rocking the bed and making the iron bars creak. She hardly noticed, for the pleasure was so intense and her world was filled with heat and salty skin and that delicious coiling feeling that rose and rose until she shattered again with a cry.

He groaned, an erotic sound of relief and accomplishment that sent another flutter of heat brushing her insides. He moved sharply, one last time, then stilled. She felt him pulsing against her and inside of her, and a deep, sensual shiver shuttled through her. When she opened her eyes and looked up, Macey caught her breath at the image of this man: broad-shouldered, damp skin, flexed pectorals, lips parted in passion, hair mussed, eyes closed.

Something inside her shifted.

He opened his eyes and looked down at her. Before she could do or say anything, he swooped to press a sweet, gentle kiss at the corner of her mouth.

"And now you've done it," he murmured into her ear as he eased onto the bed, still touching her.

"What do you mean?"

"Now I'm not ever going to be able to stop thinking about you, Macey Denton. Not ever."

Fourteen

Wherein Three Becomes a Crowd

MACEY WAS AWAKE LONG BEFORE she opened her eyes or even stirred next to Grady.

Paralyzed by her thoughts, by the knowledge that her life had irrevocably changed—that the moment she rose from this oasis of comfort and pleasure, reality would intrude sharply—she lay there for a long time. Basking as long as she dared.

Grady was warm and solid beside her. She felt the soft tickle of his thick, shiny hair against her temple, the easy thump of his heart beneath her palm. The smooth warmth of the top of his foot and ankle was wedged beneath her heel, where their legs had settled, entwined.

Each body adhered gently to the other, warm and moist due to the heat generated from their activity and the result of skin-to-skin slumber. She listened to him breathe, measured her own indrawn breaths against his, considering how they mingled and then separated.

Mingled…and then separated. Just as Macey must separate from Grady, both physically and emotionally. The thought of him ending up like Chelle or Mrs. G, the realization that, despite crosses of silver etched into threshold floors and windowsills, he'd never be safe, gave her the resolve she'd need.

He was smart. Oh, Grady was too smart. Too bold, too determined. He knew too much and was determined to know more. He was a good man, a strong one. He was everything she'd want in a lover, a partner.

And like his aunt had done, he could be so easily caught in a crossfire— of vampire and Venator. He wasn't equipped to face the undead. He wasn't part of that world, and she couldn't expose him to that danger any more than she'd already done.

It's a damned lonely life, being a Venator.

The phone rang in the living room below, breaking the silence with a shrill chime. Macey's eyes flew open. The interlude was over.

Grady sighed and broke away from her, rolling off the bed onto his feet. "Linwood, probably," he said, shoving his legs into his pants. "If it's a call not a visit, it's likely good news."

He started to leave, then turned suddenly and came back to the bed. He bent and kissed her on the mouth, gentle and filled with promise, then backed away reluctantly as the telephone continued to ring. "Don't move."

Macey sat up as he left the room. Low beams of sunlight spilled across the bed as she climbed off and located her skirt. Still daylight; the vampires wouldn't be out and about yet. This gave her only a minor sense of relief. She looked around the room as she buttoned her blouse, knowing it would be the last time she'd see this place.

Moments later she walked down the stairs, ready to face her changed life.

When she reached the living room, Grady was just hanging up the phone. Dressed only in half-fastened trousers, he was all sleek and muscled and rumpled, with his unruly hair and five o'clock shadow. When he turned, his attention swept her from head to toe. The expression in his eyes made her heart give an extra, off-rhythm bump.

"Was that your uncle?" she asked, ignoring the fluttering in her belly and the sudden intense desire to head back upstairs.

"Flora was home sleeping when they got to her boarding house today. She's been working at a cabaret at night, according to her landlady, which is probably why you haven't heard from her."

Macey's tension eased a little. "What about Dottie?"

"She was more than happy to answer the questions from the beat cop Linwood sent over. And…you're dressed."

So her friends were both safe. For now. But how much longer? And how much longer for him? "Thank you for doing that, Grady." She kept the sofa positioned between them, because she knew if he got close enough to touch her, she wouldn't say what she needed to say. "I've got to go."

He stilled. "It's Sunday afternoon. Where do you have to go?" He edged to one end of the sofa.

"I've got things to take care of."

"I'll come with you." He slipped around the sofa faster than she realized, and all at once was there, taking her hand. His eyes were cool and determined. "Don't think I don't know what you're trying to do."

She pulled away. "Grady, I have to go. You don't know the whole story, you don't understand. You can't. You can't be part of this—or part of my life."

"What are you talking about? I can't be part of your life?"

"You read the book. You know about it—more than you should. More than is safe for you to know."

"Christ, Macey, that's not—"

But she had to barrel on, to get it all out before she lost her nerve. "I'm sorry. I shouldn't have stayed. It was selfish of me to do so—"

"I wanted you. To be with you. It was me more than it was you."

She shook her head. "It was selfish. And wrong. I led you on. And I'm sorry. So it's best if I just leave now."

"Macey." Now there was a hint of anger. "Don't be playing a fool. You're safe here. They can't get in. I made sure of it."

She had to blink away the sudden stinging in her eyes. "I know. But that's what you don't understand, Grady. I can't stay here. I can't be safe. I have to go out there and…stop them."

She thought he'd argue. She even, deep inside, hoped he'd drag her into his arms and kiss her senseless, convince her to stay.

And maybe she would…for a little while longer. But he merely looked at her, his expression unreadable. Except for those eyes: the steady, glittering blue of a stormy lake.

"I have to stop them before they hurt anyone else I care about. Like you."

His jaw moved and tension rolled off him into the space between them. "I suppose you mean that as a compliment."

"Grady—"

Someone pounded loudly on the door.

Grady flung her a dark look, then strode to the foyer. He'd hardly opened the door when a familiar voice demanded, "Where is she?"

Macey turned when she heard Chas. She couldn't see anything but his legs, for Grady blocked the entrance. A little shaky, she drew in a calming breath and walked over.

"I need to find Macey. Do you know—oh, *bloody* hell." Chas had seen her.

"It's probably best if you let him in." Macey looked from one to the other, then outside to make sure no one else was lurking. "We don't need to have this conversation on your front stoop."

Grady gave the newcomer a measured look, but stepped back to allow him entrance. Macey led the way into the living room as Chas hissed, "This is just bloody great. I've been looking all over the damned place for you, and here you are, hiding out in a fucking love nest. What the hell are you thinking?"

"Mrs. Gutchinson is dead. They killed her too. Tortured her." She kept her voice steady and hard, even as the horrific images threatened to swarm her thoughts. "I found her."

Chas didn't give an inch. "I'm sorry about that, and about your friend, but we've got a bigger bloody damned problem on our hands. Vioget is missing."

Her breath caught. "Sebastian's gone? Since when?"

"No one's seen him since this morning. He never came back from his visit to the church."

"They took him. Alvisi and Iscariot."

"Of course they did. He's either dead and they have the rings, or he will be shortly. Which is why the last thing I needed to be doing was wasting my goddamned time looking for you."

"Maybe you should have been looking for this Vioget person instead."

They both turned to Grady. Chas's expression held a glint of dangerous humor. "Indeed. But now that I've found Macey, there will be two of us doing the work."

"Three of us." Grady gave her a meaningful look.

"Goddammit, I knew you were trouble." Chas vibrated with impatience and anger.

"Grady, I told you—"

But before she could finish her sentence, Chas moved. His fist connected sharply with Grady's jaw at the perfect angle, and the man dropped like a stone.

Macey turned on him in fury. "That wasn't necessary."

"The hell it wasn't. Let's go." He spun her toward the door and, as he led the way he said over his shoulder, "Fix your damned blouse. The buttons are wrong."

"I can't keep coming after you and saving your arse," Chas said as they got out of a cab.

After leaving Grady's, Macey had gone with Chas to The Silver Chalice to make sure Sebastian hadn't returned. To their increasing concern, he hadn't. So she'd changed into clean, comfortable clothing, and she and her partner prepared themselves to venture into the den of vampires—a place known as The Blood Club.

Rather than call attention to herself by wearing men's clothing—which would have been very comfortable and provided excellent range of movement—Macey had chosen to wear a frock. But it was short and light of weight, and would allow her to be as active as she needed. No heeled Mary Janes for her tonight; she'd chosen comfortable flats for footwear, and without stockings that needed to be pulled up or kept in place with a garter.

"I don't expect you to keep coming after me, Chas." Macey looked around. She didn't recognize the street they were on.

He gave her a dark look. "Obviously." He gestured for her to turn the corner. "You can't see him again, you know."

Not that Grady would want to see her again, even if she could. She gritted her teeth. "My private life is my business."

He laughed. "Not when you're a Venator. Not when there are lives at stake. I told you—it's a hell of a lonely life. If you want... companionship, it has to be with someone who understands our world."

"That sounds suspiciously like an invitation, Chas."

"It's not—"

"And like someone sticking his nose somewhere it definitely doesn't belong."

He shook his head and made a sound of disgust. "Have it your way. You're as stubborn as your father was."

Macey faltered, but kept walking. "Stubborn. I wouldn't think that'd be a liability for a Venator."

"There's stubborn, and then there's blindly stubborn. Max Denton made the tragic mistake of thinking he could have it all—a wife, a family, and a life as a Venator. And you know what happened."

"My mother was killed. By the vampires." *And he sent me away.* For the first time, Macey felt a twinge of sympathy for her absent father, a glimmer of understanding. She'd seen firsthand what violence the undead could visit upon someone she cared for. How much worse would it have been for him?

"They were unusually vicious and brutal with her." Chas's voice was flat. "And Max...well, it might have been just as well he sent you away. For a number of reasons. And here we are."

Macey looked up at the neat sign. Rico's Tailor Shop. "So this is where the Tutela congregates."

"Among others. Those who are part of the society frequent this place, sure, but The Blood Club caters also to those who wish to dabble in the pleasures of the fanged. And it's a way for the undead to find their prey. Alvisi is the proprietor, and he runs it as slickly as Capone runs his saloons. He employs mortal and undead, men and women, in order to provide a wide range of entertainment." He stopped. "It's best if we aren't seen together. I'll go first; you circle the block then come in."

She nodded, for that was the plan they'd discussed. But when he went into Rico's, leaving her to continue on, she felt a spike of apprehension and fear. Walking into a den of vampires and vampire lovers was a daunting prospect.

But she was well prepared, with stakes and other tools hidden all over her person, and Chas would be there as well. Plus Temple had seemed confident her student was capable of protecting herself, and was actually eager to let Macey employ the skills she'd learned in the past weeks. Infiltrating The Blood Club was the best and easiest way to find out what had happened to Sebastian—for if he'd been abducted or killed, surely all of the undead and their Tutela would be talking about it.

Still. Macey had only staked one vampire. And her most recent experience—that horrifying interlude in the back of Iscariot's limousine—had left her shaken more than she wanted to admit. Not to mention the haunting sight of Mrs. Gutchinson's ruined body.

But when it was time for Macey to go inside Rico's and make her way into the dim club, she did so without hesitation. Even before she was inside, the icy chill at the back of her neck was nauseatingly strong, sending eerie prickles down her spine.

She curled her fingers around the small pocketbook that held nothing but a stake, a vial of holy water, and a few dollars for cab fare. The place was just as she'd pictured it: dim, smoky, and filled with tables of people. But there was the scent of blood in the air, and when she looked more carefully at some of the patrons in the booths, she saw kissing and sexual petting, as well as wrists and throats being fed upon. The facial expressions of the victims ranged from ecstatic to pained to bored. She didn't spot Chas yet.

"What a pleasant sight," said a voice next to her. "What brings such a lovely being in to The Blood Club tonight?"

Macey turned to see a young man with his hair slicked back, wearing a provocative smile. It took her a moment to confirm that he was a vampire—and that was fine with her. "It's my first time," she confessed, trying to appear wide-eyed and hesitant. "A friend of mine told me about it. She said the sensation is…"

Her voice trailed off as she noticed the man who could only be Count Alvisi. He sat at a small table that was surrounded by women, and he was deep in conversation with another man. His entourage of females were all dressed in blue with matching headdresses. Silver and white feathers erupted from the round, blue emblem on the front of each headband, and they were dusted with something glittery.

"Who's that?" she asked, suppressing a sickly shiver. Even from this distance, she could feel the strength of pure malevolence.

"That is the boss."

Macey widened her eyes. "Oh. I thought…" She leaned closer, pitching her voice into a low whisper. "I thought Al Capone was the boss here."

Her companion laughed in derision. "Capone? Not at all. In fact, Big Al has been angling to join us—for, you realize, he's nothing without his machine guns. Alvisi wields the true power in Chicago—power that will soon be greater than you can fathom." He took her hand and raised it to his lips, pressing them against it in a soft kiss. Soft, dry lips: one cold as ice, one warm, in an awful, strange sensation. When he looked up, his fangs were just barely visible and his eyes burned soft ruby, tugging at her with their thrall. "Perhaps you might someday be asked to join us. Alvisi prefers blondes, but he would likely make an exception for one as lovely as you. I'm certain I could convince him. And then you would be young and beautiful forever."

"Oh." Macey fluttered her lashes and tried to appear flattered. "Do you truly think so? He would make an exception for me? How would that happen?"

He tucked her hand around his arm. "Permit me to show you, my lovely."

Macey allowed him to lead her off, but when he attempted to sit her at a table, she remembered the warning Chas had given her. *Don't do anything in sight of anyone else, or we will be discovered.* "I…isn't there somewhere private we could go? I don't think I want my first time to be here." She gave him a shy look. "In front of people."

"Why of course." His eyes gleamed with pleasure, leaving her uncertain as to whether it had always been his plan to get her alone, or whether he was merely delighted with an unexpected turn of events.

Conscious of the extra stake strapped to a thigh beneath her skirt, and of the long chain holding a silver cross beneath her frock, Macey went willingly with her escort. When they neared Alvisi, she angled her face down in order to keep from being recognized. Her slick vampire guide led her through an exit at the far end of the club, and beyond it was a small hallway studded with more doors.

A brothel for the undead, where the customers—or, more accurately, victims—might or might not be left alive.

He opened a door and bowed her gallantly through, then closed and locked it behind him with an ominous click. When he turned, his fangs were at full extension, and his eyes burned unholy red. "Now then." He advanced on her, no longer smooth and easy but openly intent. "Did you say this was your first time?"

"Yes." Macey already had her stake in hand, clutching it behind her back as he shoved her toward the large bed in the center of the compact room. She tumbled onto it, keeping her gaze averted from his powerful, enthralling one as he surged onto the mattress next to her.

He held her by the throat, his body wedged onto one side of hers. "You surprise me, my lovely. I thought I'd captured myself a frightened flower. But I see no fear in your eyes. This could be even more enjoyable than I expected."

Macey's stake was hidden beneath her hip, cloaked by the bedclothes mussed from her fall. He was intent on her bare throat and neck and didn't notice when she inched it free. "I don't think it's going to be very enjoyable for you at all," she said, and whipped her hand around to jam the stake into the center of his back. She stopped short of shoving it home, but definitely pierced through cloth and flesh. Precisely above the location of his heart.

He stilled, his eyes wide. His fangs retracted, then surged forth again. "Who are you?"

"Never mind who I am. I need information, and if you give it to me, I *might* not turn you into a cloud of dust. If you don't, I definitely will." She pushed harder.

"Yes, yes, all right. Don't do that. What do you want to know?"

"First, get off me. And don't try anything," she warned, pulling the long silver chain from beneath her dress. The sight of the large cross had him rearing away, his movements slow and awkward. "Very good. Now, back up slowly." She followed his movements, sitting as he eased away, all the while aiming the cross at him.

While the holy object wouldn't kill or maim him, its presence would slow and weaken the vampire. And although its effect would wear off eventually, it gave her the opportunity to pin him against the wall with her stake.

"Where's Sebastian Vioget?"

His eyes popped wide. "Vioget? I don't know."

She drilled the stake deeper, and blood began to seep from beneath his shirt. "Remember when I said this was my first time? I lied."

"Who are you?" He shrank back against the wall. His fangs had all but disappeared and his eyes were a flat, frightened brown. "Are you the new Venator? The woman?"

"I'm asking the questions. And I won't repeat this one. Where's Vioget?"

"I don't know." He winced and his voice squeaked higher. "By the fates, I *don't know.*"

She eased up a little; didn't want to accidentally explode him too soon. "Sebastian's missing. Either dead or abducted. If Alvisi had him, where would he put him?"

"He's not dead—or if he's dead, Alvisi doesn't know. We'd all know if Sebastian Vioget had been fried. Come to think of it, I'm certain we'd know if Alvisi had captured him too. Not the sort of thing he'd keep to himself. The boss likes to brag."

"Has he been after Sebastian? Trying to find him?"

"Who hasn't? Everyone wants the rings." He shook his head. "But believe me, if Vioget was under Alvisi's control, we'd know it."

"Great. Thanks." Macey shoved the stake home.

His eyes widened, his mouth gaped in protest...then he poofed.

She stepped away, a little shaky but exhilarated now that it was over. Her second vampire, slain. Easy as pie—well, as long as she was in control and had a weapon in hand.

Dusting off the ash from her clothing, Macey considered her next move. She didn't know where Chas was, but they had a time and place to meet up in order to exchange information and decide on their next steps. She had time to try and find more information—or at least, remove a few more vampires from Alvisi's clan.

She and Chas had discussed the fact that they'd be walking into a club filled with the undead they were supposed to kill, but that it was foolhardy and impossible to try and slay them all. They would be outnumbered, and their identities would be discovered. So the plan was to be low-key and get as much information as possible without being discovered.

Macey decided not to return to the club but to do some snooping around here, in the back rooms of Alvisi's joint. Just as she reached for the knob, the door flew open.

Three vampires blocked the way: red-eyed, long-fanged, and clearly very angry.

Fifteen

Our Heroine Unleashed

M ACEY DIDN'T EVEN NEED to think about it. She simply reacted, slamming her stake into the heart of the undead closest to her.

Her fighting arm jackknifed back, and she twisted away and down as his ash exploded. Temple's instructive voice singing in her head, Macey sprung back up, shoving the second vampire into the third one, and lashed out with her stake once more.

This time she missed, stabbing a shoulder, and her would-be victim caught himself and lunged toward her. On his impact, Macey flew through the air, crashing into the bed. Her breath knocked out of her, she rolled to the side and off the mattress, stumbling to her feet as she gasped for air.

The other vampire caught her by the arm and yanked her toward him. Macey lost her balance and fell against him, then hooked her foot around the back of his ankle. As he grabbed her by the throat with one hand and held her arm with the other, she used her stable foot to pivot her insubstantial weight into him. He staggered, but the hand around her throat was tightening and he remained upright as they twisted around in a macabre dance.

Black spots danced before her eyes, and Macey found herself weakening. She couldn't breathe. Another hand grabbed at her stake arm—the second vampire—and she felt the sharp, unexpected pain of brutal fangs in her wrist. Her grip loosened and the stake fell from her fingers. She couldn't breathe. Her knees trembled.

She was losing.

No.

She wouldn't.

Gathering all her strength, dragging in the little air she could, Macey jammed up with a knee, then, when the grip at her throat lessened, she rammed her forehead up into the nose of the undead. He howled and released her. She swooped down with her free hand, yanked the stake from beneath her skirt, and spun like a dancer in the arm of her other attacker.

Slam.

Into the heart of the undead who was feasting on her wrist. Gasping, still weak with polka-dotted vision, she pivoted just as the third one recovered from her attack. He lunged, but she was ready and the point of her stake found its home—right in his gut. Blood spurted.

Damn. Missed again.

He grunted with rage and pain, but he was still moving a little slow. She ducked when he swiped for her, diving for his knees. Macey hooked her arm around him and pulled him off balance as he grabbed a handful of her hair. They tumbled to the floor, pain roaring at her scalp as he held on. But as he rose up over her, using his grasp on her curls to slam her head to the ground, Macey twisted to the side, jamming her knee into the side of his gut. Her arm followed and she slammed the wooden pike into the back of his torso…

And he froze.

Thank God.

She collapsed on the floor, tears streaming from her eyes, completely out of breath, room spinning. Then he exploded.

It was another moment before she dragged herself to her feet. Her head pounded. Knees and hands trembled. But she was filled with grim satisfaction. *I did it.*

The air was thick with ash-scent, and it clung to her eyelashes and arms. Some still filtered through the air like dust mites. Oh, *damn*.

She vaulted toward the door, flinging the bolt. In the midst of the fight, she hadn't had the chance to wonder what had happened—why the vampires had suddenly shown up—but now she realized. The scent of ash in the air had drawn them to investigate, just as the sound of gunshots would warn mortals of a threat.

I have to find Chas.

She listened, waiting. The only sounds were distant—laughing, cries of pleasure, conversation. The chill at the back of her neck was present, but not insistent or foreboding. She opened the room's small, high window, hoping some of the heavy smell of vampire dust would disseminate before any others noticed it.

After a moment, she unlocked and peered around the door. No undead in sight. Before leaving the room, she replaced one stake in her garter, the other in her pocketbook, and tucked the silver cross back down into her dress.

Now to locate Chas. And maybe do a little snooping. It was safer, now that she wasn't in the room with the remains of a vampire, waiting to be found.

And she'd slain *three* of them. All at once. All on her own.

Macey couldn't help the thrill of excitement and relief at her success. *I can do this.*

Listening for the sounds of anyone approaching, Macey went down the hallway, stopping at each door. Silence, silence, silence. But behind one there was the unmistakable sound of pleasure and pain. She hesitated at the door. It would be easy to break in and kill the vampire—particularly if he or she was in the throes of feeding, or other erotic play—but Macey wasn't certain if it was the best thing to do: making more noise, sending more ash in the air.

And then there would be the mortal left behind, who might shout or call warning, or worse, need an explanation if he or she had been a willing participant. Because, yes, there were those

Tutela members Chas had told her about. They desired to be fed upon. They craved it, sought it out.

Still…what if the mortal was in danger? Unwilling?

Macey had no way of knowing, but her job, her calling was, above all, to protect and save.

She made the decision and, hand inside her pocketbook, ready to yank out her weapon, she carefully tested the doorknob. It turned soundlessly. Carefully, she pushed it open a crack. The deep sounds of pleasure sent a little shivery twinge in her belly, but then she recognized slurping and suction, and the flutter turned into an uncomfortable twist.

Neither occupant sounded in distress, but Macey peered through the crack anyway. The sight that met her eyes was disturbing and, shockingly, erotic.

A female vampire bent over the bare, muscular shoulder of a man. Her hands curled into his skin, covering his bare torso from behind, and the tendons and veins in his neck were distended as his head tipped to the side. Even through the skinny crack, she could see his chest rising and falling rapidly, the muscles in his arms bunching. His hands were fisted on the bed, making no move to fight off the vampire.

Macey swallowed hard and was just about to close the door when the man shifted and she saw his face, taut with arousal and pain. *Chas.*

Without thinking—without *allowing* herself to think—Macey shoved open the door and launched herself into the room. Both faces whipped up at her entrance, but it was too late—she had her stake in hand and was on the female in an instant.

One sharp thrust, and the undead was gone.

Macey spun away to catch her breath, not certain she'd seen what she thought she'd seen…not ready to face him and find out. Her heart pounded and her insides were in turmoil. But the image of his expression was burned into her mind. Stark, beautiful, and filled with pain.

She heard him behind her—rising, pulling on his shirt. When she finally turned, it was to find him facing partly away. His mouth tight, his movements sharp and quick.

"I—"

"Any news about Vioget?" He had a stake in his hand, and his eyes were cold and dark.

"No. I don't think Alvisi has him. But I killed four vampires—now a fifth—and I think the others might know something is happening."

He nodded curtly. "The smell of ash—it can spread like smoke. That's why it's not the best idea to stake them here."

Was he *criticizing* her for killing that vampire? Macey shook her head but held her tongue. She knew what she'd seen. She just wasn't sure what to make of it.

"Let's go."

"Where to?"

"Out of here. You're obviously leaving a trail behind you, and we'll soon be discovered if we don't leave." He started toward the door.

She had no choice but to follow him. "Back to the club?"

"For now."

But two steps later, the sound of voices approached, and the back of Macey's neck grew icy cold. She and Chas looked at each other at the same time, and without speaking, ducked into one of the rooms.

"Alvisi," he breathed into her ear as they peered out the crack of the door.

Sure enough, the count and a trio of his female attendants in their blue frocks and feathery headdresses were heading down the hall toward them. Macey sniffed, wondering if the scent of ash was still heavy enough in the air for the undead to notice. Chas was very still, standing behind her to look out above her head. She could smell the iron scent of his blood, still clinging to his throat and shirt.

Alvisi and his group strolled closer, the women giggling and the count bragging vociferously about something. A large male undead followed behind, obviously a bodyguard of sorts. None of them paused, and Macey felt some of her tension ease…to be replaced by a stab of disappointment.

What a coup that would be…to kill Count Alvisi. One of the most powerful vampires in Chicago—in the world, at least according to Sebastian. It would be so easy. He was right there, walking right past. Hardly guarded at all. She'd handled three on her own, and Chas was here now.

Macey's hand or body must have tensed, preparing to throw the door open and bolt out after the vampire count, for Chas clamped a firm hand onto her shoulder. A clear warning.

She shook off his grip and eased the door open a smidge wider. By now, the group had passed by and disappeared around a corner of the hall.

"Don't make a scene," Chas muttered, his words hot and barely audible against her ear. "We're outnumbered."

She pulled away and glared up at him. "We can get Alvisi. Now's our chance."

"Possibly. But—"

They both stilled and looked back out the crack. Two voices, two figures were approaching. One male, one female. At least one of them undead, based on the chill over the back of her neck. Macey peered out through the awkward opening and her belly dropped. She went cold.

Chas must have felt it, for he gripped her arm—but she was already throwing the door open. "Flora," Macey cried, stumbling out into the corridor. "*Flora?*" It couldn't be.

It was. Her redheaded friend, dressed in a sparkling blue frock with a feathery blue headband—ornamented in front with a blue circle, just as the landlady had described—and long white gloves. She was with a pale-skinned man dressed in a suit with a matching blue tie and handkerchief.

There were fresh bite marks on her neck.

"Macey!" Flora came to a dead stop.

She didn't think. Macey lunged at Flora's companion, aiming for the center of his chest, but before she shoved it home, someone grabbed her arm and whipped her through the air.

Crash. She slammed face-first against the wall and crumpled to the ground. Breathless, dragging herself to her feet, Macey whirled just in time to see Chas slam his stake into the man's torso.

Ash exploded and, with smooth, lethal movements, the grim-faced Chas spun toward Flora.

"No!" Macey screamed, and launched herself off the wall. She hurtled into her friend just as Chas thrust the stake down.

Macey cried out as the sharp point drove deep into her shoulder. Pain exploded through her torso. Chas shouted a curse and yanked the weapon back, but she hardly noticed through the chaos that ensued. Running footsteps, shouts, and others came on the scene.

Clutching at the wound, gushing with blood, Macey stumbled against Flora. "What…happened?" she managed to say. "When?" From behind her, Macey heard Chas struggling with a new assailant.

Her friend stepped back, looking at her with cool, emotionless eyes. "I wanted something more. Something I was never going to get working in a pool or in a damned garment shop."

Someone jostled Macey and she bumped against the wall. Her vision was flashing with black and white lights, and her hand was covered with warm, slick blood. "Flora…" Her knees buckled. *Am I going to die?*

"I'm happier now. I have a place. My sire adores me, and I'm very valuable to him. The friend of the new Gardella. I had no idea you were so…important, Macey."

A great force sent Macey sprawling onto the ground. Someone shouted, something slammed into the back of her head, and everything went dark.

Sixteen
Of Guilt and Devastation

T HE PAIN WAS WHAT DRAGGED HER back to consciousness. The pain radiating through her shoulder like a deep, continuous thud. That, and the block of ice covering the back of her neck.

Macey remembered everything just before she dragged her eyes open. But when she did so, she was surprised to find she was alone. The room was dark, lit only by a single, naked bulb. Small, close, and windowless. Little more than a closet.

She was on a cold, concrete floor, lying on her side in a pool of her own sticky blood. Gingerly, she used her right hand to push into a sitting position; the left side of her body was in too much pain. As she sat up, she felt at the wound below her left collarbone. Sticky, globular bits of blood clung to her hand and frock.

"Macey."

The gritty voice came from behind her, and she recognized it as Chas. Staggering to her feet, she used the wall as a support and turned to find him crumpled in the corner. A large bookshelf pinned him in place.

Though every movement was agony and her knees trembled, Macey still had her strength. She pulled the bookshelf off him, and the exertion caused blood to start flowing from her injury again. Chas groaned with relief as the heavy wooden piece was maneuvered away. He was bound with his arms behind his back and legs together. With the weight of the bookshelf on him, he obviously hadn't been able to move near Macey or even find a way to loosen his bonds.

But now the weight was gone, and he was already struggling with the ties around his wrists. "How are you?" he grunted. "Need a doctor, probably. Ugh." This last was the sound of triumph as the ropes loosened. He whipped his arms free.

Macey had already fumbled open the knots around his ankles and now sat, leaning against the wall. Her vision was mottled with black dots and her head felt as if it were spinning. She pressed a hard palm to her wound, trying to stop the renewed bleeding. "What happened? Where are we?" Chas moved into the small circle of light, and she saw blood on him. Everywhere. Throat, arms, the front of his torso. Someone—or several someones—had feasted. Her insides shriveled. "You're lucky to be alive."

His smile was humorless. "Both of us are. Left for dead. But they don't know how strong we are, Macey. That's one of their weaknesses." He edged closer. "Let me look at that."

She reluctantly moved her hand, and he pulled away the torn edges of her silky dress. He hissed something dark and short, then looked up at her. "You're lucky to be alive. Two more inches…"

Macey pulled away. "You had no business going after her like that." A wave of despair and anger flooded her, washing away the dull, throbbing pain. God, no. Not Flora too. *Not* Flora.

"You had no business interfering like that. What were you thinking? You could have been killed."

"Flora is my *friend*. My best friend." Her words were choked and tears welled in her eyes.

"Not anymore." His voice was flat. "Goddammit, Macey, you better understand that right now. She's not your friend anymore."

"You don't know that. It's *Flora*. She wouldn't…do something like that."

He thrust a bloodied arm in front of her. "This is her work."

Macey turned away. "*No*." She shook her head. Tears spilled freely, and her belly was an awful, churning mess. Not Flora. Never. Rage and disbelief warred inside her, and she wanted to roar with pain, to lash out at someone. Destroy them.

Who'd done this? Who was to blame? *Who?*

But she knew… in the pit of her conscience, she knew.

Chelle. Mrs. G. And now Flora. Macey had no one to blame but herself. And…

"*Alvisi.*"

Chas looked up at her voice, his expression taut. He'd poured something on his wounds—holy water, from the small vial in his hand. She heard the hiss of pain as he dumped another small dose on his chest.

Macey dragged herself to her feet. Her head wasn't as frothy, and the bleeding seemed to have stopped. Her jaw was tight as she ground out the words. "I'm going to kill him. Do you know where he is?"

For a minute, she thought Chas would argue. Or try and talk her out of it. But he replied, "I have a suspicion. But don't forget Vioget. We have to find him."

"*No.* Alvisi first."

"Macey. You can't put your personal retributions ahead of the good for all. If the undead get those rings, we—"

"Alvisi," she said from between clenched teeth. Tears burned her eyes.

And what about Flora? What will you do when you see her again? Her insides roiled alarmingly. Drive a stake into the heart of her best friend?

Never.

You must.

She stilled. The sounds and sensation over her neck told Macey undead were approaching. They exchanged glances, then wordlessly got into position on each side of the door. Macey had the stake from beneath her skirt, and Chas pulled one from some hidden location on his person.

When the door opened, they moved in tandem. *Slam. Thrust. Shove.* She got the first undead, Chas the second—and he would have gotten the third on his backhand swing if she hadn't yanked the startled vampire out of the way.

Despite the pain in her shoulder, and the fact that she barely reached the lanky vampire's chin, Macey whirled him against the wall. "Where's Alvisi?" Her stake hovered over his heart. Chas made a sound that resembled a surprised laugh, but she didn't spare him a look. Anger and resolve boiled inside her. There was no room for levity.

"Uh…he's in his private…quarters." The vampire looked as if he might have been barely twenty when he was turned—and a skinny, gawky young man. "Don't…push that." His goggling eyes focused on the wooden pike settled on his chest.

"I won't. If you take me there." Macey pulled out the silver cross from behind her gown for added insurance.

"I will."

"What were you doing here?" Chas interrupted. "Coming to get us?"

"We were…she told us we could feed." The vampire's eyes darted about. "We haven't fed in three days. She said you'd be easy."

Macey didn't want to ask who "she" was. She didn't want to know if it was her dear, clumsy, funny Flora. Surely it couldn't be. Surely Flora wouldn't say something so crass. Macey avoided looking at the telltale wounds on Chas's arms. Her stomach was still upset, still churning, and a sensation of dread cloaked her as she and Chas ushered the vampire out from what was, indeed, little more than a storage closet.

"No funny business," Chas warned. "No detours, and keep away from populated areas. Or instead of staking you, we'll throw you out in the goddamned sun to fry. Slowly."

Their guide seemed to take Chas at his word, for he led them quickly and efficiently through back hallways. They encountered no one. Macey was glad, for she was still weak, and her injury bothered her. It would slow her on the left side, her fighting arm. Chas seemed to be himself, however, despite the great loss of blood. Or perhaps he was just better at hiding his deficiency.

The ever-present frigidity at the back of Macey's neck was nearly unbearable when they approached a set of double doors. "No guards?" She poked the stake into the vampire's back.

"No. Not here. He doesn't need them. This is his private quarters."

The sound of raucous laughter from beyond the door indicated three or four, maybe five people. Mostly female from the sound of it.

Macey whipped her captive around to face her. "What's your name?"

"Ricky."

"All right, Ricky. Here's what's going to happen. You are going to bring me in there as if I'm still your captive. My hands will be behind me, and you'll make it look as if I'm still tied. You stay out here," she added, looking at Chas. "You can join us at the appropriate moment."

Her companion nodded, pursing his lips. "Go on."

Turning back to Ricky, she tucked the silver cross back down inside her dress. "If you get me close enough to take a strike at Alvisi, I'll let you escape unscathed. And so will he." She gestured to Chas, who rolled his eyes but nodded agreement. "*If* you leave and don't come back. If I see you again anywhere in the vicinity of The Blood Club or Alvisi, you're dust. Understood?" She ground the stake deeper, poking through his shirt.

Ricky nodded, his Adam's apple bobbing and his eyes wide. Macey might have had a flicker of sympathy for him if she were in a better mood—and if he hadn't chosen to become an immortal, blood-sucking fiend.

"Let's go."

Chas moved out of sight of the door. Ricky opened it, then shoved Macey through. The gawky undead did a good job playing his role, holding onto her arm, directing her toward the vampire count. She kept her hands behind her back, with a stake hidden up her sleeve and pressed against her spine. She knew she looked beaten and bedraggled, bloody and exhausted as she was.

Attempting to appear cowed and weak, Macey took stock of the room. The scents of lavender, blood, and oil paint mingled. Apparently, Count Alvisi fancied himself an artist, for he stood in front of an easel in one corner of the chamber lit by electric bulbs—presumably to give him the best artificial lighting for his work. He brandished a palette and brush, and a nearby table held pots of paint. Two female vampires were arranged on a divan, draped in diaphanous white clothing. The filmy, toga-like attire did nothing to hide sharp pink nipples, the dark shadows at the juncture of their thighs, and a myriad of bite marks in intimate places.

In two armchairs, with a small table between them, Flora and a fourth female vampire sat. They had goblets filled with something red. Macey suppressed a shudder and looked away, but not before she caught Flora's eye.

Macey quickly averted her gaze, unable to bear what might be in her friend's expression. Focusing on creating a devastated facade, she allowed herself to be manhandled toward Alvisi.

"She wanted to see you," improvised Ricky.

Count Alvisi looked up. "The Venator." He sounded pleased. "A pleasant surprise."

Macey was close enough to see the mole on his cheek, and that he had begun to turn gray at the temples before he was turned. Close enough.

With a glance at Ricky, she threw him off and launched herself at the count. His palette and brush went flying, and the other vampires shrieked as she grabbed Alvisi by the collar and poised her stake over his heart even as her wound twinged in warning. The sound of a door slamming open behind her told Macey Chas had appeared, right on cue.

"How's this for a pleasant surprise?"

The count's eyes were wide with shock and fear. Macey pressed her advantage, aware that Chas had already dispatched one of the undead. She didn't turn to see whether it was Flora.

"I hear you're one of the most powerful undead in the world," she taunted. "You could have fooled me." He shrank inside his shirt, tried to brighten his eyes with a glowing thrall, and failed when she flexed her fingers, tightening the stake against him. "Where's Sebastian Vioget?"

"Vioget? I don't know."

"I don't believe you." Amid the sound of feminine grunts and flesh pounding flesh, Chas staked another vampire behind her. But Macey heard shouts and running footsteps in the distance. Damn.

"I don't know where he is. Haven't seen him."

"Have you heard anything about him? Iscariot? Does he have him?"

"Iscariot." At this Alvisi showed emotions other than fear: disgust and hatred. "I wouldn't know. We don't mingle."

Macey's control, which had been teetering for days, slipped. "Why did you take my *friend*? Why did you do that to her?" Her voice was too high.

"Who? What? I don't know what you me—"

Disgusted with him as much as herself, she piked him with the stake. "Goodbye, Count Alvisi."

Brushing off his ash, she turned to find Chas holding his own with Flora and the other female.

"Macey!" Flora cried.

Holding her stake at the ready, Macey advanced, slipping behind Chas. She grabbed her friend by the arm and yanked her from the melee. "How? How did this happen?" Though her friend was taller than she and an undead, they were evenly matched in strength now that Macey wore the *vis bulla*.

"You killed him," Flora said, panting as she looked down at her. "Alvisi. You killed him. Just like that."

Macey hefted the stake in her hand. The running footsteps were nearly at the room. She knew what she had to do. Her mouth was dry. "He sired you. How…just tell me. Did you *know* what you were doing? *Why?* How could you do this?"

Flora tilted her head and smiled, and for a moment, Macey saw her old friend. Funny, silly, awkward, happy Flora. Pain lanced through her, from her heart down to her gut. *How? Why?*

"The night at The Gyro. Antony found me—he ran outside with me, or at least, he was waiting outside. He saved me. He was so handsome and attentive. I never had a fella treat me like that. At first, I didn't know he was one of them. Then he introduced me to the pleasures of their kind—and then I found out who you were. *What* you were." Her eyes flashed red and the sweet Flora was gone. "And I realized Antony only wanted me because of you."

"Antony? Do you mean Alvisi?" Macey could hardly breathe. She had to do this. Reinforcements were coming.

"Yes. And now you've freed me from him. I do owe you for that, at least." Flora smiled, and the sweet girl was back, sending another dull stab into her gut.

But Macey gripped the stake. "I'm sorry, Flora. I don't want to do this, but—"

Vampires burst into the room behind her, and Macey swung her arm up, slamming the wooden pike into her friend's chest.

Flora screamed. Her eyes went wide and bloodred, her mouth open, fangs gleaming. "You *bitch*!"

Macey staggered back and saw the blood on her stake, saw the red blossoming on her friend's blue dress. *No.* She swung again, wildly, sick at heart, but Flora moved. Eyes narrowed with fury, teeth bared, she shoved with all her might, and sent Macey spinning into the wall. Her bad shoulder crashed into it and she cried out, stumbling back up and pivoting around after her friend.

But another vampire jumped between them, and Macey had to adjust her strike at the last minute. *Thud.* Right into his chest. *Poof.*

She whirled, staggering into a chair, and saw Chas swinging as he fought off three undead. Vaulting over the chair, Macey landed unsteadily on her feet, then surged into the hip of the nearest one. They tumbled to the floor, and she bit back a cry of pain as blood spurted from her injury once more. The undead rolled her onto her back, swiping down over her throat and chest with a long-nailed hand. Sharp pain seared as she bucked and twisted, unseating the vampire enough so she could swing up with her stake.

Poof. Gone. Macey pulled to her feet just as another somersaulted over a table and crashed into her. Back to the ground, air knocked out, stake falling from her hand. It rolled across the floor, and the vampire looked down at her. With a vicious grin, he curled a hand around her throat and squeezed. She couldn't breathe. His knee was in her bleeding shoulder. Her stake was out of reach.

Just as he swooped, fangs at the ready, Macey saw a shadow behind him. Then suddenly, he was gone in an explosion of ash.

And the room was still.

Chas offered her a hand and yanked her up. Macey was panting, ill, and her wound throbbed like a flame. "I didn't think you'd do it," he said, hands on his hips as he tried to catch his breath. "I didn't think you would."

"I missed."

"But you *did* it."

"Did you—did she…?"

Chas shook his head. "She's gone. Slipped away in the fracas. But you did what had to be done. You proved yourself, Macey. Well done."

The churning in her belly surged harder. She'd tried…but she'd missed. She'd missed her chance.

And Macey wasn't altogether certain she hadn't meant to.

Seventeen

Reality in the Light of Day

M ACEY EMERGED INTO THE BRIGHT LIGHT of day, leaving Alvisi's lair behind her. Chas was behind her, but she didn't want to talk. She stayed ahead of him.

The warm sun should have been a welcome sensation after such darkness, death, and destruction, but it only served to remind her of light, of normalcy, of happiness. Of life *before.*

Dejected, exhausted, and sick at heart, she trudged down the street in silence, weaving among and between other passersby who had no idea what evil lived beneath their streets. She'd found a coat to hide the bloodstains on her dress, but there were splatters of blood on her face and throat. No one seemed to notice.

Children gathered in parks, swinging, chasing each other, playing catch. Girlfriends linked arms and laughed at the soda fountain. Men jested on street corners while eating hot dogs. Mothers held the hands of dancing toddlers, pushed strollers, gave orders. Fathers carried children on their shoulders, managed dog leashes.

And so life went on. So utterly *normal.* And good.

Alvisi was dead. Flora lived. No, *existed.* Existed…owned and beholden to the devil. But lost to her. The look in her eyes told Macey there was no chance for redemption.

What was left of her friend was well and truly gone.

And Sebastian was still missing, but at least she knew who had him. Iscariot.

Macey glanced up as she crossed the street and saw the huge *Chicago Tribune* sign emblazoned on its building. Another stab of grief tore through her belly, superseding the aching wound in her shoulder, the scratches and cuts and bites on the rest of her. Those would heal much sooner, and much more easily, than the loss of Grady in her life.

J. Grady.

She'd probably never learn his real name—unless it was someday listed on a byline in the paper—or, knowing him, even the masthead. If she could, if she hadn't committed her life to her family legacy, she would keep walking…all the way to that Irish neighborhood where he lived, with his embedded silver crosses and dark, velvet eyes and soft, welcoming bed.

But she was a Venator.

Damned lonely life, being a Venator.

Macey glanced over her shoulder. Chas was still there. Their work was not yet done. It would never be done.

They had to find Sebastian. Somehow extricate him from Iscariot.

Just as she was about to turn and suggest hailing a cab, a long, black automobile pulled up along the curb. Macey's heart skipped a beat, but hell, she'd been through so much in the last few days. How could this be any worse?

Since it was broad daylight, and three suited men were getting out of the vehicle—plus her neck was toasty warm from the sun— she knew vampires were not the current threat. However, bullets and knives could be a problem.

"My boss has been waiting to meet with you," said one of the men. He gestured to the open door. The bulge of a firearm was clearly visible from beneath his suit.

"I appreciate the invite," Macey said, hardly slowing her pace, "but it's not a good time. I'm not in the best of moods."

But the man and his cohort blocked the way, and she was forced to stop. Other pedestrians crossed the street, unwilling to witness—much less be involved in—such a conflict.

"Move," Chas growled. One of the men stepped between him and Macey, producing a firearm, which he aimed boldly at Chas. Apparently, a handgun was going to have to be added to her vampire hunting tools.

"Get in da car," said the goon blocking her way. "I don't wanna have to make a scene." He shrugged sorrowfully as he showed her his gun. "But my finger's twitchy."

Macey glanced at Chas, but it appeared she had no other choice. And the invitation was clearly for her, and her alone.

"I hope you have something to drink in here," she muttered, climbing into the limousine.

To her surprise, the inside was empty. The doors closed and before she could wonder why the goons weren't joining her, one climbed in the front seat, and the driver took off.

"Who's your boss?" she asked, checking to make certain her stake was still tucked in her garter. Her silver cross was long gone. Not that either would be of much help against Nicholas Iscariot, if that was indeed where she was going.

Macey investigated the inside of the vehicle and found a small cooler with whiskey, glass tumblers, and—wonder of wonders—a large bottle of water. Half she used to clean up a little, and the other half she glugged down. Her wound from Chas's stake had stopped bleeding again. She hoped it would finally have a chance to heal.

By the time she'd dabbed at the rest of her injuries and eased her parched throat, the automobile pulled up to the backside of a tall, ornate brick building. The alley was narrow and deserted except for the man who waited at the door. He opened the vehicle to help her out.

No one spoke other than to direct her inside and then aboard an elevator. Macey had never ridden in one that went so fast, and she swore it left her belly on the ground.

Or perhaps it was nerves. For now she entered the den of a lion, alone and barely armed.

The lift stopped at the floor labeled "Penthouse," and that was when Macey realized it wasn't Nicholas Iscariot who'd summoned her.

Now she was really up a creek without a paddle. A stake wasn't going to do any damage to a mortal…

The twinge in her shoulder reminded her that wasn't precisely the case. If she hadn't been a Venator, Chas's stake would have killed her.

A set of double doors opened into the penthouse suite, which was beautifully and expensively appointed. Sofas and chairs were clustered at one side next to a set of French doors covered by filmy curtains. A large desk filled with papers, photos, and a container of writing implements stood to the right. There was a small grand piano with a cluster of silver candlesticks, a compact fireplace with a mantel displaying pictures and a vase of roses, and a hall that led, presumably, to bedrooms and a lavatory. Next to the door was a coat and umbrella rack with a mirror and half-moon table.

A stocky, sleek-haired man of thirty stood next to the French doors. He was dressed in a dapper white suit and neat spats. He had a red rose tucked into his buttonhole.

"Miss Denton. Welcome to my humble abode." He smiled as she entered.

"Mr. Capone." Though her heart was lodged in her throat, Macey kept her voice cool and her gaze steady. "We meet again."

He smiled and beckoned jovially. "You're a difficult broad to get at, you know."

"Most *broads* don't appreciate being summoned into a vehicle at gunpoint."

"A guy's gotta do what a guy's gotta do," said Capone.

She stepped farther into the room, casting about for potential weapons, escape, and information. Two dark-suited men stood in the corner, watching silently. They were going to make things more difficult. "What do you want? I'm in a really bad mood and I don't have any desire to spend my time with you or your Tutela friends."

"Tutela?" He laughed heartily. "You aren't as well informed as I believed."

"I doubt that." In the back of her mind, Macey could hardly believe she was challenging and baiting Chicago's most dangerous criminal. Only a month ago, she would have been trying to hide tears of terror—or at least be holding herself up on trembling knees—if she'd been brought into his presence like this. Now, she simply didn't care. She knew her abilities. And she knew the risks she'd taken on.

And she didn't *care*.

Capone looked at his three goons, one of whom had been her escort. "Go."

Their exit left her alone with the infamous gangster. It was a perfect opportunity to—well, to do something. After all, how often was the man at such a disadvantage—and in the presence of someone who could beat him? Take him into custody?

She looked around. A heavy wooden chair. A metal urn. Maybe there was a pair of scissors or a letter opener on the desk. No. The silver candelabra. She edged toward the piano.

"You would use my hospitality against me?" he said, obviously reading her mind. His Brooklyn accent was strong, even though he'd been in Chicago for more than three years. "That would be a mistake. Especially since we can be of use to each other."

"Since I'm not in the market for a prostitute—male or female—and I don't gamble, nothing could be further from the truth, Mr. Capone."

"I prefer Snorky."

"Snorky. Big Al. *Scarface.*" She purposely used his despised nickname. "I've heard them all. You're wasting my time—and yours. You and I have no reason to do anything together."

"You're going to be my personal bodyguard."

Macey gaped, then she could only laugh. "You're delusional. As if I'd ever work for the likes of you. In any capacity."

"I ain't got no problems with the fuzz or the law, or hardly with other gangs anymore. But it's the vampires. They're my problem," he said, as if she hadn't spoken. "And yours too."

"Well, that's one thing we can agree on. But I'm not going to be your bodyguard."

"I pay very well. You'll be dressed…" He sneered, then flapped his hand as if he couldn't bear to see the state of her current attire. "Well, much better than that. I serve the best food, the best drink, and have the best entertainment. And you'll have your own private suite—for when you aren't on the clock."

"And you get shot at, you're wanted for murder, bootlegging, racketeering, gambling, money laundering, and God knows what else." Disgust dripped from her voice. "Why would I join your club?"

Capone waved again. "They can't pin none of that on me. An' they won't try. But the undead are a concern. They could put me outta business. Competition."

"And so the most powerful man in Chicago—oh, we both know you are; let's not beat around the bush—is asking a woman—a *broad*—who's half—no, a *third* your weight to be your bodyguard?"

"Not just any broad. A Venator. The daughter of Max Denton." He seemed delighted by her surprise.

"So you've done your research. But that doesn't change anything."

"You'll be my bodyguard." He directed her to the French doors. "This way, Macey." He smiled coldly, and a streak of fear stripped down her spine. "Since you'll be my employee, I think a first-name basis is acceptable."

Capone threw open the French doors to reveal an enclosed rooftop aerie with waist-high walls, outfitted like an outdoor living room. Chairs and benches were arranged on an area rug. Potted trees and red geraniums gave it the feel of a garden. Half the space was in the light, and the other half was shaded by a large umbrella. Once the sun moved across the sky, the entire rooftop would be covered by its bold heat.

Macey stilled. In the shaded area, on what appeared to be a large, round table, was a man.

Wearing only trousers hacked off at the knees, he was spread-eagled over the table, bound by wrists and hands. He was still in the shade, but the edge of the sun was only inches away from his right hand—where five copper rings glinted dully.

Sebastian.

Eighteen
A Battle Lost

DAMNED GOOD THING MY MEN found you when they did. Another ten, fifteen minutes and Mr. Vioget—he'd be very uncomfortable." The pungent scent of cigar smoke wafted through the air as Capone wandered across the rooftop.

Macey was already at Sebastian's side. His head hung upside down from the table, and he blinked groggily when she touched his arm. Bruises and cuts battered his bare torso and muscular arms. They'd sure as hell worked him over—they would have had to, in order to subdue a man with his cunning and strength. Even so, he was still strong and beautiful, like a golden lion ready to roar to action. And there was his *vis bulla*, settled like a tiny silver pool in the hollow of his navel. For a moment, she couldn't take her eyes off it.

"A pleasure to see you, Macey," Sebastian said, lifting his head to look at her with a crooked smile. Despite his obvious discomfort, his amber eyes were warm, glinting with levity and resolve. "No offense, but I was rather hoping you wouldn't make it in time. Then he'd have nothing with which to hold you."

She was already working on the knots at the wrist nearest the sun, but froze when something poked her in the back. The barrel of a gun.

"Let's not get ahead of ourselves." The cigar smoke curled around her. "Your friend will be freed as soon as you agree to my terms."

"Forget it, Macey. It's time. I'm ready to go—though, admittedly, it's not the way I'd have chosen. I have an aversion to pain, you know." Sebastian's voice was wry and strong. He grabbed at her hand with his left fingers, squeezing hard. "But it's best you're here to see it. And to take these." She knew he meant the Rings of Jubai, on that very hand.

"You aren't going to fry," she said, squeezing back and surreptitiously picking at the knot. "I won't let you, and neither will Mr. Capone."

The gangster had eased back around to face them while keeping the gun trained on her. "That's up to you, Miss Denton. Step away now or I'll use this. One bullet won't kill you, especially where I'll put it—but it'll slow you the fuck down."

Macey edged away, her attention darting about the roof. Nothing looked promising—the chairs were flimsy and wooden. The flowerpots too ungainly.

"Do you accept my proposal or not?" her host pressed.

"No." She moved like lightning, grabbing a chair and spinning at the same time. She slammed it into Capone's gun arm, and the chair splintered as the weapon tumbled to the ground, skidding across the concrete floor.

To her surprise, instead of going after it, he lunged toward her. But Macey dodged and he caught only a fragment of her dress. It tore and she spun away, dashing into the penthouse. Candles went flying as she grabbed the metal candelabra from the piano and swung back to face him, holding it like a baseball bat.

The French doors slammed shut and Capone stood there, between her and the rooftop. "I suggest you reconsider. I might give you time to think, but the sun won't wait."

Macey gritted her teeth. *Sebastian.* "Why? Why do you want me? I'm just a weak broad. Won't you look ridiculous with itty-bitty me standing next to you, protecting you?"

"Cut the shit. I don't know who you're tryin' to fool, Macey Gardella. You're the one. And your friend out there—he might have a death wish, but I doubt your boyfriend does. Or your other friend. Or…well, take a look." He gestured to the desk.

Cold and numb, Macey walked over to find a slew of photos strewn over its surface. Pictures of her—with Mrs. Gutchinson, with Chelle and Dottie…and Grady. Coming out of the Harper Library, talking to her co-worker Leena. And more.

"I hate it when people get caught in the crossfire," Capone commented as he poured himself a glass of whiskey. "But it happens."

It happened with Grady's aunt.

It happened, in an entirely different but even uglier way, with Chelle and Mrs. G.

And Flora.

Her stomach rebelled and it was all she could do to hold back the bile.

She was trapped.

Capone had put down his gun and now held the whiskey. He was no longer standing in front of the French doors. "I trust you're convinced?"

"You're even more cold hearted than they say."

He smiled thinly. "Don't believe the damned gossip, Macey Gardella. Believe the prophecy."

She frowned. "Prophecy?"

"As written by Rosamunde Gardella. The mystic."

Macey was bewildered, but she nodded. "Yes. But how do you…"

"She wrote a verse I found most interesting. *'From the deepest bowels of madness and grief shall the dauntless one root, who shall go forth to lay bare from the earth this condemned evil. The dauntless one shall make the half of the whole, and the whole shall be formidable as the ocean and unyielding as the mountain.'* You, doll, are the dauntless one. And I," said Capone as he began to unbutton his shirt, "am the other half of the whole."

Macey stared in astonishment as the gangster pulled the white cotton apart, revealing his bare belly. It was surprisingly muscular and tighter than she'd expected, but that wasn't what caused her to snatch in her breath.

For, in the midst of the thatch of thick, dark hair was a tiny silver cross, pierced through the skin of his navel.

Macey couldn't speak for several long moments. Then finally, she had to say it aloud. "You're a Venator."

"Alphonsus Gardella Capone. Don't tell me my name isn't listed in the family Bible." His smile was half sneer, half bravado.

Just then, Macey noticed the bright sun filtering through the curtains on the French doors. It was brighter than before; its reach broader. "Sebastian!"

Capone moved faster than she'd expected, catching her by the arm and spinning her up against the entrance in one smooth flow. The doors crashed and rattled with the force, and the wind was knocked from her lungs. "Do you accept my proposal?"

She closed her eyes, drew in a deep breath. Thought not only of Sebastian, but of Grady. And Dottie. And anyone else she'd touched. Dammit…Flora too.

"Yes," she hissed in agreement.

Capone released her. She flung open the doors and was halfway across the brilliant sunlit roof by the time she realized Sebastian was gone. The ropes lay in empty crumples amid the remnants of the chair she'd flung at her captor.

The space was silent and still. No copper rings. No ash filtering through the air. She released a long, slow breath.

Macey turned to see her new employer—no, *partner*—standing in the doorway.

Al Capone had won this battle. They would work together to stop the undead, and God help her, she'd do her best to protect the man as well.

But she was going to make damned certain he didn't win the war.

Epilogue
A Damned Lonely Life

MACEY WAS STILL WEARING HER TATTERED dress and the coat she'd taken from Alvisi's hideaway.

Weighted with grief and despair, she walked and walked and walked. More passersby, more children, more families, more friends and colleagues and lovers.

These were the people she had sworn to protect.

These were the people of whom she must think…not herself. Not her losses. Not her fears and loneliness.

And that was when she understood what her father had done. Why he'd sent her away. To protect himself as much as to protect her.

Her eyes burned suddenly and she blinked rapidly. If only he were still here…still here, for her to talk to.

Oh, God, she needed *someone*.

She stopped and looked up. The red and white *Tribune* sign rose above her, and she blocked the sidewalk, but she couldn't make herself move. How had she ended up here? In all of Chicago, after all the blocks…why here?

"Macey."

She spun, startled. "Grady." And why *now*?

He took her by the arm before she could turn away. Or maybe she purposely didn't move fast enough. The coat shifted and he saw the front of her—a dress that had once been light blue was now stained mahogany. But she hardly felt the pain anymore.

"My God, you need a doctor. Something. Macey. Let me take you…somewhere." He should have been angry and put off. Furious with her. But his voice sounded tight and devastated. His eyes were a stormy, tortured blue. "Please."

She steeled herself to be cool and remote. But she faltered when she saw the purple and green bruise on his chin. *I'm sorry, Grady.* "It's nothing. I was on my way—"

"You can't just leave like this. Like you did last night."

Had it only been last night, late yesterday, that she'd been skin to skin with him? Sleeping, innocent, sated in his arms?

"I'm sorry, Grady. I can't…I told you, I can't do this. I shouldn't have…" *Stopped here. Waited to see you. Hoped to see you.*

Damn me. "I have to go."

"Macey."

"Take care of yourself, Grady. Please take care." She turned and gestured, blinking rapidly. The black automobile that had been following her for blocks pulled up to the curb.

Grady's eyes went to the vehicle, to the man who stepped out and opened the door, and then back to Macey. Comprehension dawned. "Macey, what are you doing? Do you know what you're doing? With *him*? With *them*?"

Nearly the same words she'd spoken to Flora. In the same confused, repulsed tone. How utterly, horribly ironic.

Macey swallowed hard and turned to the car. "Goodbye, Grady," she said as she climbed in.

The door closed.

And Macey sealed the deal with her own devil.

Author's Note

History buffs and experts on Chicago gangsterology (my own made-up word!) will note I took a bit of artistic license in *Roaring Midnight*: Al Capone didn't actually move into the Lexington Hotel until 1926.

And for those of you who'd like to know more about Chas Woodmore and his ill-fated affair with Narcise Moldavi, I refer you to *The Vampire Narcise*, as well as the other two books in my Regency Draculia trilogy, *The Vampire Voss* and *The Vampire Dimitri*.

The official reading order of the books is *Voss, Dimitri,* and then *Narcise*, but you will lose very little if you read them out of order—or just the third one—for they all overlap. Chas plays a major role in *The Vampire Narcise*.

Thank you for reading!

Colleen Gleason

Don't miss the next installment in the
Gardella Vampire Chronicles…

Roaring Shadows
Now Available!

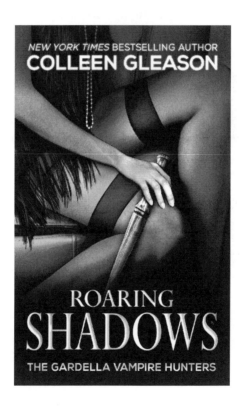

Excerpt from Roaring Shadows

November 1925
Chicago

"YOU'VE HEARD NOTHING from Macey, then. It's been nearly a week, and you've heard nothing." Chas Woodmore paused with the whiskey glass halfway to his lips. "And so do you simply intend that we *leave* her with Al Capone?" The glass slammed back onto the bar, its contents sloshing dangerously.

Sebastian Vioget didn't have any such compunction. He swallowed his drink—a gorgeous fifteen-year-old bourbon—in one hot gulp. Its heat rushed pleasantly through him, reminding him that he could, indeed, still feel.

If Woodmore had been an undead, his eyes would have been a blazing inferno. As it was, they nevertheless leapt with roaring fury and disdain. "You're simply going to stand back and let this happen?"

Sebastian tightened his fingers around the whiskey bottle and considered how pleasurable it would be to smash it over the other man's head. In the end, he didn't. Not because he feared injuring Woodmore or starting a fight—but because it would have been a waste of good liquor.

And he would have to clean up the mess, because Temple sure as hell wouldn't.

Aside from that, with Prohibition still limping gallantly along, it would have been costly to replace the bourbon.

If only Chas Woodmore could be replaced...by someone less difficult and angry. Why Wayren had brought the man here a few years ago—literally *brought* him, through some sort of time warp Sebastian didn't quite understand—was a question to which he had yet to learn the answer. He contented himself with trust in Wayren, and the knowledge that she never did anything without a reason.

So he gritted his teeth and responded with deceptive mildness. "Let precisely what happen?"

Woodmore's jaw moved. "I know you don't believe Al Capone wants Macey for simple window-dressing. What I don't understand, frankly, Vioget, is how it happened that *you* escaped and left her behind."

"Capone's thugs caught me as I came out of the church—just as dawn broke. I had no choice but to accompany them if I didn't want to fry in the sunlight. Perhaps you feel differently, Woodmore, but the last thing I want is for Big Al to be the one who retrieves these from my damned ashes." Vioget flexed his right hand, showing off the five copper rings that had been fused to his fingers since the day he removed his hand from the enchanted pool at Munţii Făgăraş.

Woodmore's gaze sharpened. Some of the belligerence faded from his face, replaced with interest. "So if Capone wanted the Rings of Jubai, he could have ordered his men to allow you to burn right then and there on the sidewalk. Curious."

"I agree."

"Then what did he want from you? And what does he want with Macey?"

Sebastian poured himself another glass and gestured to Chas's untouched one. "Not rotgut enough for your taste, Woodmore? I can't remember the last time a full glass—let alone a bottle—remained intact in your presence. Don't tell me you're cutting back. Have you joined the Temperance movement now? You wouldn't hear any complaints from me if you had. It would save me a lot of money, since you've yet to settle a bill since you arrived here."

Woodmore picked up his glass and sipped, nonchalance in his movements. "Why are you prevaricating, Vioget? What did Capone want if it wasn't the rings?"

Sebastian pursed his lips, then allowed his prickly mood to ease. "It wasn't me. It's clear he wants Macey."

Woodmore's expression darkened. "Wants her...how?"

"As his...moll. Or, more accurately, as his personal bodyguard. But one would suspect there will be other duties involved as well." Vioget kept his voice bland, carefully watching his companion.

But Woodmore's face closed up. "He knows she's a Venator."

Sebastian inclined his head. "Don't ask me how he discovered this bit of information—unless he learned it through your escapades at The Blood Club. You do tend to be a little lax while under the influence."

Both men knew precisely what Sebastian was referring to by "influence"—and it wasn't merely to alcohol—but to his surprise, Woodmore chose not to react to the dig other than to reply, "Capone has never had anything to do with The Blood Club, as you well know. And now that Count Alvisi has been dusted—thanks to Macey—Nicholas Iscariot has taken over the establishment."

"Perhaps Capone wants the club for himself. It is a very lucrative venture," suggested Sebastian innocently. "It would fit right in with his prostitution and gambling rings. Women, cards, and immortality. Pleasure for an infinity."

"Perhaps." Woodmore remained silent, possibly in reflection, and looked down into his glass. "Capone's goons did a number on you with their blackjacks. Doesn't it bother you Big Al had you worked over but didn't try for the rings? Surely he's heard about them. It must be widely known among the Tutela that Iscariot would do anything to have them in his possession."

"There's no indication Al Capone has joined the Tutela," said Sebastian. "And he's certainly not been turned. It's possible he doesn't know about the rings. Perhaps we were wrong that he's intending to ally himself with the undead."

Chas lifted his face suddenly, spearing Sebastian with cold, dark eyes. "Perhaps we were."

What does he know?

It was rare for Sebastian Vioget to be put off his game—especially since he'd been alive for more than 140 years, and immortal for more than a century—and during that time, he'd found it his particular gift to woo and manipulate and guide the people around him to get what he wanted. But at this moment, by not being completely forthright, he knew he was taking a risk that could turn Chas Woodmore from an ally to an enemy.

A more formidable enemy than he'd wish to engage—unless it came down to it.

Yet Sebastian had secrets he must keep if he ever hoped to finish the "long promise" he'd taken on 105 years ago. And so he remained silent, pouring himself another glug of bourbon with a very steady hand. Then he replaced the bottle on its shelf next to an array of decorative objects, including a marble Buddha, a jade dragon, and a square cut-glass bottle with its blue-black pyramid topper.

"And so what do we do about Macey?" asked Chas after a long, heavy silence.

Sebastian gave an insouciant shrug. "We let her do what she must do. After all, she is a Venator."

Now Available!

Colleen Gleason is an award-winning, *New York Times* and *USA Today* best-selling author with more than twenty novels in print. Her international bestselling series, the Gardella Vampire Chronicles, is a historical urban fantasy about a female vampire hunter who lives during the time of Jane Austen. Her first novel, *The Rest Falls Away*, was released to acclaim in 2007.

Since then, she has published more than twenty novels with New American Library, MIRA Books, Chronicle Books, and HarperCollins (writing as Joss Ware). Her books have been translated into more than seven languages and are available worldwide.

Visit Colleen at:
colleengleason.com
facebook.com/colleen.gleason.author

Or sign up for new book release information from Colleen Gleason here:
http://cgbks.com/news

Printed in Great Britain
by Amazon